ROOT SLEEP

STONEBOUND
BOOK 3

N.B. CROSS

For what remains when the struggle ends.

CHAPTER
ONE

The mud sucks at Vincent's boots with each step, a rust-colored mire that spreads between the temporary trailers like blood pooling in snow. Morning fog clings to the plywood ramps connecting each unit, and diesel fumes from the construction site mix with the smell of wet cedar until his throat burns with it. Beside him, Mira picks her way through the worst of the puddles, her dark hair catching droplets of mist that make her look wrapped in spider silk.

"Three more months of this," Vincent says, gesturing at the cluster of white trailers squatting on cinder blocks. "Then we get a real school again. One that doesn't rock in the wind like we're on a boat."

"Better than the town hall," Mira says. After the fire, they'd spent two weeks crammed into city's overflow building while the district scrambled for these rentals. At least here they have actual desks, even if they wobble on the uneven floors.

Mira touches his arm lightly, a gesture so natural now it barely registers except as warmth through his jacket. "The ground feels different today."

Vincent knows better than to dismiss her observations.

Since Marrowick, since The Adversary opposed her and made her something more than just Mira, she feels things before they happen. Not prophecy exactly, but a kind of listening that goes deeper than ears.

"Different how?" he asks, but she's already stopped walking, her amber-gray eyes focused on something beyond the visible morning.

A metal door slams somewhere in the maze of trailers, the hollow thud echoing between units. Other students trudge past them, shoulders hunched against the damp, backpacks dark with moisture. Someone's playing music from a phone speaker, tinny hip-hop that cuts through the fog before another door swallows it. For a moment, Vincent can almost pretend this is just another miserable Monday at Duswood High's temporary campus, that the worst thing ahead is Ms. Sanford's chemistry quiz.

Then the ground moves.

Not a tremor, not the sharp jolt of tectonic plates grinding. This is something else, something organic. The earth lifts beneath them in a slow roll, like the chest of something massive drawing breath. The sound comes with it, not the crack of breaking stone but a wet crushing, like gravel being ground between enormous teeth. Vincent's knees buckle slightly, his body trying to adjust to solid ground that suddenly isn't.

"Get back," Mira says, her voice carrying that strange authority it holds now, the voice that made grown men listen during the worst moments in Marrowick. She grabs Vincent, pulling him toward the nearest trailer.

The parking lot fifty feet away begins to buckle. Asphalt cracks in a spider web pattern, pieces lifting and tilting. Steam rises from the gaps, carrying that familiar metallic smell Vincent remembers from the aftermath of the pizzeria attack.

Then the world explodes.

A column of deep red-orange flame punches through the

rain-soaked asphalt with a sound like tearing metal. The blast catches Vincent mid-step and flings him backward into the side of a trailer. His shoulder hits first, then his head, stars bursting across his vision. Glass shatters somewhere above him, the windows of three trailers simultaneously giving way. The shards rain down, some still glowing with heat, hissing as they hit the puddles around him.

His ears ring with a high, painful whine that drowns out everything else. Through the confusion, he sees rather than hears the chaos erupting. Students pour from trailer doors, some falling on the slick ramps, others frozen in place as their minds try to process what's happening. A teacher stands in a doorway with his mouth open in what must be a shout, though Vincent hears nothing but the endless ringing.

The flame column wavers, thick and almost liquid, more like molten metal than fire. It throws shadows that stretch and contract independent of the light source. Where it touches the trailer roofs, the metal immediately glows white-hot and begins to sag.

Vincent tries to stand, his legs unsteady, hands sinking into mud that feels too warm. Through the ringing, other sounds begin to penetrate; screaming, the crash of collapsing metal, and underneath it all, that grinding sound continues, the earth still chewing on something deep below.

Through the haze of pain and ringing ears, Vincent sees Hale Ness emerge from the smoke. The construction foreman moves with purpose, his work boots finding solid ground where others slip and stumble. His mouth moves in what must be shouts, though Vincent catches only fragments through the whine in his head. Hale grabs a girl who stands frozen, steering her away from the burning trailers with hands that know how to move people without hurting them.

The south trailers catch fire first, flames spreading across their roofs in patterns that make no sense. Rain still falls, droplets visible against the orange glow, but the fire races through the water like it isn't there. The metal walls buckle and pop. One trailer's door warps shut, trapping whoever might be inside.

Vincent forces himself upright, using the trailer wall for support. His vision swims, doubles, then snaps back into focus. Twenty feet away, Hale drops to his knees beside a twisted section of metal ramp. A younger student, maybe a freshman, lies pinned beneath it, eyes wide with terror. Hale's own fear shows in the tight line of his jaw, but his hands are steady as he works to lift the metal. The ramp must weigh more than both of them combined, but Hale manages to raise it enough for the kid to scramble free, his legs scraped bad but working.

"Move! Everyone move!" Hale's voice finally breaks through the ringing, distant but clear. He stands between the students and the growing inferno, arms spread wide like he's herding cattle. "North gate! Stay together!"

The exit of a nearby trailer is blocked. Vincent can see it from here, the doorway to that trailer crimped shut by the blast's pressure wave. Students press against it from inside, their palms visible through the narrow windows, mouths open in screams that blend into the chaos.

Then Mira is there.

She appears through the smoke like something summoned, her slight frame moving against the tide of fleeing students. Her hands find the jammed door's edge, and Vincent watches her pull. Not with the desperate yanking of panic, but with something deliberate, measured. The door groans, metal protesting, then tears free from its frame entirely. She tosses it aside like cardboard, and students pour out, some falling to their knees in the mud, others running without looking back.

"Vincent!" Her voice cuts through everything else, not because it's loud but because something in it resonates in his bones. He turns toward her, and the world tilts again. The air between them shimmers with heat waves, and he tastes metal on his tongue, iron and salt, hot enough to sting.

His throat burns as he breathes, each inhale bringing more of that metallic taste. Students stream past him, some crying, others silent with shock. A teacher half-carries a boy whose leg won't support his weight. Someone's backpack burns in a puddle, the synthetic fabric melting into toxic smoke.

Sirens wail in the distance, growing closer. Through the gaps between trailers, Vincent sees the red and white of emergency vehicles racing down Kipling Avenue. But even as they arrive, even as firefighters leap from their trucks with hoses already unrolling, something changes in the fire itself.

It begins to collapse inward.

Not dying naturally, not starved of fuel or smothered by water. The flames pull back like something recoiling, drawing into themselves. Steam rises in massive billows, thick enough to turn the morning into twilight. The heat that seconds ago threatened to melt the trailer walls suddenly vanishes, leaving only the ghostly afterimage of warmth on Vincent's skin.

The firefighters slow their approach, hoses still ready but uncertain what they're fighting. The fire hasn't just gone out; it's been swallowed, pulled down into the crater where it began. Vincent can see the hole now through the clearing smoke, a perfect circle of absence in the parking lot, edges glowing faintly red like the rim of a volcanic vent.

Students cluster in groups, some sitting in the mud, others standing with blank expressions of shock. Vincent has his arm around the kid Hale saved, both of them staring at the destruction. Teachers try to count heads, voices calling names that echo strangely in the steam-thick air.

Vincent finds Mira again, or she finds him. Her hand touches his face, checking for damage, her fingers cool against his heated skin. The ringing in his ears has faded to a low hum, and through it he hears her say something that makes his stomach clench with recognition.

"It wasn't trying to hurt us," she says, looking not at him but at the crater. "It was trying to tell us something."

In the aftermath, what remains disturbs Vincent more than the explosion itself. The parking lot has become a moonscape of melted asphalt and standing water that glows faintly red, as if lit from below. Rain continues to fall, steady and cold, but where it hits certain puddles, it bubbles and steams. The physics of it aren't natural, like watching water boil in reverse.

Emergency personnel move through the scene with practiced efficiency, stringing yellow tape between sawhorses, taking photographs of the crater. But Vincent notices how they avoid stepping too close to the hole itself, how their voices drop when they pass near it. Even professionals recognize when something exceeds normal disaster.

Joe Bullit arrives fifteen minutes after the fire dies, his old field jacket dark with rain. Vincent watches him push past the tape without hesitation, that military bearing still evident in how he moves through chaos. Joe kneels beside the crater's edge where Hale Ness stands with his hands on his hips, both men studying the hole like it might provide answers.

"Gas main?" Hale asks, though his tone suggests he already knows better.

Joe touches the mud with two fingers, brings them close to his face, sniffs. His expression doesn't change, but something in his shoulders tightens. He wipes his hand on his jeans, leaving a rusty smear.

"Gas main didn't do this," he says, loud enough for Vincent to hear from twenty feet away. "Gas mains don't leave glass."

Vincent looks closer and sees what Joe means. The crater's sides gleam in places, earth fused into smooth, dark glass by impossible heat. But the glass has veins in it, red threads that pulse faintly like capillaries. Like something organic transformed rather than simply melted.

The sirens have mostly faded now, only the occasional ambulance departing with students who need treatment for smoke inhalation or cuts from flying glass. The temporary campus stands evacuated, doors hanging open, homework and backpacks abandoned in the mud. One trailer lists badly to one side where its cinder block foundation partially collapsed. Another has a hole burned straight through its roof, edges still glowing faintly orange despite the rain.

Steam rises from the entire lot, thick and white, carrying the scent of hot metal and something else. Burning cedar, Vincent realizes, though there are no cedar trees near the trailers. The smell comes from below, from whatever the explosion opened. It's the same scent that haunted the pizzeria, the same smell that clung to Mira's hair after her episodes near the old Hearthstone Chapel's mission ruins.

Vincent takes a step toward the crater, and that's when he feels it.

Not an aftershock. Not the sharp crack of settling earth or the groan of shifting stone. This is a pulse, deliberate and deep, traveling up through his boots and into his bones. Like standing on the chest of something breathing. The rhythm is too slow for a heart, too regular for random geological movement. It comes again, and this time Vincent sees others feel it too. Joe stands abruptly. Hale takes a step back from the crater's edge. A firefighter pauses mid-conversation, looking down at the ground with confusion.

"Everyone back," someone shouts, probably the fire chief. "Clear the area until we can get the state engineers out here."

But Vincent knows no engineer will explain this. No building inspector or insurance adjuster will have forms for what grows beneath Duswood. They didn't two years ago when Carl was killed in the swamp. No one was there to explain why or how Marrowick succumbed to malevolent mycelial.

Mira stands beside him, appearing with that quiet way she has of moving without sound. Her dark hair hangs wet against her face, and rain traces lines down her cheeks that could be tears but aren't. She watches the crater with those amber-gray eyes, and Vincent recognizes the look. It's the same expression she wears when things don't make sense, half present and half listening to something beyond normal frequency.

"It's starting again," she says, voice barely above a whisper. The words carry anyway, reaching him clearly despite the distance and noise. "Only this time, it's underneath us."

Vincent wants to ask what she means, but part of him already knows. The creature they returned to the swamp, the presence they held back in Marrowick, were just parts of something larger. Something that now runs beneath all of Duswood, connecting the town and beyond in ways they don't yet understand.

The afternoon light struggles through smoke that still hangs over Duswood. Vincent sits in the back of Elias's sedan, watching the town slide past the window in muted shades of gray and rust. Beside him, Mira's hand rests on the seat, fingers spread as if feeling for vibrations through the leather. Up front, Elias drives with both hands on the wheel, knuckles white, jaw set in that particular way that means he's grinding his teeth.

They pass the temporary school lot, now wrapped in yellow tape that flutters like trapped birds. Two news vans cluster at the perimeter, their satellite dishes aimed at nothing. A reporter stands before a camera, gesturing at the destruction while carefully avoiding any angle that might show the crater itself. Vincent catches fragments of her rehearsed explanation through the cracked window: "...underground gas pocket... electrical malfunction... no serious injuries, thankfully..."

"They're calling it a gas leak," Elias says, his voice flat and clinical, the way he sounds when reading post-operative instructions to patients. "The official statement will blame aging infrastructure. Maybe some story about mineral deposits affecting the pipes or the disruption from the construction."

Vincent watches a firefighter in the background shake his head at something the reporter says, but the camera has already turned away. The truth sits heavy in the car, unspoken but present as the smell of smoke that clings to their clothes.

The familiar streets of their neighborhood appear unchanged, as if the morning's explosion happened in some other town. Mrs. Henderson sweeps her porch. The Kemp boys shoot baskets in their driveway, the rhythmic bounce of the ball carrying through the quiet afternoon. But Vincent notices the subtle fragmentation: curtains drawn in houses that usually welcome light, dogs that should be barking now silent behind fences, the absence of children's voices from the park.

Angela waits on their porch, wrapped in the quilt from their couch though the afternoon isn't cold. She must have been sitting there since the first news reports, since the principal's automated calls went out telling parents not to panic, that all students were accounted for, that counselors would be available tomorrow at the community center. Her face turns toward them as Elias pulls into the driveway, and Vincent sees the hours of worry etched in the lines around her eyes, the way her hands clutch the blanket like it might keep her from floating away.

She stands as they approach, the quilt falling from one shoulder, and Vincent notices she hasn't changed from her night clothes. Coffee stains dot her sleeve. Her hair, usually carefully arranged, hangs loose and tangled. The smell of smoke precedes them up the porch steps, and Angela's nostrils flare slightly, her body tensing as if the scent confirms fears she's been nursing all day.

Inside, the house feels too quiet, too still. The television murmurs from the living room, news coverage on mute, images of the destroyed trailers cycling endlessly. Angela moves to the kitchen, starts pulling plates from cabinets, her hands shake enough that one plate rings against another. Elias catches her wrist gently, stills the tremor.

"You don't have to," he says.

"I need to do something." Her voice cracks on the last word.

They end up in the living room, not quite sitting, not quite standing. Angela perches on the arm of the couch, the blanket pulled tight around her shoulders again. Elias stands by the window, looking out at nothing, his reflection ghostlike in the glass. Vincent finds himself in the doorway, neither fully in nor out of the room. Mira has disappeared somewhere upstairs, probably to her room where she can listen without the weight of their eyes on her.

The silence stretches, elastic and suffocating. On the muted television, the reporter from earlier points at a diagram of underground gas lines, red arrows indicating theoretical leak points. Vincent watches Angela watch the screen, sees the moment she stops believing the comfortable lie.

"Something else is happening, isn't it?" Her voice comes out soft, trembling, but the question lands solid.

Elias answers too quickly, the words escaping before thought can temper them. "It's nothing like before. This was an infrastructure failure. Old pipes, unstable ground from all the construction." He turns from the window, and Vincent sees him trying to arrange his face into something reassuring. "The fire department confirmed it. Gas pocket, nothing more."

But his denial hangs in the air, unconvincing as smoke. Angela's shoulders hunch forward, curling in on themselves like she's trying to become smaller, to take up less space in a world that suddenly feels too large and dangerous. Elias's spine stays rigid, too straight, the posture of someone holding themselves together through will alone. Between them, Vincent feels the weight of their unspoken knowledge: that the unnatural reality of Duswood never really ended, just went quiet for a while, waiting.

Night settles over the house like a wet shadow, and the casserole Angela made sits untouched on the table, its surface developing a skin that catches the overhead light. Vincent pushes green beans around his plate with his fork, creating patterns he doesn't mean to make. Across from him, Angela's place remains empty, her food cooling while she stands at the sink, washing the same glass for the third time. Elias sits rigid in his chair, cutting his portion into smaller and smaller pieces without eating any of it.

Mira stands by the back door, so still she might be part of the house itself. She's been there for twenty minutes, watching rain pool in the ruts the construction trucks left in their yard last month when they were surveying for new utility lines. The puddles glow faintly red in the darkness, not reflecting the emergency lights but producing their own sullen luminescence. Vincent watches her from his seat, noting how her breath fogs the glass in slow, deliberate intervals, as if she's matching her breathing to something only she can hear.

"You should eat something," Angela says to no one in particular, but her voice lacks conviction. She sets the glass in the drying rack with excessive care, as if sudden movements might shatter more than dishes.

"I'm not hungry," Mira says without turning from the door. Her words carry that weight they've held since Marrowick, not commanding but impossible to argue with.

The doorbell rings, sharp in the silence. Through the front window, Vincent sees Joe Bullit on their porch, his boots caked with clay that looks black in the porch light. He stamps them on the mat, but the clay clings stubbornly, as if it doesn't want to let go.

Elias rises to answer, his movement careful and controlled. Vincent hears the door open, the low rumble of Joe's voice mixing with the rain. Without deciding to, Vincent finds himself moving toward the stairs, positioning himself where he can listen without being seen.

"Come in," Elias says, though his tone suggests he'd prefer otherwise.

Joe's boots sound heavy on the entryway tile, leaving prints that will stain no matter how much they're scrubbed later. The two men move to the kitchen, their voices dropping to that register adults use when they think minors might be listening.

"Coffee?" Elias offers, already reaching for the pot.

"Sure." Joe's jacket rustles as he removes it. "Been at the site since noon. They've got state engineers coming tomorrow, but..." A pause, the sound of ceramic against counter. "Elias, I need to tell you what I saw down there."

Vincent edges down two more steps, the third one from the bottom that creaks if you step on the left side. He avoids it, settling his weight carefully.

"The crater goes deeper than they're saying," Joe continues. His pragmatic voice carries a note Vincent has never heard before, something between confusion and unease. "Thirty feet at least, but that's not the strange part. There are roots down there, fused to metal pipes. Old pipes, from when the school was first built. The roots are grown right through them, like the metal was soft when they passed through."

"Root systems can be aggressive," Elias says, but his clinical tone wavers slightly. "The construction probably disturbed..."

"They're still warm." Joe's words cut through the attempted rationalization. "Hours after the fire, rain pouring down, and those roots are warm to the touch. And the smell coming up from the bottom, it's not gas. It's cedar. Burning cedar, but there's no char, no ash. Just that smell, rising up like breath."

Vincent can't see them from his position, but he hears a chair scrape against the floor, someone sitting down heavy.

"I don't think it was gas," Joe says, quieter now. "I've smelled gas leaks, dealt with them in the field. This was something else. Something that wanted out."

Elias's response is too low to catch, but Vincent sees his shadow on the wall, shoulders drawn tight, head bowed like someone receiving bad news they've been expecting. The rain intensifies outside, drumming against the windows, and beneath it, Vincent swears he hears something else: a rhythm, patient and deep, like the earth itself learning to breathe.

———

The house finally goes still as midnight approaches, that peculiar quiet that comes when even the walls stop settling and the pipes cease their complaints. Vincent lies on his back, still dressed in jeans and t-shirt, staring at the ceiling where water stains form patterns like fossil remains. Joe left an hour ago, his truck growling away into the rain, but his words linger in the house like smoke. Warm roots. Metal pipes. Something that wanted out.

Sleep feels impossible. Every time Vincent closes his eyes, he sees that column of fire punching through asphalt, sees the crater's glass-veined walls pulsing with their own light. His shoulder throbs where he hit the trailer, a bruise blooming purple and green beneath his shirt. The pain keeps him anchored to his body when his mind wants to drift toward panic.

Rain continues its steady patter against the roof, a sound he's known all his life. Tin eaves creak in the wind, another familiar voice in the darkness. The refrigerator hums downstairs, cycling on and off with mechanical regularity. These are the sounds of home, of safety, of ordinary life continuing despite the day's horrors.

But beneath them, Vincent detects something else.

At first, he mistakes it for his own pulse echoing in his ears. The rhythm is so close to a heartbeat that his brain tries to categorize it as internal sound. But when he holds his breath, the thrumming continues, steady and patient. It comes from below, not just beneath his room but beneath the house itself, beneath the foundation and the soil, rising up through layers of earth and stone.

Vincent rolls onto his stomach, lowers himself to the floor. The hardwood feels cold against his palms, colder than the air temperature suggests. He presses his ear to the boards, the way he used to as a child, listening for conversations, and arguments, in the kitchen below when his dad came home too late. But this isn't voices he hears. It's that pulse, clearer now, transmitted through wood and nail, through joint and beam.

The rhythm is deliberate, too regular for settling earth or distant machinery. It sounds like something breathing, if breath could move through stone. Each pulse sends a subtle vibration through the floor, barely perceptible but undeniably present. Vincent spreads his hand flat against the wood, feeling the tremor travel through his palm, up his arm, into his chest where his own heart beats its familiar pattern.

Then something shifts.

The underground pulse slows, adjusts, finds a new tempo. Vincent's breath catches as he realizes what's happening. The rhythm from below is synchronizing with his heartbeat, matching it beat for beat. When his heart speeds up from fear, the underground pulse accelerates too. When he forces himself to breathe slowly, to calm his racing blood, the deep rhythm follows, patient and attentive.

His breath fogs in the suddenly frigid air, each exhale visible in the darkness. Ice crystals form at the edges of his window, spreading in patterns that look almost organic. The cold seeps through his clothes, through his skin, settling in his bones. But he can't move, can't pull away from the floor where he lies listening to something vast and ancient learning the rhythm of his life.

Vincent thinks of the roots Joe described, warm despite the rain, growing through metal as if it were soft earth. He thinks of Mira standing at the door, listening to sounds only she can fully hear. He thinks of the crater's red glow, of flames that pulled back into the earth like something swallowing its own scream.

The pulse continues, steady as a metronome, as certain as sunrise. It's not threatening, exactly. It's worse than that. It's patient. It's aware. And it's rising.

Vincent remains there on the cold floor, ear pressed to wood, listening to the synchronized heartbeats: his own, small and frightened and human, and the other, vast and deliberate, ascending through Duswood's soil with the slow certainty of roots seeking light. His limbs grow stiff with cold, his bruised shoulder aches, but he can't bring himself to move. Because moving would mean acknowledging what he's hearing. Moving would mean accepting that beneath their ordinary town, beneath streets and houses and lives built on solid ground, something has been sleeping. And now, terrible and patient and older than memory, it's starting to wake.

The rain continues outside, washing the smoke from Duswood's air. But deep below, where root meets stone meets the buried history of a town that has always been stranger than it admits, that rhythmic pulse grows stronger. Not louder, but more present, as if the space between the surface and the depths is gradually collapsing, bringing the buried closer to the light.

Vincent closes his eyes, still listening, still feeling that synchronous beat through floor and bone. Tomorrow, there will be explanations and emergency meetings and official stories about gas pockets and infrastructure. But tonight, in the darkness of his room, he knows the truth that Joe suspected, that Mira feels, that even Elias can't quite deny: Duswood's real truth has always been growing underground. It has always been there, feeding on everything.

CHAPTER
THREE

The streets of Duswood smell acrid two days after the explosion, a mix of wet ash and iron. Vincent drives his mother's sedan through neighborhoods where hardened snow lines the driveways. Beside him, Mira sits with her window cracked despite the cold early Spring drizzle, breathing in the damaged air like she's trying to identify each perverse component.

They pass the grocery store where Mrs. Kellerman stands at her register, scanning items like it's her only purpose until her hand pauses mid-reach, hovering over a can of corn as if she's forgotten what comes next. Through the window, Vincent watches her stare at nothing for three full seconds before continuing, the fluorescent lights above her flickering in a pattern that matches no electrical rhythm he knows.

The mailman, Peterson or Patterson, Vincent can never remember which, holds letters at the corner of Elm Street, but his eyes keep darting to the puddles gathering at his feet. When a drop of water falls from his coat and lands in one, sending ripples outward, the man takes a full step back, clutching his mail bag like a shield. The puddle settles, reflecting the gray sky, but Peterson-Patterson doesn't move closer, choosing instead to deliver to the houses across the street first, giving the water a wide berth.

"Everyone feels it," Mira says in a tone that's not quite prophecy but weighted with understanding that goes deeper than observation. "They're trying not to know what they know."

Vincent turns onto the street where St. Clement's bell tower rises against clouds that hang too low, too thick, as if the sky itself has grown heavier since the explosion. The pastor, Father Morrison, stands in the doorway despite the misting rain, his black cassock spotted with water. He watches each car pass with an intensity that suggests he's counting them, or perhaps blessing them, he greets Vincent and Mira as they enter the parish.

The parish office sits separate from the main church, a brick building that somehow looks older than its construction date suggests, as if time moves differently within its walls. Rainwater drips against the stained glass windows in a rhythm that sounds almost like morse code, though Vincent knows that's just his mind trying to find patterns in chaos. The colored glass throws strange shadows on the wet pavement, reds and blues and golds that shimmer and shift independent of any light source.

Mrs. Driscoll stands in the reception room wearing her cardigan that smells of candle wax and cedar polish, her silver hair pulled into its familiar tight bun.

"Thank you for coming, Mira. I thought seeing for yourself is easier than sending texts," she says. Her voice carries its measured calm, that musical cadence that makes even mundane statements sound like liturgy, but when she reaches to light a candle on the entry table, her fingers tremble just slightly, a vibration so small Vincent might have missed it if he wasn't watching.

The office interior feels suspended in amber light from old lamps, though overhead fluorescents hum their presence.

Brass fixtures gleam with recent polishing, and the scent of lemon oil mingles with something older, the smell of paper aging slowly in humidity. Water stains pattern the ceiling in shapes that remind Vincent of the fossil impressions in his old geology textbook, and the shelves sag slightly under the weight of ledgers and records dating back decades, their spines marked with dates that precede the town's official incorporation.

In the corner, Owen Driscoll sits sorting hymnals with one earbud in, the other dangling loose against his Michigan Tech sweatshirt. He glances up when they enter, and Vincent catches something in his expression that isn't quite surprise but rather confirmation, as if their presence validates a hypothesis he's been forming. The young man's fingers are stained with graphite, and a notebook lies open beside him, filled with diagrams that look more like geological surveys than anything related to church music.

"My grandson," Mrs. Driscoll says, though they all know Owen from when he was younger, from summers when he'd visit and spend his time mapping the town's elevation changes for fun. "He's been helping me organize the old records. I don't know what that old cackle did before me. Finally, seemed like the right time to put things in order."

Owen offers a slight nod, his attention split between them and whatever plays through his single earbud. There's a tension in how he holds himself, the careful attention of someone who's noticed things that don't add up and is waiting for someone else to confirm he's not imagining them.

Mrs. Driscoll moves to a cabinet Vincent hasn't noticed before, its wood so dark it seems to absorb light rather than reflect it. She opens it with a key that looks older than the lock it turns, and inside, rows of ledgers stand like tombstones, their covers water-stained and warped but still intact.

"There are things about this town," she begins, then stops, choosing her words with the care of someone defusing a bomb. "Things that were here before this church, before the schools, before the houses. The ground has a memory, you understand. And sometimes, when we dig too deep or build too heavy, it reminds us what came first."

The water continues its coded tapping against the stained glass, and Vincent notices how the colored light falls across Mira's face, painting her in beautiful moments of rose and gold before shifting away, as if even the light recognizes something in her that demands both reverence and caution.

From the cabinet's depths, Mrs. Driscoll withdraws a ledger that looks like it's been drowned and resurrected, its leather cover warped into ridges that resemble topographical maps. The spine bears faded gold lettering: Great Northern Rail & Ore, 1941-1953. Years of natural elements and humidity has transformed parts of the cover into something that feels organic under her fingers, as if the ledger itself has started growing roots.

She carries it to the oak table with the ceremony of someone handling a relic, setting it down where the afternoon light, filtered through water rivulets and stained glass, can illuminate its damaged pages. Vincent and Mira draw close, their shadows falling across the ledger like wings.

"The company built freight vaults beneath the town before the high school ever existed," Mrs. Driscoll explains, her voice dropping to that low, almost musical register that makes Vincent think of prayers spoken in empty churches. Her fingers hover over the cover without quite touching it, as if even now she's reluctant to disturb what lies within. "They needed somewhere to store ore during the winter months, when the lakes froze and shipping stopped. Before the USCGC Mackinaw maintained reliable shipping lanes. So they dug. And dug. And dug."

She opens the ledger with care, and the smell that rises from its pages fills the room with dampness and age and something else, something mineral and foul. The first page shows a survey map of Duswood from 1941, but it's a Duswood Vincent doesn't recognize. Where the high school should be, there's nothing but forest. Where downtown stands now, the map shows only scattered buildings around a massive rail depot. And lines resembling an octopus with too many arms, marked in blue ink that's bled into purple with age, a network of trails spread like veins.

"The ground never wanted them here," Mrs. Driscoll adds, almost to herself, the words escaping like an involuntary confession.

Vincent traces the ledger's margins with cautious fingers, feeling the paper's texture change where water damage has made it soft, almost flesh-like. His touch follows the trail lines as they branch outward from the depot, spreading through what would become the school, the church, the neighborhood where he's lived his whole life. The trails don't follow any logical pattern for transportation. They curve and spiral in ways that remind him of the root systems Mira draws in her notebooks, organic and searching.

Beside him, Mira's touch lingers on the pages differently, not tracing but pressing down gently, as if she's feeling for a pulse beneath the paper. Her breathing has slowed to match that deep rhythm they've both been sensing since the explosion, and Vincent watches her eyes lose focus.

The next page contains construction notes, written in a tight, worried hand. The ink has run in places, but certain phrases remain legible: "unexpected resistance at forty feet," "tools fouled by organic matter," "workers reporting dreams of breathing earth." One entry from November 1942 describes a tunnel collapse that killed three men, though the cause listed isn't structural failure but "aggressive root infiltration at depths where no roots should exist."

Vincent turns the page to find diagrams of a tunnel system outside of town from different angles. The main vaults appear as rectangular chambers, but around them, smaller passages branch off in patterns that weren't planned, marked with question marks and notes like "formed naturally?" and "do not pursue." One branch extends directly toward what Vincent recognizes as the swamp's location, and beside it, someone has written in red ink: "FLOOD VULNERABLE" and below that, in a different hand: "ORGANIC INTER-FERENCE."

Owen has abandoned his hymnals entirely now, moving closer to peer over Vincent's shoulder. His earbud dangles forgotten against his chest, whatever music was playing now just a tinny whisper in the quiet room. He studies the diagrams with the intensity of someone who understands topography, who can read elevation and depth in simple lines.

"These measurements," Owen says, pointing to numbers in the margins. "They're recording settlement, but it's backwards. The tunnels aren't sinking. They're rising. Like something's pushing them up from below."

Mrs. Driscoll nods slowly, unsurprised. "The company abandoned the vaults in 1953. Said it was due to economic factors, the decline of ore production. But the last entries in this ledger tell a different story."

Vincent finds the final pages, where the neat construction notes give way to increasingly frantic scrawls. "Walls breath-ing," one entry reads. "Johnson claims he saw faces in the clay. Mitchell won't go below anymore, says the tunnels hum at night." The last dated entry, December 5, 1953, contains only one line: "The land resists."

Vincent sees a note scrawled in the margin, undated and in different ink. The handwriting looks fresher, maybe from the 1970s, and it says: "They built the school on top of it. God help them, they built the school on top of it."

Owen straightens, and Vincent sees him processing this information like data points in an equation. "Sounds like they hit something alive," he says, his voice carrying the careful neutrality of scientific observation, but underneath Vincent hears the tremor of recognition.

Mira's finger stops on a page near the back, where someone has drawn not a map but something that looks almost like an anatomy diagram. Curved lines suggest something massive, something that exists in parts throughout the tunnel system. Her pulse quickens visibly in her throat, and when she speaks, her voice comes out as barely more than a whisper, but it fills the room like smoke.

"Or something that remembers."

The words hang in the air, and Vincent feels them settle into his bones like the cold that's been creeping through Duswood since the explosion. Because memory implies consciousness, and consciousness implies intent, and intent means that whatever lies beneath their town isn't just reacting to their presence. It's been waiting for something. Maybe waiting for them.

Vincent can see puddles in the parish parking lot through the stained-glass windows, and they shimmer with that faint red luminescence he's been noticing everywhere since the explosion, as if the construction lights from the damaged school site have somehow infected all standing water in Duswood. The color pulses gently, matching that deep rhythm he felt through his bedroom floor two nights ago.

Mrs. Driscoll walks back to the ledger's cabinet, but her movements have taken on a ceremonial quality, each gesture deliberate and weighted with meaning Vincent doesn't fully understand. She reaches for her ring of keys, and he notices how many there are, far more than a parish office should require. Some look ancient, their metal dark with age, their teeth worn smooth. Others appear newer but somewhat corrupted, as if they've been cut to fit locks that time forgot.

She selects one particular key, darkened brass, and fits it into the ledger's cabinet lock. The mechanism turns with a sound like grinding stone, though Vincent knows the lock was oiled recently because he can smell the WD-40 beneath the lemon polish and old paper. Mrs. Driscoll turns the key three times, not once, and with each revolution Vincent hears something deeper than mechanical tumblers falling into place. It sounds like roots breaking, or maybe roots taking hold. The cabinet is now sealed, locking the other ledgers in.

"We'll be closing early today," she says, though it's barely past three in the afternoon. Her hands move to the bank of light switches near the door, but she pauses, fingers hovering over the plastic toggles. Vincent watches her face shift through micro-expressions of decision before she swipes her hand down, extinguishing the electric lights.

"Electricity feels funny lately," Mrs. Driscoll says by way of explanation, though her tone suggests this explains nothing and everything. "Since the explosion. The current runs different. Makes the walls hum in frequencies I've never heard."

Owen has been packing his things, sliding his notebook into a backpack that's seen better days, coiling his earbuds with the careful precision of someone who's particular about wire management. He looks up at his grandmother's words, and Vincent sees understanding pass between them, the kind of shared knowledge that comes from living in a house together where both occupants have noticed things they don't discuss at dinner.

They move toward the door, Vincent carrying the weight of new knowledge that feels heavier than the ledger Mira has tucked into her bag. The book has left marks on the oak table, wet rings that form a pattern Vincent doesn't want to interpret. Mrs. Driscoll notices them too, running her finger along one curved water stain before pulling her hand back as if burned.

At the doorway, Owen calls out to them, abandoning his usual scientific detachment. "Hey. Text me if you find anything weird." He attempts a half-smile that doesn't quite hide the worry creasing his forehead. "Weirder, I mean. Than underground tunnels with breathing walls."

His fingers drum against his thigh in a nervous pattern, and Vincent recognizes it as the same rhythm they've all been feeling, that underground pulse that's been growing stronger since the explosion. Owen doesn't seem aware he's doing it, his body unconsciously synchronizing with something his mind is still trying to rationalize.

"We will," Mira says, and her voice carries that weight of certainty that makes promises feel like prophecies.

Vincent glances back at the parish building as they step into the mist that has gotten heavier to the point it feels like proper rain, and that's when he notices something that makes his neck prickle with recognition. The raindrops slide down the regular windows in normal patterns, racing each other to the sills in the chaotic way water always moves. But on the stained glass, it's different. The rain seems to avoid the colored panes, sliding around rather than over them, as if the glass itself repels water. Or as if the water recognizes something sacred and to be feared in those windows and chooses a different path.

The ledger in Mira's bag has a weight that seems to increase with each step they take toward the car. It's not just the water-logged paper and warped leather cover. It's the weight of documentation, of proof that what they've been feeling since the explosion has roots that go back decades. The town they thought they knew sits on top of something else, something that was here first and has been waiting with the patience of stone and root and deep earth.

They don't speak as they hurry to the car, but their eyes meet across the roof as they open their doors, and in that glance Vincent sees his own understanding reflected. They're carrying more than a ledger. They're carrying evidence of Duswood's true foundation, built not on solid ground but on something that breathes and dreams and remembers.

In the distance, toward the school site, the construction floodlights pulse once, a brief dimming and brightening that could be a power fluctuation. Could be. But Vincent knows better now. He's heard the rhythm at night, felt it in the tremor of the earth, seen it in the pulse of red light in standing water. The lights steady again, but the damage is done. He's seen it breathe.

The town itself is breathing.

As they drive away, the parish office recedes in the rearview mirror. The rain continues to fall, and every puddle they pass reflects that faint red shimmer, as if the very water is carrying messages from below. The ledger sits heavy between them on the center console, its damaged cover still damp to the touch, and Vincent can't shake the feeling that by taking it, by learning what it contains, they've started something that's been waiting decades to continue.

Evening settles over Duswood like sediment in still water, each layer of darkness heavier than the last, and the sidewalks outside Cedar Lagoon Pizzeria gleam with a slickness that isn't quite rain. Vincent watches through the front window as streetlamps flicker on in sequence down Kipling Avenue. The images in puddles waver but don't break, even when a car drives through, tires spraying water that falls back into perfect mirrors.

Inside the pizzeria, the air carries its familiar weight of flour dust and oregano, but tonight there's something else beneath it. Vincent tastes copper on his tongue when he breathes too deeply, the same metallic flavor that's been haunting the town since the school explosion. Joe moves behind the counter with practiced efficiency, pulling cash from the register with hands that have performed this ritual a thousand times. The bills whisper against each other as he counts, and Vincent notices how Joe pauses between twenties, his fingers hesitating as if the paper feels different tonight.

"Sixty, eighty, one hundred, ten," Joe mutters, rubber-banding the stack. His field jacket hangs on the hook by the kitchen door, still damp from the afternoon's mist that eventually turned into rain. "Grid's been acting up all week. Power company says it's the substations overloading from the construction equipment."

Vincent nods, though they both know the construction site has been lit only by the auxiliary lights for three days now, wrapped in yellow tape and silence. He moves to the prep counter, gathering the plastic containers of toppings to carry back to the walk-in cooler. The pepperoni glistens too brightly under the fluorescents, oil on its surface catching light in rainbow patterns that shift when he looks directly at them. He blinks, and the colors normalize, but the image lingers in his peripheral vision like an afterburn.

The cooler door opens with its familiar pneumatic wheeze, and cold air rushes out carrying the scent of cheese and vegetables and something underneath that Vincent can't name. It reminds him of the smell from the ledger at the parish office, that mineral dampness that speaks of things buried too long. He slides the containers onto their designated shelves, noting how his breath fogs more densely than the temperature warrants. The condensation on the metal shelving has formed patterns, delicate fractals of ice that look almost like writing in a language he doesn't recognize.

"You coming down with something?" Joe's voice carries from the dining room where he's wiping down tables. "You've been standing in that cooler for five minutes."

Vincent realizes he's been staring at the ice patterns, trying to parse meaning from their crystalline geometry. He backs out, letting the door seal with a soft thump, and returns to find Joe spraying the red vinyl booth seats with cleaner that smells sharp enough to cut through the copper taste in the air.

"Just tired," Vincent says, though tired isn't the right word for the electric current he feels running beneath his skin, the sense that his nerves are tuned to a frequency that wasn't there before.

They work in companionable silence, Vincent pushing the

mop bucket across black and white checkered tiles while Joe counts down the register. The soda machine hums its constant note, punctuated by the occasional shift and fall of ice in its reservoir. These sounds are as familiar as his own heartbeat, the soundtrack of working evenings here, saving money and finding something like peace in the routine.

Then the lights flicker.

Not a quick blink but a long, slow dimming that makes the shadows stretch and breathe. The refrigerator compressor stutters, stops, starts again with a grinding sound Vincent has never heard before. For three seconds, maybe four, the pizzeria exists in a twilight state where the neon OPEN sign provides the only steady light, casting everything in arterial red.

The power returns with a surge that makes the fluorescents buzz angrily overhead. Joe doesn't look up from the register.

"Substations," he says again, but his jaw tightens the way it does when he's choosing not to acknowledge something.

Vincent wrings the mop, watching gray water spiral down the drain. The water sloshes and circles down as he thinks about the diagrams in the ledger, those spiraling tunnels that seemed to follow their own logic north Duswood. He forces himself to look away, to focus on the simple task of cleaning floors that will be dirty again tomorrow.

Outside, fog has begun to creep along the street, but it's not moving the way fog should. Instead of rolling in from the lake or settling in the low places, it rises from the storm drains in thin columns that twist and merge at shoulder height. Vincent watches through the window as the street-lamps become isolated islands of light in an ocean of gray. A couple hurries past, hunched against air that shouldn't require hunching, and their footsteps echo too long after they've passed from view.

"Leave the trash," Joe says, though taking out trash is always the last task. "I'll get it in the morning."

Vincent understands the subtext: Joe doesn't want him walking to the dumpster out back, not with the fog moving like something aware. He peels off his apron, hangs it on its designated hook, and notices his hands are trembling slightly. Not from fear exactly, but from that electric charge in the air that makes his skin feel too tight, too sensitive to invisible currents.

The thermometer by the door reads sixty-eight degrees, unseasonably warm for April 2nd, but Vincent's breath still fogs when he exhales. The moisture hangs in the air longer than it should, forming shapes that almost resolve into meaning before dissipating. Joe clicks off the lights in sequence, each switch accompanied by a small spark that's brighter than normal, blue-white and sharp.

They stand at the door, looking out at the transformed street. The fog has thickened to the point where the building across the way exists only as a vague suggestion of brick and shadow. Somewhere in that gray mass, a dog barks once, then cuts off abruptly, as if remembering that making noise might not be wise tonight.

"You need a ride home?" Joe asks, his hand on the door handle but not turning it yet.

"I can walk," Vincent says, though the span of blocks to his house seem like a vast distance through whatever the fog has become.

Joe nods slowly, his fingers drumming that underground rhythm against the door frame. Vincent wonders if Joe feels it too, that pulse rising from below, or if his body has simply learned the beat through proximity.

The door opens with a soft chime, and the fog immediately reaches for them with tendrils that feel almost solid, almost purposeful. The air outside carries more than moisture; it holds that same electric charge Vincent's been feeling all evening, strong enough now to raise the hair on his arms. His shoes splash through puddles that weren't there when he arrived for his shift, water that reflects not the streetlamps above but something deeper, something red and pulsing far below the surface.

Cedar Lagoon Pizzeria's neon sign clicks off behind them, the second to last OPEN sign on the street going dark, and Vincent thinks about the tunnels, about breathing walls and roots that grow through metal, about Mrs. Driscoll's fear of electric current. The fog swallows Joe's truck as he drives away, taillights visible for only a moment before the gray claims them.

Vincent turns toward home, toward streets he's walked a thousand times but which feel foreign now, transformed by fog and that electric potential that makes the air itself feel conscious. His breath continues to fog despite the warmth, each exhalation a small ghost that the larger fog eagerly absorbs. He walks through air that tastes of copper and stone and something anciently patient.

He begins walking down Kipling Avenue, and the fog closes behind him like water, like earth, like something that's been waiting to embrace him all along.

The Porchlight Café appears through the fog like something remembered rather than seen, its windows glowing amber against the gray weight of evening, and Vincent stops on the sidewalk outside, drawn by the warmth that seems impossible after the electric cold of the streets. Steam clouds the glass from inside, turning the figures within into watercolor suggestions of people, but he recognizes Mira immediately by the way she tilts her head when she laughs, that particular angle that makes her dark hair fall across one shoulder.

The fog presses against his back like something eager to move him along, but Vincent stays rooted to the wet sidewalk, watching through the steamed glass. Inside, the café exists in its own pocket of normalcy, untouched by the strange electricity that charges the air outside. The espresso machine hisses its familiar rhythm, and he can hear the faint jazz that always plays here, Duke Ellington or something close, the notes muffled but still sweet through the door's imperfect seal.

Mira sits at the corner table, the one with the wobbly leg that requires a folded napkin for balance. June Everhart sits across from her, that dinged-up camera she carries everywhere resting beside two cups that send up parallel columns of steam. June's copper-blonde hair catches the café's warm light as she gestures at something, her hands painting shapes in the air that make Mira laugh again. The sound doesn't quite penetrate the glass, but Vincent knows it anyway, has memorized its particular music and kept it in his heart.

Owen Driscoll occupies a nearby booth, hunched over a small notebook with the same intensity he brought to the parish records. His pencil moves in quick, precise strokes, and every few seconds he glances up at the girls, then back to his page. Not drawing them, Vincent realizes, but drawing something they're describing. His other hand rests flat on the table, fingers spread like he's feeling for vibrations through the wood.

The tableau they create feels almost staged in its perfection: three teenagers hanging out in a coffee shop, sharing stories while the world outside dissolves into fog and the dark night. June lifts her camera, aims it at Mira, and the flash illuminates the steam between them like frozen breath. Mira doesn't flinch from the light but leans into it, her amber-gray eyes catching the flash and holding it a moment too long, the way cat eyes hold light in darkness.

Vincent's hand finds the door handle, the metal shockingly cold even through the ambient warmth that radiates from inside. Through the glass, he watches June show Mira something on the camera's display screen, probably the photo she just took. Mira studies it with an expression Vincent can't read, something between recognition and surprise, as if she's seeing herself for the first time.

Then she looks up and slightly turns her head. Her face wears an inquisitive grin. As if she's heard something that wasn't spoken.

Her face brightens with genuine pleasure, and then she continues listening to June's story. Her lips move and June turns towards Owen who pauses mid-sketch. June offers a small wave, and Owen nods in that careful way he has, acknowledging presence without committing to opinion. He's apparently content on listening to the conversation without wanting to be a part of it.

Vincent's fingers tighten on the handle, but something makes him pause. Maybe it's the way the fog seems to recoil from the door, pulling back like something burned. Maybe it's the copper taste that intensifies on his tongue, sharp enough now to make him want to spit. Or maybe it's the reflection in the door's glass, the way it shows the café's interior but also shows the street behind him, and how those two images don't quite align with reality.

In the reflection, he can see himself, pale and fog-dampened, standing at the threshold. He can see the café's interior, warm and inviting, with Mira still listening to June at their table. But he can also see the street behind him, and there's someone standing there, directly across from the café, beneath the streetlamp that flickers between orange and something colder.

It's Mira.

Not a trick of the glass, not his imagination painting her face on a stranger. It's Mira, complete and perfect and impossible, standing in the fog with her dark hair hanging wet against her green jacket, the same jacket she's wearing inside the café. She stands perfectly still, arms at her sides, watching him with those amber-gray eyes that don't blink, don't shift, don't acknowledge anything except his presence.

Vincent's breath stops in his throat. His eyes flick between the Mira inside, animated and warm, actively conversing with June, and the Mira outside, static as a photograph, observing him with the patience of stone. Both are equally real, equally present. Inside, Mira laughs at something Owen says, her hand reaching for her coffee cup. Outside, Mira doesn't move except for the barely perceptible rise and fall of her chest, breathing in rhythm with something Vincent can feel through the sidewalk under his feet. Vincent's hand falls away from the door handle.

Inside, the warm Mira's expression loses its glow that was there a minute ago. She shifts in her chair and Vincent takes a step back. The outside Mira doesn't move, doesn't react, just continues her perfect stillness. The fog between them thickens, and for a moment both Miras exist in Vincent's vision simultaneously, superimposed like a double exposure.

Then he blinks, and the outside Mira is gone.

Not walking away, not fading into fog. Simply absent, as if she was never there at all. The streetlamp burns steady now, illuminating nothing but empty sidewalk where she stood. A puddle remains, perfectly circular, reflecting deep red light that has become common now in Duswood.

Through the door's glass, the inside Mira rises from her chair. She leans across the table toward June, examining something on the camera's display. The steam from their cups mingles between them, creating a momentary veil that distorts their features. Vincent's fingers leave patterns on the handle that fade almost immediately in the ambient warmth. Outside, a car passes, its headlights cutting through the fog and briefly illuminating a puddle near his feet.

Vincent backs away from the door, his shoes splashing through puddles that weren't there moments ago. The fog welcomes him back, wrapping around him with something almost like comfort. Behind him, the café's warmth recedes, its amber light swallowed by gray. He doesn't look back, doesn't want to see if Mira still laughs with June, doesn't want to know if she's inside or outside or both.

He walks through fog that tastes of childhood playgrounds and carries the electric potential of storms. His mind tries to process what he saw, he's been aware of her bilocation and she seems to be in control of it more now. But deeper than thought, in the same place that feels the underground rhythm through Duswood's streets, Vincent understands that it isn't a random occurrence.

It was practice.

Mira is learning to be in more than one place, testing the boundaries of what she's becoming. And somewhere in the fog, in the spaces between where she is and where she appears to be, something vast and patient takes note of her progress.

———

The kitchen light spills into the hallway as Vincent closes the front door behind him, and through the archway he can already see Mira at the sink, her hands submerged in water that catches the overhead fluorescence like liquid glass. She stands with her back to him, sleeves rolled past her elbows, working a sponge across the surface of a plate in slow, methodical circles. Elias stands beside her with a dish towel, accepting each clean dish with the careful precision he brings to everything, as if dropping a plate might fracture more than ceramic.

The impossibility of her presence here stops Vincent at the threshold. He looks at her with a playfully suspicious eye. The walk from the café took him five minutes through fog-thick streets. Even if she'd left immediately after he backed away from the door, even if she'd run, she couldn't have arrived before him. Yet here she stands, hair dry, clothes unmarked by the night, as if she's been washing dishes for an hour. Which Mira is this? He considers she might be using her gift as a means to teleport.

"Vincent," she says without turning, her words spoken as if underwater. "You're home."

The kitchen smells of green apple dish soap and something else, something earthen and alive that seems to emanate from the water itself. Vincent watches the soap bubbles catch and hold the light, each one a tiny prism that splits white into component colors he doesn't remember seeing in bubbles before. They rise from the sink in lazy spirals, taking too long to pop, hanging in the air like questions.

"June showed me some old photos of the swamp," Mira says, her hands never stopping their circular motion on the plate. "From before the development, when it was just cedar and water. You should've come in."

The casual nature of the statement strangely enough relaxes Vincent. She speaks as if their encounter at the café was normal, as if she wasn't simultaneously there and not there, as if her presence in two places at once was no stranger than choosing between coffee or tea.

Elias glances between them, and Vincent sees the concern written in the careful way he dries each dish, the deliberate attention that keeps him from having to acknowledge what floats unspoken in the kitchen air. His shoulders carry a tension that's become permanent since the explosion, since the world started revealing its hidden nature again. He sets a dried plate in the cabinet with the same precision he must use placing temporary crowns, aware that one wrong move might cause collapse.

"The power went out twice while you were gone," Elias says, his voice maintaining that clinical distance he uses to avoid feeling things too deeply. "Only for seconds. The lights came back different."

Vincent understands what he means. The fluorescent overhead doesn't buzz quite right anymore, its frequency shifted just enough to be noticeable without being nameable. It makes shadows that fall at angles that seem wrong for the light source, as if the room exists in two slightly different versions of itself, superimposed but not quite aligned.

Mira pulls the drain plug, and the water spirals down with a sound like distant thunder. She dries her hands on the towel Elias offers, her movements unhurried, deliberate. When she turns to face Vincent, her amber-gray eyes hold that quality they've developed since Marrowick, seeing him but also seeing through him to something beyond.

"We should talk," she says, and it's not a question.

They climb the stairs together, leaving Elias to his careful arrangement of dishes. The hallway is dim, the only light coming from below, and their footsteps are soft against the worn carpet. They pass Vincent's room first, the door half-closed and shadowed, then Danny's room, the soft glow of an animated show coming from his TV. Mira takes Vincent's hand, familiar and sure, and he is content to follow her lead. When she pauses at her own bedroom door, he feels the quiet invitation in her posture.

Her bedroom door opens on hinges that don't creak anymore, though Vincent remembers them creaking last week. Inside, a single lamp casts amber light across walls that hold the ghost shadows of posters recently removed. The space feels transitional, caught between the teenager's room it was and whatever it's becoming. Rain has started again, tracing silver lines down the window glass that catch the lamplight and throw it back in patterns that remind Vincent of the ice formations in the pizzeria's cooler.

They sit on her bed, backs against the wall, shoulders touching but not quite. The contact point between them feels electric, not uncomfortable but charged with potential, as if current could flow between them given the right conditions.

The rain intensifies, drumming against the roof with enough force to create a white noise that swallows smaller sounds.

"June's photos," Mira says, her voice soft enough that Vincent has to lean closer to hear. "They show things that aren't there when you look directly. Shadows that don't match the objects casting them. Reflections in water that show skies we don't have."

"We graduate in two months," he says, the mundane future feeling both impossible and inevitable. "I keep thinking about the caps and the gowns and the speeches about new beginnings. People acting like it means something's ending, like we get to choose a next chapter. But it doesn't feel like that. Not for us. It just feels like... whatever's waiting, it's already started. So what are we supposed to do? Pretend we're still just students, or start acting like we're not? Then what?"

"Then we become what we're becoming anyway," Mira answers, and her hand finds his, fingers interlacing with the ease of long practice. Her skin feels cooler than it should, but not unpleasantly so.

They talk about smaller things for a while, letting the larger questions circle unspoken. About Owen's maps and his growing obsession with the tunnel patterns. About Joe's quiet vigilance, the way he watches the fog like a soldier expecting ambush. About the town's collective pretense that gas leaks and power fluctuations explain what everyone feels in their bones: that Duswood exists on top of something that's waking up.

"I keep thinking," Mira says eventually, her head finding its familiar rest against Vincent's shoulder, "what if we're not on top of something? What if we're inside it, and we just don't know it yet? Like we're already swallowed, already digested, and what we think is living is just the dream of whatever ate us?"

The thought should terrify him, but Vincent finds an odd

comfort in it. If they're already consumed, then the fear of consumption becomes pointless. If they're already transformed, then resistance is just denial of what they've become.

Through the rain-streaked window, their reflection wavers on the glass. Two teenagers sitting on a bed, haloed by amber light, ordinary in every way except for how the reflection holds for a moment after they move, except for how it seems to expand slightly with each breath, as if the image itself is learning to breathe.

"Maybe that's not wrong," Vincent says, watching their reflection pulse with subtle life. "Maybe we've always been inside something. Maybe Duswood was never separate from what's below it."

Mira's hand tightens in his, and he feels that current flow between them, not electricity but something older, something that moves through root and stone and the spaces between what's real and what's possible. The rain continues, and their reflection continues its subtle breathing, and somewhere beneath the house, beneath the street, beneath the whole of Duswood, that patient rhythm continues its rise toward the surface.

"I can feel it all the time now," Mira whispers, and Vincent doesn't need to ask what she means. "Like there's no difference between me and it anymore. Like boundaries are just things we invented to feel separate."

Vincent turns to respond, but stops when he sees their reflection again. For just a moment, brief as a blink, there are three figures in the glass: himself, Mira beside him, and Mira also standing by the lamp, watching with eyes that hold too much patience for anything human. Then the image settles back to normal, just two teenagers in lamplight, holding hands against whatever their town is becoming…or what it's always been.

CHAPTER
FIVE

The third morning after the explosion brings no sun to Duswood, only a gray weight of clouds that press down on the construction site like a palm against fevered skin. Vincent rides in Joe's truck through streets still slick from pre-dawn rain, pizza boxes stacked between them releasing steam that fogs the windshield from inside. The smell of melted cheese and breakfast sausage mingles with diesel exhaust as they turn onto the access road where yellow tape flutters against chain-link fence like trapped birds trying to escape.

Joe parks beside a cluster of work trucks, their beds loaded with shovels and wheelbarrows that gleam wet in the diffused light. Through the fence, Vincent can see Hale Ness directing three men in reflective vests, their movements careful as they navigate the churned earth. The crater itself yawns fifty feet away, its edges crumbling inward where rain has softened the soil. Water pools at its bottom, dark and still, reflecting nothing.

"Grab the coffee," Joe says, already hefting pizza boxes from the truck. His field jacket bears new stains from the past few days, rust-colored marks that won't wash out no matter how hard he scrubs them. Vincent takes the two thermoses, their weight familiar from other of similar deliveries to work sites, though never to one that looks like this.

The gate stands open, its lock unlocked and dangling from the chain. Vincent follows Joe through, their boots squelching in mud that clings with unusual persistence. The ground here doesn't feel solid; it gives too much with each step, as if the earth beneath has gone soft all the way down. Hale looks up from where he's examining a twisted piece of rebar, his expression shifting from concentration to something like relief.

"Thought you might need fuel," Joe calls out, setting the boxes on a relatively dry patch of plywood someone has laid across two sawhorses.

"Been here since five," Hale says, pulling off work gloves that are already black with whatever coats everything here. "Insurance company wants preliminary cleanup before their inspectors arrive tomorrow. Like we can make this look normal."

The other workers gather around the makeshift table, accepting paper plates and coffee with mumbled thanks. Vincent recognizes two of them from around town: Murphy who runs the hardware store, and a younger man whose name he doesn't know but who sometimes drinks at the Porchlight. Their faces wear the same expression, a careful blankness that suggests they're trying not to think too hard about what they're doing.

Vincent pours coffee while Joe distributes slices, the ordinary ritual feeling like a ward against the absurdity of the place. Steam rises from the cups, and for a moment the workers stand in a loose circle, eating in silence while the construction site sprawls around them like something diseased. The temporary trailers, those that didn't burn, list at odd angles where the ground has subsided beneath their supports. One has a hole punched through its side, edges melted and re-solidified.

"You helping or just delivering?" Hale asks, though his tone suggests he already knows the answer.

Joe nods toward a trailer being used for debris collection. "Got time before the lunch prep. Point us where you need bodies."

Hale hands them each a shovel from the truck bed, the metal cold even through work gloves Vincent pulls from his jacket pocket. They follow him toward the fence line, where twisted chunks of asphalt lay scattered like broken teeth. The explosion threw them here with enough force to embed some pieces inches deep in the earth. As they walk, Vincent notices something that makes his steps falter.

The ground is seamed with red.

Not everywhere, not in obvious patterns, but in thin veins that web through the dark soil like capillaries. They catch what little light filters through the clouds, gleaming with a wet sheen that doesn't match the surrounding mud. Vincent's shovel blade cuts through one as he begins working, and the severed ends weep something viscous and warm that immediately soaks back into the earth.

"Don't touch it directly," Hale says without looking up from his own work. "Whatever it is, it stains. Murphy got some on his hand earlier and it won't wash off."

Vincent glances at Murphy, who's working twenty feet away. The man's right palm bears a rust-colored mark that looks almost like a burn, though he handles his shovel without apparent pain. The mark seems to pulse faintly, or maybe that's just Vincent's eyes playing tricks in the gray light.

They work in rhythm, the scrape of shovels against asphalt and earth creating a percussion that almost masks the other sounds: the distant hum of morning traffic on Kipling Avenue, the drip of water from damaged gutters, and underneath it all, something else. Vincent doesn't recognize it at first, mistakes it for his own pulse echoing in his ears. But when he pauses to wipe sweat from his forehead, the sound continues, a low thrumming that comes from below rather than around.

Joe stops shoveling, his posture shifting to that alertness Vincent remembers from stories about his military days. He moves toward the fence line where the red veining grows more pronounced, the lines thicker and more numerous. Here they branch and merge in patterns that suggest intention rather than random geological formation. Joe squats beside a particularly vivid patch, where the red threads converge into something almost like a node, a knot of glowing tissue embedded in the soil.

His weathered fingers hover over the surface, not quite touching. "It's warm," he says, voice carrying that measured tone he uses when something demands careful attention. "Ground should be cold after all this rain."

He pulls a work glove off and holds his palm an inch above the node. Vincent watches Joe's expression shift from curiosity to concern as he lowers his hand closer. The air between skin and soil shimmers slightly, the way it does above hot asphalt in summer, though the morning carries a damp chill that makes Vincent's breath visible.

"Sap burns when it's dry," Joe says, more to himself than anyone else, "but this warmth's coming from below." His brow furrows as he tests the heat with his palm, careful not to make actual contact. "Deep below."

Across the street, movement catches Vincent's eye. Mira stands beneath the dripping eaves of what used to be a flower shop, closed since the previous winter. Beside her, June Ever-hart raises her camera, adjusting the lens with quick, practiced movements. They're far enough away that Vincent can't make out their expressions, but something in Mira's posture, the absolute stillness of her stance, tells him she's aware of more than just the visual scene.

June's camera clicks repeatedly, the sound carrying across the empty street. She's shooting through the chain-link fence, and Vincent realizes she's focused on the red veining, on Joe's careful examination, on the way the ground seems to pulse with its own circulation. Her copper-blonde hair catches what little light exists, but it's Mira who seems to glow faintly in the shadows of the eave, as if she's gathering light from somewhere else.

Hale approaches Joe's position, his boots crushing smaller red veins that immediately begin seeping back together behind him. "State inspector called this morning," he says. "Wants to know if we've found any gas line markers, any sign of what fed the explosion."

"This isn't gas," Joe says, standing slowly. His knees pop with the movement, but his attention remains fixed on the ground. "Gas doesn't grow."

The word hangs in the air, acknowledging what they've all been avoiding. These veins aren't deposits or chemical reactions. They're growing, spreading through the soil with purpose, reaching toward something or away from something else. Vincent thinks of the ledger in Mira's bag, the mentions of breathing walls and organic interference, and wonders if this is what those long-dead workers encountered in the tunnels below.

One of the workers, the young man Vincent doesn't know, backs away from his section of debris. His shovel drops from his hands, clattering against a chunk of asphalt. "It's moving," he says, voice tight with controlled panic. "The red stuff. It's moving."

They all turn to look where he's pointing. At first, Vincent sees nothing unusual, just the same web of red veins they've been working around all morning. Then his eyes adjust, or maybe the veins become more active, and he sees it too. A slow, peristaltic motion, like watching blood move through vessels in slow motion. The veins pulse in sequence, drawing something up from deep below or pumping something down, Vincent can't tell which.

Across the street, June continues photographing, her camera capturing each pulse of the veins. Beside her, Mira hasn't moved except to tilt her head slightly, as if listening to something only she can hear. The morning light, such as it is, seems to bend around her, creating a pocket of clarity in the gray morning.

"It's moving," June whispers, though Vincent shouldn't be able to hear her from this distance. The words carry anyway, threading through the chain-link fence and across the muddy ground to where he stands.

Mira responds with a single nod, her stillness a stark contrast to June's restless documentation. Her amber-gray eyes remain fixed on something beyond the visible scene, seeing patterns the rest of them can only glimpse. The ground between them thrums with that underground pulse, connecting the construction site to the street to the closed shops to the whole of Duswood above and below.

Hale moves toward a section of ground near the collapsed trailer, where rainwater has pooled in depressions. His shovel rises and falls in practiced rhythm, each bite into the earth measured and efficient. Vincent watches him work, noting how the man's shoulders carry a different tension now, no longer the casual wariness of dangerous construction but something deeper, more primitive. The kind of tension prey animals carry when they sense predators but can't see them.

The shovel blade descends into a patch of mud darker than the rest, almost black in the gray morning light. It should sink easily into the waterlogged soil, should slice through with the wet sound of earth parting. Instead, it stops abruptly, the handle jarring in Hale's grip. The mud around the blade doesn't behave like mud at all. It quivers, contracts, pulls back from the metal intrusion like muscle beneath skin.

Hale freezes mid-motion. His hands maintain a firm grip on the shovel handle, but he doesn't push down or pull back. He stands absolutely still, and Vincent can see him processing what he's just felt, his mind trying to reconcile the sensation with anything that makes sense. The mud continues to quiver around the blade, little tremors that radiate outward in patterns that look almost like breathing.

Then Hale straightens his back with deliberate slowness, drawing the shovel out with the same careful motion someone might use to extract a knife from a wound. The mud releases it with a wet, sucking sound. Where the blade emerged, the ground immediately seals itself, the depression filling in as if it was never there.

"We're done here," Hale mutters, voice flat but final. He doesn't raise his voice, doesn't shout or panic. He simply states it as fact, the way someone might announce that rain is coming or that the workday has ended. But underneath that flat tone, Vincent hears something else: the kind of certainty that comes from recognizing danger that can't be reasoned with or worked around.

No one argues. No one asks questions. The young worker who dropped his shovel earlier is already moving toward the trucks, his steps quick but controlled. Murphy sets down his wheelbarrow with exaggerated care, as if sudden movements might wake something. The third worker, whose name Vincent still doesn't know, begins gathering tools.

Vincent finds himself helping without conscious decision, his hands collecting shovels and depositing them in truck beds. The metal tools clang against each other, the sound sharp in the morning air, and everyone winces at each impact. Joe moves alongside him, and Vincent notices how the older man's eyes keep scanning the ground, watching for movement, for changes, for signs of whatever lies beneath deciding to surface.

The cleanup becomes a retreat disguised as organization. They load equipment with the kind of focused intensity that speaks of suppressed fear, the way people move when they're trying very hard not to run. Hale directs the loading with terse gestures, ensuring nothing important gets left behind, but Vincent can see him counting seconds in his head, measuring how long they can maintain this pretense of calm before someone breaks.

That's when the humming begins.

At first, Vincent mistakes it for machinery, some piece of equipment left running in one of the damaged trailers. It's low, steady, almost below the range of hearing, felt more than heard. It travels up through his boots, through the bones of his legs, resting in his chest where it creates a counter-rhythm to his heartbeat. The sensation is neither painful nor pleasant, just unsettling, like swallowing water that's the wrong temperature.

Joe moves to the generator with swift purpose, the only piece of equipment still running. It powers work lights that aren't even on in the gray morning, but protocol demands it run during work hours. His hand finds the kill switch, and the generator coughs once, twice, then dies. The sudden absence of its familiar rumble should bring quiet.

The humming continues uninterrupted.

If anything, it grows clearer without the generator's noise to mask it. The sound doesn't come from any single source but rises from everywhere at once, from the ground itself like ice cracking on the expanse of a lake, as if the earth beneath the construction site has developed its own frequency. Vincent watches Joe's expression shift from confusion to understanding to something approaching fear, though Joe would never name it that.

"Everyone in the trucks," Hale says, still maintaining that forced calm, but his voice carries new urgency. "Now."

The chain-link fence begins to tremble. Not shaking like it would in wind, but vibrating in place, each metal link clicking against its neighbors in a rhythm that matches the underground hum. The sound builds, dozens of tiny metal impacts creating a percussion that sounds almost like music, if music could be made of warning. The fence posts, sunk deep in concrete, transfer the vibration to the ground around them, creating little circles of disturbance in the mud where puddles ripple outward in perfect rings.

Vincent looks toward Mira and June, still watching from across the street. The vibration must reach them too, because June lowers her camera, her expression shifting from fascination to concern. But Mira remains still, and in that stillness, Vincent sees something in her. She's not surprised. She's not afraid. She's listening with the attention of someone hearing a familiar voice calling from very far away.

The workers pile into trucks with barely controlled haste. Doors slam, engines start, and Vincent feels the vibration change, disrupted by the rumble of diesel engines. But it doesn't stop. It adapts, finds spaces between the mechanical noise, threading through like water finding cracks. Murphy's truck pulls away first, tires spinning briefly in the mud before finding purchase. The young worker follows, his vehicle fishtailing slightly as he accelerates too quickly toward the gate.

Hale does a final visual sweep of the site, his eyes cataloging what they're leaving behind: wheelbarrows, some smaller tools, a cooler someone brought and forgot. His jaw works like he's chewing on words he won't let escape. Then he climbs into his truck, the door closing with finality.

"Time to go," Joe says, but he doesn't move immediately toward his truck. Instead, he stands perfectly still, head tilted slightly, listening to something Vincent can't quite hear. Or maybe he can hear it but his mind refuses to process it: beneath the hum, beneath the fence's metallic percussion, something else. A sound like breathing, but too big, too deep, coming from somewhere that shouldn't have lungs.

They walk to Joe's truck with measured steps, not running but not dawdling either. The ground squishes beneath their boots, and Vincent notices the red veins have spread since they arrived, creating a network that extends beyond the fence line, disappearing beneath the street, beneath the closed shops, beneath all of Duswood. He wonders how far they go, how deep, whether they're spreading or whether they've always been there, waiting for the right conditions to become visible.

Joe starts the engine, and they pull away from the construction site. Through the rear window, Vincent watches the abandoned site recede. The yellow tape continues its trapped-bird flutter against the fence, which still trembles in its mysterious rhythm. The crater sits at the center, its dark water reflecting nothing but gray sky.

As they turn onto Kipling Avenue, Vincent glances back one more time. The site looks almost peaceful from this distance, just another failed construction project in a town full of abandoned ambitions. But he can still feel the vibration through the truck's frame, transmitted through rubber tires, through asphalt, through layers of earth and stone from whatever moves beneath.

The last thing he sees before they round the corner is the puddles scattered across the lot. They're settling now that no one disturbs them, the ripples from footsteps and vehicle tracks gradually fading. But they don't settle the way water should, with smaller and smaller ripples until stillness. Instead, they stop all at once, every puddle going perfectly still at the exact same moment, surfaces flat as glass.

Too still. The kind of stillness that comes before something breaches from below. The kind of stillness that isn't peace but preparation, not rest but the pause before action. The puddles wait, dark mirrors reflecting gray nothing, and beneath them, beneath the mud and the red veins and the damaged earth, something vast and patient draws in breath.

CHAPTER
SIX

Morning frost turns the construction site into something almost beautiful, each twisted piece of metal wearing a skin of ice that catches what little sunlight penetrates the clouds, and Vincent helps Joe unload equipment from the truck while three figures in reflective vests move through the wreckage like priests performing last rites over something they refuse to name. The state inspectors from Lansing arrived twenty minutes ago in a government sedan that still idles at the gate, exhaust mixing with ground fog that clings to the fence line despite the hour.

Vincent pulls work gloves from his jacket, the leather stiff with cold and yesterday's mud. The site looks different now, sanitized by frost that covers the disturbed earth like bandaging over a wound. No trace remains of the red veining that pulsed through the soil yesterday. The ground presents itself as innocent clay and construction debris, frozen into stillness that feels more like held breath than peace.

Sheriff Brennan stands beside the inspectors, his uniform pressed sharp despite the mud caking his boots. He gestures at the crater with one hand while the other stays planted on his hip, near his service weapon. His voice carries across the lot, each word precise and hollow.

"The initial assessment suggests a localized ignition event," Brennan says, and Vincent watches how his mouth shapes the words like they taste sour. "Underground gas pocket, likely disturbed by the construction activities. Natural accumulation over decades, possibly centuries."

One inspector, a woman with steel-gray hair pulled into a bun so tight it stretches her features, makes notes on her clipboard without looking at what Brennan indicates. Her pen moves in neat lines across the paper, recording words that will become truth simply by being written in an official report. The two men flanking her nod at appropriate intervals, their faces carrying the practiced neutrality of people who've learned not to see things that complicate paperwork.

Hale Ness stands thirty feet away at the fence perimeter, arms crossed over his chest. His work jacket bears new stains from this morning's preliminary cleanup, and his eyes track the inspectors with the wariness of someone watching a magic trick where the deception is obvious but pointing it out would ruin everything. He doesn't speak, doesn't move except to shift his weight when the frozen ground makes his feet ache. His presence feels like testimony without words, a silent record of what really happened here.

Joe hands Vincent a pry bar, and they move toward a section of twisted trailer siding that needs to be broken down for the dumpster. The metal resists at first, welded by heat into shapes that shouldn't be possible from a simple gas explosion. Vincent works the bar beneath an edge, feeling how the metal has been transformed at a molecular level, made into something between solid and liquid and frozen in that impossible state.

"Safety protocols were followed to the letter," Brennan continues, his voice rising slightly as if volume might make the words more believable. "The evacuation was swift and orderly. No serious injuries reported."

The female inspector moves closer to the crater, her polished shoes incongruous against the churned earth. She pulls a thin metal probe from her equipment case, the kind used to test soil density and composition. Her movements are efficient, professional, the actions of someone who's done this hundreds of times at hundreds of sites that were exactly what they appeared to be.

She selects a spot ten feet from the crater's edge, where the ground looks undisturbed beneath its frost coating. The probe slides in easily for the first six inches, then meets resistance. She adjusts her grip, prepares to push harder, and that's when Vincent notices the frost beginning to melt in a perfect circle around the probe's entry point.

The detection device clipped to her belt chirps once, a sharp electronic sound that cuts through the morning air. The display flashes numbers that Vincent can't read from his distance, but he sees her eyebrows draw together slightly. She pushes the probe another inch deeper.

The device dies.

Not a gradual power-down or a fritzing of circuits. Complete electronic death, the screen going black, the small LED indicator lights extinguishing simultaneously. A thin curl of steam rises from the hole left by the probe, delicate as breath but carrying an acrid scent. Metal and earth and something else, something organic that's been heated past the point of recognition.

The inspector withdraws the probe in a smooth motion. She glances at the dead device, shakes it once as if it might be a loose battery connection, then clips it back to her belt. Her foot moves to cover the hole, and she scrapes clay from her shoe against a chunk of concrete, the gesture casual, automatic, as if she's simply cleaning her shoes rather than concealing evidence.

No one speaks. Brennan's explanation has paused mid-sentence, his mouth slightly open as if he's forgotten what comes next. The other two inspectors continue making notes, their pens moving across paper with the same automatic motion, recording nothing about the probe, the dead device, the steam that still rises faintly despite the inspector's attempt to cover its source.

Joe's hands never stop working, but Vincent feels the older man's attention sharpen, cataloging everything while appearing to focus only on the twisted metal they're dismantling. The pry bar bites deeper into the trailer siding, and the sound it makes, metal screaming against metal, provides cover for the silence that wants to acknowledge what just happened.

The inspectors converge near their sedan, comparing notes that will match perfectly because they've agreed without speaking what story they'll tell. The woman tucks her clipboard under her arm, and Vincent catches a glimpse of the top sheet. Neat boxes checked, standardized phrases about structural integrity and gas line infrastructure. Nothing about electronic devices dying on contact with the soil. Nothing about steam that smells like heated metal and decay.

"We'll have our initial report filed within forty-eight hours," the woman says to Brennan, her voice carrying the kind of authority that makes lies into policy. "I don't anticipate any complications with the reconstruction timeline."

Brennan nods, but Vincent notices how he shifts his weight from foot to foot, a nervous gesture that wasn't there before the steam rose from the ground. His hand moves to his radio, fingers drumming against its case in a rhythm that Vincent recognizes. It's the same pulse they all feel now, the underground heartbeat that's been growing stronger since the explosion. Brennan doesn't seem aware he's doing it, his body responding to a frequency his mind refuses to acknowledge.

The inspectors climb into their sedan, doors closing as

though the case has already been sealed. Through the windshield, Vincent watches them remove their reflective vests, transforming back into ordinary people who will drive back to Lansing and file reports that explain everything while explaining nothing. The sedan pulls away, tires crackling over the frozen ground, leaving tracks that will melt within the hour as the earth beneath continues its slow, patient warming.

————

The kitchen table bears the remnants of Vincent's homework, calculus problems abandoned in favor of his phone screen where the Duswood Press website loads in stuttering increments, the economy server struggling as half the town presumably seeks the same comfortable lies he's about to read. Evening light slants through the window, colored amber by the setting sun filtered through whatever still hangs in the air from the explosion, turning the familiar kitchen into something that belongs to a different house, a different life.

The headline appears first, bold black letters against the newspaper's simple web design: "State Inspectors Confirm Gas Main Rupture at School Site." Below it, a photo of the construction site from this morning, carefully angled to show only the administrative trailer that survived intact, not the crater or the warped metal or the ground that refused to behave like ground should. Vincent scrolls with his thumb, the gesture automatic, though part of him doesn't want to read what comes next.

The article unfolds in measured paragraphs of official language. "Following comprehensive assessment by state infrastructure inspectors, the disturbance at Duswood High School's construction site has been identified as a gas main rupture, likely caused by aging pipeline infrastructure and recent construction activity." The words flow past like water, clean and clear and seemingly pristine. "Reconstruction efforts are expected to resume pending further safety review. School district officials express confidence in the continued timeline for completion."

Vincent reads it twice, the second time focusing on what isn't mentioned. No explanation for the blast pattern that threw debris in every direction. No mention of the heat that melted metal into new shapes. Nothing about the red veining that spread through the soil like infection, or the vibrations that still pulse beneath the town at night. The article constructs reality through omission, building truth from the spaces between words.

His thumb continues scrolling, past quotes from the principal about student safety, past reassurances from the construction company about enhanced protocols. Almost at the bottom, where most readers would have already stopped, a single paragraph stands apart from the rest. "Owen Driscoll, a geology student at Michigan Tech conducting fieldwork in the area, noted that 'preliminary data remains inconsistent with state report findings.' Driscoll was unavailable for further comment."

The words sit on the screen like a crack in glass, small but suggesting the possibility of complete fracture. Vincent stares at them, understanding what Owen has done. It's not quite dissent, not quite accusation, just a careful placement of doubt that anyone looking for truth might notice. He pictures Owen hunched over his notebooks, comparing soil samples to official explanations, finding the gaps where reality doesn't align with narrative.

"I see he doesn't accept the narrative," Mira says, and Vincent feels her presence behind him before her voice registers. She leans over his shoulder to read, her hair falling forward to brush against his cheek. The contact carries warmth but also something else, that electric charge she seems to generate now, as if her body runs on different currents than before. Her breath stirs the air near his ear as she reads Owen's quote again, and when she smiles, he catches it in his peripheral vision, equal parts affection and worry.

The smile acknowledges what Vincent already knows: Owen has made himself visible to whoever monitors these things, whoever ensures the official story remains unchallenged. In a town learning to pretend nothing happened, Owen has refused to play along, even if his refusal comes wrapped in academic language and buried at the article's end.

Angela moves through the kitchen with deliberate care, every motion precise, as if each step could tip her balance. She lifts the casserole dish from the oven, a weighty vessel packed with shepherd's pie, steaming and golden. No one has much appetite for it, but it stands for something solid: the comfort of routine, the hope of ordinary evenings. Her hands tremble as she sets the dish down, the ceramic landing harder than she meant, sending the silverware clattering on the tabletop.

"Dinner," she announces, though everyone can see what she's brought. The word seems to mean something else in her mouth, maybe "I've made everyone's favorite dish."

Elias comes out of his study, still in his white coat even though it's well past seven. He looks tired, moving with the slow caution of someone whose back acts up after a long day on his feet. He drops into his chair and rubs at his eyes, not bothering to change or say much.

"The report seems thorough and, well, official," Elias says, nodding at Vincent's phone. His tone carries that clinical detachment he uses for everything now, the voice of someone reading symptoms from a chart. "Gas infrastructure in this part of Michigan is notoriously outdated. The state's been warning about potential failures for years. At least there's some logic to it."

He serves himself a portion of shepherd's pie with

geometric precision, cutting a perfect square that he transfers to his plate, then scooping up the remaining creamed corn. The performance of normalcy requires such exactitude, each gesture calculated to maintain the illusion that they live in a normal town discussing the news over dinner.

"It's good they… settled on something so fast," Angela says, her voice carefully steady. She passes the salad bowl to Mira. "Now they can continue rebuilding the school. At least, that's the hope."

"Owen seems to have concerns," Vincent says, keeping his voice neutral, just noting a fact from the article.

Elias's fork pauses halfway to his mouth. "Owen's young. Eager to find anomalies where simple explanations suffice." He completes the motion, searching for the right thoughts. "Occam's Razor. If the lights flicker, it's probably a loose bulb. Not ghosts. I'm surprised he wouldn't live by that principle. It's a cornerstone of rational thinking. A reminder that simplicity is usually a better starting point than speculation."

But his words carry no conviction, only the hollow echo of someone reciting lines they've memorized. Vincent catches the glance that passes between Elias and Angela, quick as a blink but loaded with shared understanding. They both know the official story is fabrication. They both decide to accept the official story, because the alternative would mean facing the truth that Muldrath and Marrowick had shown them their lives, their relationship, this fragile attempt at family, have always stood on ground shaped by things they cannot explain.

Mira shifts beside Vincent, her hand finding his beneath the table. Her fingers are cool against his palm, and he feels her pulse through her touch. She doesn't speak, doesn't need to. Her presence alone contradicts every comfortable lie the adults try to believe. She is proof that the world has shifted, that boundaries between possible and impossible have dissolved like sugar in rain.

The kitchen fills with the sounds of eating, forks against plates, the gulp of water being swallowed. Outside, street-lights flicker on in sequence down Kipling Avenue, their illumination catching on windows across the way where other families presumably share similar meals, similar conversations, similar desperate grasps at normalcy. The Andersons discussing their son's baseball practice. The Kemps planning their weekend trip to Green Bay. All of them agreeing without coordination to accept the official story, to let the gas main explanation cover the impossibility like frost covering disturbed earth.

Elias clears his throat and sets down his fork, glancing at the others before speaking with cautious precision. "I spoke with one of the site managers this afternoon," he says, keeping his tone neutral. "They told me the damage was mostly superficial with just debris and some charred siding. Nothing structural, at least by their assessment. They're still confident the new school will open on schedule." He pauses, the words heavy with unspoken doubt, then looks back down at his plate, as if the conversation is settled by repetition.

Night settles over the house like sediment. Vincent lies on his back in the darkness of his room, still dressed in jeans and a t-shirt because something about this evening makes the vulnerability of pajamas feel unwise. The ceiling above him holds patterns of shadow that shift when cars pass on the street, their headlights painting brief geometries across the plaster before abandoning the room to darkness again. He counts these passages of light like sheep, but sleep remains distant, held at bay by something more than restlessness.

The rhythm starts so gradually he doesn't notice it at first, mistaking it for his own heartbeat echoing in his ears. But when he holds his breath, the pulse continues, steady and deep, traveling up through the foundation, through the walls, through the bed frame and mattress into his spine. It's not quite sound and not quite vibration, but something between the two, a presence felt deep within rather than heard with the ears.

Vincent presses his palm flat against the mattress, feeling the pulse more clearly through direct contact. The sensation travels up his arm, a warmth that isn't quite warmth, a pressure that isn't quite pressure. It reminds him of standing too close to the massive speakers at a concert Jayce dragged him to last year in Saginaw, that full-body thrum that made his organs feel like they were rearranging themselves. But this is deeper, more patient, rising from somewhere far below the basement, below the foundation, below the frost line where things should be still and cold and dead.

The house responds to the rhythm with its own language of wood and nail. A beam in the ceiling creaks, the sound longer and lower than temperature change would cause. The walls tick like cooling metal, though the furnace has been steady for hours. In the corner where his bookshelf meets the wall, a gap appears and disappears with each pulse, as if the house is breathing, expanding and contracting in time with whatever moves beneath.

Footsteps pad softly past his door, and through the gap beneath it, Vincent sees the interruption of hallway light that means his mother is awake. She pauses outside his room, and he can picture her there in her robe and slippers. The footsteps continue after a moment, heading downstairs where she'll make chamomile tea and stand at the kitchen window, looking out at the street while pretending everything is normal.

"It's the furnace," she says to no one, her voice carrying up the stairs with the hollow tone of someone trying to convince themselves. "These old houses, the heating systems need adjustment."

The furnace kicks on as if in response, its familiar rumble joining the deeper rhythm without masking it. The two sounds layer uncomfortably, mechanical noise over organic pulse, creating a particular dissonance. He understands his mother's need to name it, to assign the sensation to something fixable, something a repair technician could solve with the right parts and labor. But the furnace will cycle off in twenty minutes, and the deeper rhythm will continue, patient as erosion.

The vent in Vincent's room breathes harder for a moment as Elias adjusts something in the system. Warm air flows out carrying the scent of dust and metal and something else, something that reminds Vincent of the morning's construction site, that organic smell that rose from the probe hole before the inspector covered it. The air itself seems infected with whatever grows beneath Duswood, carrying spores of impossibility through the ventilation system.

Through the thin wall that separates their rooms, Vincent feels more than hears Mira's presence. She isn't moving around like their parents, isn't trying to assign blame to furnaces or pressure changes. He pictures her sitting cross-legged on her bedroom floor, palms flat against the wood like she's reading braille written in grain and varnish. Her stillness has weight to it.

He knows she feels it more clearly than any of them. Since Marrowick, since the thing that changed her or revealed her or made her more herself, she's been tuned to frequencies the rest of them only catch in fragments. Where Vincent feels a pulse, she probably hears symphony. Where he senses something vast and patient beneath the town, she likely sees its full anatomy spread through soil and stone like a medical diagram of something that shouldn't exist.

The lights flicker.

Not the quick blink of electrical interruption, but a slow dimming that makes the darkness seem to press inward from the corners of the room. Vincent's desk lamp, which he'd left off, glows faintly anyway, its bulb producing a brown-orange light that shouldn't be possible without electricity flowing through it. The illumination lasts three seconds, maybe four, just long enough for him to see his own shadow on the wall, distorted and stretching toward the ceiling like it's trying to escape.

When the lights return to normal, when the lamp goes properly dark again, the air carries new scents. Cedar, sharp and resinous, though there are no windows open in the house. Warm dust, like summer afternoons in abandoned buildings. And beneath both, that metallic tang that's become Duswood's new perfume, the smell of something vast and iron-rich stirring in the deep.

Vincent sits up, feet finding the floor, drawn by an impulse he doesn't examine. The floorboards feel warm through his socks, warmer than the furnace could account for. He stands, and the rhythm travels up through his legs more insistently now, as if proximity to the ground strengthens the connection. His hand reaches for the doorknob, though he doesn't remember deciding to leave his room.

The hallway stretches before him, lit by the nightlight his mother bought last week, claiming it was for safety but really for comfort against the dark that feels darker lately.

Halfway down the hall, Mira's door stands open.

She appears in the doorway without crossing the space between, or maybe Vincent just didn't see her move. The hallway light creates a corona around her silhouette, making her edges indistinct, as if she's partially dissolved into the darkness of her room. She stands perfectly still, arms at her sides, head slightly down as if listening to instructions only she can hear.

"It's not done," she says, her voice soft but certain, carrying the weight of prophecy without the drama. The words aren't threatening or ominous, just factual, like announcing rain when you can smell it coming.

Vincent wants to ask what she means, though he already knows. The official story, the gas main explanation, the inspectors' reports, none of it matters. Whatever caused the explosion, whatever spreads through the ground in red veins, whatever makes the earth pulse with its own heartbeat, it hasn't gone away. It's just paused, perhaps gathering strength, perhaps waiting for the right moment, perhaps simply being patient in the way only geological things can be.

"Can you feel it getting stronger?"

CHAPTER
SEVEN

Within a week, new classroom trailers line the south parking lot, hastily delivered from somewhere in Wisconsin and anchored into the still-soft earth. School officials insist the disruption will be temporary. By Monday morning, the lot buzzes with the churn of buses and anxious voices, the smell of fresh plywood and paint fighting to mask the lingering memory of burnt cedar and steam. Teachers are determined to pretend that nothing has changed except the address of first period.

The temporary campus spreads before Vincent like a violation, its white trailers squatting on mud that never quite dries despite three days without rain. Morning frost still clings to the metal railings, but it melts at his touch, leaving his fingers wet and somehow warmer than they should be. The air tastes of diesel exhaust from the buses pulling away, mixed with something else that coats the back of his throat like medicine. Beside him, Mira picks her way across the plywood walkways with careful grace, as if she's walking on something more fragile than wood.

Students flow around them in practiced patterns, navigating the maze of temporary structures. Their voices carry that bright edge of forced normalcy, conversations about homework and weekend events that ring hollow against the industrial backdrop of their displacement. A sophomore Vincent recognizes from his history class laughs at something her friend says, but the sound cuts off too quickly, as if she caught herself being too loud in a place that demands quiet.

The walkways bounce slightly under their combined weight, a sensation Vincent has grown used to but which still makes his stomach tighten. Each footstep creates a small vibration that travels through the plywood, into the cinder blocks, down into earth that feels less solid than it should. He watches a freshman ahead of them stumble slightly where two sections of walkway don't quite align, the gap between them stuffed with newspaper that's gone soft and gray from moisture.

They pass between trailers where condensation has formed on the windows despite the morning chill, the glass fogged from inside with the breath of too many bodies in spaces too small. Through one clear patch, Vincent glimpses a teacher writing on a whiteboard that's been bolted directly to the trailer wall, the surface rippling slightly with each stroke of the marker. The normalcy of the gesture, the careful formation of letters and numbers, feels like a magic spell.

June Everhart stands at the intersection of two walkways, her camera raised to capture something Vincent can't identify. The morning light catches on her copper-blonde hair as she adjusts the focus, her fingers moving with the unconscious precision of long practice. The shutter clicks, the sound sharp and metallic in the morning air, and she lowers the camera to check the display. Whatever she sees makes her frown slightly, she gets that expression when the world presents itself differently through the lens than to the naked eye.

"Morning documentation," she says as they approach, not quite a greeting but an acknowledgment of shared presence. Her voice carries that careful neutrality they've all adopted, the tone of people who've agreed not to discuss what they all feel. She shows them the camera's display: a perfectly ordinary shot of students walking to class, except for how the shadows fall wrong, stretching in directions that don't match the sun's angle.

Vincent wants to ask what else she's captured, what other impossibilities her camera reveals, but the warning bell rings from a speaker mounted on a light pole. The sound crackles with static that wasn't there yesterday, little pops and hisses that make it sound like the bell is ringing underwater. Students begin moving faster, their casual clusters breaking apart as they head for their designated trailers.

———

Vincent attends his last class of the day inside the math trailer. The fluorescent lights hum at a jagged frequency as he finds his seat, the desk wobbling on the uneven floor until he wedges his backpack under one leg. The teacher, Mr. Paulson, writes equations on a whiteboard that's already stained with the ghosts of previous lessons that won't quite erase. Other students settle into their seats with the resigned acceptance of prisoners, their movements creating a symphony of creaking plastic and shifting weight that makes the whole trailer feel alive.

Halfway through Paulson's explanation of derivatives, Vincent feels it: a vibration through the floor that doesn't match any of the normal movements. This runs deeper, traveling up through the cinder blocks, through the metal frame, into his desk where his pencil begins to roll toward the edge. He catches it automatically, but his attention focuses on that pulse, familiar now as his own heartbeat. The underground rhythm has followed them here, or maybe it's everywhere now, the whole of Duswood beating in time with whatever stirs below.

Mira sits three desks over, and Vincent watches her shoulders tense, the only visible sign that she feels it too. Her pencil stops moving across her notebook, the tip hovering just above the paper as if she's waiting for something. The vibration intensifies, not dramatically but steadily, like someone slowly turning up the volume on a bass speaker. A water bottle on someone's desk begins to walk toward the edge, its progress marked by tiny plastic clicks against the desktop.

The sound comes first: a wet tearing that makes everyone stop mid-motion. It originates from somewhere outside, close enough that Vincent can hear the individual fibers of something separating, the noise somehow both organic and geological. Through the window, he sees students on the south walkway backing away from something, their faces wearing expressions of confusion sliding toward alarm.

Mr. Paulson moves to the door, his hand on the handle but not turning it yet, as if opening it might invite in whatever's happening outside. The tearing sound continues, now accompanied by a grinding that Vincent feels in his chest, a percussion that doesn't match any machinery. The trailer rocks slightly, not from wind but from something shifting in the ground beneath.

Then he sees it through the window: a crack opening along the walkway, not the clean break of splitting wood but something more like flesh parting. The edges curl back, revealing darkness beneath that seems to pulse with its own light, a deep red glow that comes in waves. The crack widens with deliberate slowness, as if savoring its own birth, and from the depths comes the sound of water moving in ways water shouldn't move, bubbling up with too much purpose.

And then they emerge.

Beetles, but not any species Vincent recognizes from biology class. They rise from the cracks in perfect spirals, their shells gleaming black with an oil-slick iridescence that catches vibrant colors. Each one is the size of a thumb joint, their legs moving in perfect coordination as they climb from the crack. The sound they make isn't the skittering of normal insects but something more deliberate: a clicking synchronization, each impact precise as a metronome.

They pour out in impossible numbers, hundreds becoming thousands in seconds, their spiral pattern never breaking even as they spread across the walkway. Where they touch the wood, they leave marks like burns, perfect circles that overlap to create larger patterns. Students scramble back, some running, others frozen in place watching the beetles move with their terrible purpose.

The clicking intensifies, becomes almost musical in its complexity, each beetle adding its voice to create profane harmonies. Vincent presses his hand to his ribs, feeling his own heartbeat trying to match their rhythm, his body wanting to synchronize with their alien percussion. Through the window, he watches one beetle pause at the edge of the walkway, its antennae moving in slow circles as if tasting the air. Then it turns and continues its spiral, adding its click to the growing symphony.

Mira stands slowly, her movement drawing Vincent's attention. Her face wears an expression he's never seen before, something between recognition and dread, as if she's watching a recurring nightmare finally manifest in daylight. She doesn't speak, but Vincent hears her thoughts anyway, transmitted through whatever connection they share: They're not coming from the ground. They're being pushed out.

The trailer door opens with pneumatic resistance, as if the air itself has thickened in response to what's emerging from the crack. Vincent steps onto the walkway where other students and teachers have begun to gather, their bodies forming a loose semicircle around the source of the distur-bance. Someone has already begun stringing yellow caution tape between the walkway posts, though the gesture feels absurdly inadequate, like putting a bandage on a severed artery.

The beetles continue their emergence, their spiral pattern extending outward across the plywood in concentric circles that remind Vincent of growth rings in a tree. The smell has intensified, that mixture of hot metal and organic decay turns the air acidic. Some students hold their sleeves over their noses, but most just stand transfixed, watching the impossible unfold with the blank acceptance of shock.

Vincent edges closer, careful to stay behind the arbitrary boundary of yellow tape that someone continues to unspool. Mira appears beside him with that quality she has now of moving without seeming to cross the intervening space. Her hand brushes his, not quite holding but establishing contact, a grounding point in the unreality of the moment. Together they watch as more beetles spiral up from the crack, their shells catching the weak morning light and throwing it back in a kaleidoscope of colors.

"They're not coming from the ground," Mira whispers, her voice pitched low enough that only Vincent can hear. "They're being pushed out."

The distinction feels important though Vincent can't articulate why. Coming from suggests intention on the beetles' part, some insect agenda that brought them to the surface. Being pushed out implies something else entirely, something below that needs the space they occupied, or perhaps something that's rejecting them like a body rejecting foreign tissue.

As if responding to Mira's words, the nearest beetle stops its spiral progression. It stands perfectly still for a moment, antennae waving in slow circles, then begins to tremble. The trembling intensifies, becomes a vibration Vincent can see in the air around the insect, a localized distortion. Then, with no warning, no sound, the beetle bursts into ash.

Not burns. Not explodes. Simply transitions from solid to powder in an instant that defies physics. The ash hangs in the air for a heartbeat, holding the beetle's shape like a ghost of itself, then drifts down to settle on the walkway. Where it lands, it leaves a mark darker than charcoal, a perfect spiral that seems to sink into the wood rather than sit on top of it.

Another beetle stops, trembles, becomes ash. Then another. The transformation spreads through their ranks like a signal passing from one to the next, each insect reaching some invisible threshold before dissolving. The air fills with fine gray powder that smells of ammonia and burnt copper, making everyone step back, coughing. But even as they retreat, Vincent notices how their eyes stay fixed on the spectacle, unable to look away from the systematic undoing of these impossible creatures.

The spiral burns they leave overlap and interconnect, creating a pattern across the walkway. It's almost like writing, like someone leaving a message in a language that predates words. Mira's breathing has slowed beside Vincent, her hand now completely in his, matching the rhythm of the beetles' dissolution, as if she's reading what they're writing with their deaths.

Sirens cut through the morning air, approaching fast from downtown. Through the gaps between trailers, Vincent sees the red and blue lights of Sheriff Brennan's cruiser racing up the access road, followed by two deputy vehicles. The remaining beetles, perhaps a hundred still moving in their spirals, all stop simultaneously. They stand frozen for three seconds, antennae moving in perfect synchronization, then burst into ash all at once. The cloud of powder rises like smoke from an extinguished fire, hanging in the air before the morning breeze carries it away, leaving only the burned spiral pattern as evidence they existed.

Sheriff Brennan's boots hit the gravel with authority, but Vincent catches the hesitation in his stride when he sees the crack and the elaborate burn patterns surrounding it. Two deputies flank him. Brennan's face wears the same expression

Vincent saw after the school explosion: carefully composed denial fighting with the evidence of his own eyes.

The sheriff approaches the crack with measured steps, his boots carefully avoiding the spiral burns though Vincent suspects he doesn't consciously realize he's doing it. He stops at the yellow tape line, pulls out a small notebook, and begins writing without looking at what his pen produces. His jaw works like he's chewing something bitter.

"Alright, everyone back up," Brennan says, his voice carrying the forced calm of someone reading from a script they don't believe. "We've got a ground subsidence issue here. Probably related to the water table changes from the construction."

Vincent watches the sheriff's face as he speaks, noting the tiny muscle that jumps in his cheek when he says "water table." The man's eyes never quite focus on the crack itself, instead sliding past it to look at the crowd, the trailers, anywhere but the source of the impossible beetles and their spiral message.

"The insects," one teacher starts to say, but Brennan cuts her off with a raised hand.

"Thaw pressure," he says, the words coming out practiced and hollow. "Ground warming unevenly can force dormant insects to the surface. The chemical reaction with the air causes rapid oxidation. It's unusual but not unheard of."

The lie hangs in the air like the ash from the beetles, obvious and choking but somehow easier to breathe than the truth. Vincent sees several adults nod slowly, accepting the explanation not because it makes sense but because it provides an exit from having to confront what they've witnessed. Even the teacher who started to object closes her mouth, her expression shifting from confusion to relief at being offered a story she can repeat.

The principal, Mr. Davidson, emerges from the administrative trailer with a megaphone that crackles to life with a burst of static. His usually steady voice wavers slightly as he announces, "Due to ground instability and potential safety concerns, we're implementing early dismissal. Buses will begin arriving in fifteen minutes. Please proceed to your designated loading areas in an orderly fashion."

The words trigger a collective exhale from the gathered students, as if they've been holding their breath since the beetles emerged. They begin moving toward the bus zones with the shuffling compliance of people eager to be else-where, to be home where they can pretend this was a strange dream or a story they'll tell wrong on purpose. Vincent notices how they all avoid stepping on the spiral burns, creating winding paths across the walkways like water finding its way around stones.

Some students pull out phones, but Vincent watches them struggle with what to say in texts to parents. How do you describe beetles that shouldn't exist dissolving into ash that burns patterns that form an archaic language? Most settle for variations of "early dismissal" and "ground problems," already participating in the collective fiction that will become the official story.

A deputy begins photographing the crack and the burn patterns, but Vincent notices he's holding the camera at odd angles, never quite capturing the full spiral design. Whether intentional or not, the documentation will show only frag-ments, pieces that don't quite add up to the whole, evidence that suggests without confirming. Another deputy takes samples of the ash that still clings to some surfaces, sealing it in evidence bags that he handles like they might explode.

"Natural phenomenon," Brennan says to no one in particu-lar, or perhaps to everyone, or perhaps to himself. "We've seen similar insect emergences in other parts of the state. Mining subsidence, geological activity. The state's sending an ento-mologist to confirm."

Vincent knows no entomologist will come. Just like the

state inspectors who came after the explosion, anyone sent to investigate will find exactly what they expect to find: unusual but explainable insect behavior, ground subsidence from construction, chemical reactions that produce ash. The spiral patterns will be dismissed as coincidence, the synchronized behavior as a flocking response, the impossible as merely improbable.

Mira hasn't moved throughout the sheriff's performance, her attention still focused on the burn patterns the beetles left behind. Vincent follows her gaze and sees what she sees: the spirals aren't random. They radiate from the crack in specific directions, pointing toward different parts of town like arrows on a map. One spiral trail points toward the old construction site. Another toward the swamp. A third toward the parish, and a fourth toward something Vincent can't identify, some location that exists in the spaces between the known landmarks of Duswood.

Students flow past them toward the buses, their voices low and careful, discussing evening plans and homework as if these normal concerns might overwrite the morning's impossibility. Vincent catches fragments of conversation, each one participating in the denial: "Weird bugs," "glad we get out early," "my mom's making tacos tonight." No one mentions the spirals. No one questions the sheriff's explanation. No one asks why beetles would emerge just to immediately turn to ash.

The yellow tape perimeter expands as deputies push everyone further back. The crack remains, dark and wet, tinged with red. The burn patterns remain too, sunk so deep into the wood they look like they've always been there, like the walkway was built with these spiral scars already in place. Vincent takes one last look before starting the walk home with Mira, memorizing the pattern, knowing that by tomorrow it will be covered, explained, or simply gone.

The living room feels smaller with three of them crowded around Mira's laptop, the screen's blue light painting their faces in shades of electronic pallor. Vincent sinks into the sofa cushions that still smell faintly of the lavender spray Angela uses to mask older, more persistent odors. June sits cross-legged on the floor, her camera connected to the laptop by a cable that coils like a black snake across the coffee table. The house around them maintains its evening quiet, punctuated only by the distant sound of Elias in his study, the rhythmic click of his calculator as he reviews patient billing.

June's fingers move across the camera's controls with practiced efficiency, navigating menus Vincent doesn't understand. The device looks expensive, all matte black metal and precise buttons, the kind of equipment that captures more than just images. She's already uploaded two dozen photos from this morning, their thumbnails appearing on the laptop screen in neat rows, each one a tiny window into impossibility.

"The sensor picks up spectrums we can't see," June explains, though her voice carries the distraction of someone focused on a task rather than teaching. "Sometimes it shows things that aren't there. Or things that are there but we can't perceive."

She clicks on the first image, and Vincent's breath catches. It's the crack in the walkway, taken moments after it opened. In person, the crack appeared dark. But in June's photo, it glows. Not metaphorically, not as a trick of light, but with genuine luminescence that extends beyond the visible wound in the ground. Tendrils of red light reach outward from the crack like roots or veins, spreading across the walkway in patterns the naked eye couldn't detect.

"That's not lens flare," June says before anyone can suggest it. "I checked. This is what the camera saw."

Mira leans forward, her face inches from the screen, studying the light tendrils. Her fingers hover over the screen, not quite touching, as if the image might transmit something through contact. Vincent watches her eyes track the patterns of light, following connections his own vision can't quite grasp.

The next photo shows the beetles emerging. In person, they appeared black with oil-slick iridescence. Through June's lens, they're surrounded by halos of that same red light, each insect carrying its own small aurora. The spirals they form aren't just physical patterns but light-paths, streams of energy that connect each beetle to the others and to something deeper, something the photo's frame can't contain.

"Look at this one," June says, clicking to an image taken seconds before the beetles began turning to ash. The insects stand frozen in their spiral formation, but above them, caught by the camera but invisible to the witnesses, hangs a cloud of something that looks like heat shimmer mixed with smoke. It has shape, form, almost like a massive hand pressing down on the beetles from above. Or rising up from below, Vincent can't tell which.

They cycle through more images. Each one reveals layers of the morning's event that their eyes couldn't process. The burn patterns the beetles left don't just mark the wood; they extend downward in the photos, visible through the walkway as if the camera can see through solid matter. The depths they reach exceed what should be possible, extending down through the ground toward something the photo's perspective can't capture.

"There," Mira says suddenly, her finger pointing at a particular image. It's an overview shot of the entire spiral pattern, taken from the slight elevation of a nearby trailer's steps. "Can you enhance this section?"

June zooms in on the area Mira indicates, the pixels resolving into clearer detail. The individual spiral burns become visible, but more than that, the relationship between them becomes apparent. They're not random dispersions but components of something larger. Vincent stares at the pattern, his mind trying to process what he's seeing. It's almost like looking at one of those Magic Eye pictures from the nineties, where relaxing your focus reveals a hidden image.

Then he sees it. The spirals, taken together, form a symbol or sigil, something that strains his eyes to perceive directly. It's not quite a shape and not quite writing, but something between the two, a form of communication that predates human language. The design pulses on the screen, or maybe that's just Vincent's vision struggling with something his brain isn't equipped to interpret.

"It's trying to show us something," Mira murmurs, her voice carrying that quality it has when she's partially elsewhere, perceiving things on frequencies others can't access. Her hand finally touches the trackpad, and she traces the pattern with one finger, following the spiral paths from their origins at the crack to their termination points.

Each spiral trail ends at a specific location relative to the crack. Vincent recognizes the directions from this morning: toward the old construction site, toward the swamp, toward the parish. But in the photo, with the enhanced detail and the invisible light made visible, he can see there are more trails. Dozens of them, so faint even June's camera barely caught them, spreading out from the crack like a root system or a neural network or a map.

"Dinner," Elias calls from the kitchen doorway. Vincent hadn't noticed him approaching, too focused on the screen and its revelations. "Angela made pot roast."

The spell breaks, or at least pauses. June disconnects her camera with careful movements, tucking it into the padded case she always carries. The laptop screen goes dark, taking with it the evidence of morning's impossibilities. They move toward the dining room with the automatic compliance of young people called to meals, though Vincent's mind remains fixed on that pattern, that sigil, that message written in beetle ash and invisible light.

Conversation at dinner stays carefully mundane. Angela asks about their day with the bright interest of someone who absolutely doesn't want real answers. Elias discusses a complex root canal he performed, the technical details serving as white noise that fills space without requiring engagement. June participates with polite responses about her photography project for school, never mentioning what her camera actually captured. The pot roast tastes like nothing to Vincent, his senses still overwhelmed by the morning's ammonia and ash.

After June leaves and the house settles into its nighttime routines, Vincent lies in bed staring at the ceiling. The pattern from the photos burns behind his eyelids when he closes them, that impossible sigil that suggests communication from something that shouldn't be able to communicate. He drifts in and out of shallow sleep, his mind wandering around thoughts he wish he didn't have.

A voice pulls him from half-sleep. Mira's voice, but strange, monotone in a way that makes his skin prickle. It drifts through the wall between their rooms, steady and rhythmic like she's reciting something. Vincent sits up, feet finding the floor before he's fully awake. The hallway is dark except for the nightlight Angela insists on keeping, its weak amber glow making the shadows seem deeper.

Mira's door stands slightly ajar, unusual for her. Through the gap, Vincent can see her silhouette on the bed, sitting upright with her back against the headboard. Her eyes are closed, but her mouth moves with a ghostly motion, releasing a steady stream of numbers.

"Four five point seven eight five nine," she says, each digit clear despite the monotone delivery. "Negative eight seven point zero nine nine six."

Vincent recognizes the pattern: coordinates. Latitude and longitude. His mind automatically tries to place them, somewhere in Michigan certainly, but the specific location escapes him. He retreats quietly to his room, grabs the notebook he keeps on his nightstand, and returns to the hallway. Settling against the wall where he can hear clearly, he begins transcribing.

The numbers continue for several minutes, some repeating, others appearing only once. Mira's voice never wavers, never speeds up or slows down, maintaining the same mechanical rhythm like she's a receiver for a signal broadcast from somewhere else. Vincent writes each set carefully, his handwriting cramped but legible in the dim light.

Then, abruptly, she stops. The silence feels sudden and complete, as if someone cut a transmission. Vincent holds his breath, waiting, but no more numbers come. Instead, Mira speaks a single word, still in that monotone but with something underneath it, some emotion trying to break through:

"North."

The word hangs in the air for a moment, then Vincent hears the rustle of covers as Mira lies back down. Her breathing immediately deepens into the rhythm of true sleep, as if the entire episode never happened. He waits another minute to be sure, then retreats to his room with the notebook clutched against his chest.

By the light of his desk lamp, Vincent studies what he's written. Seven sets of coordinates, all clustered in what must be northern Michigan. He'll need to check them online, but something tells him they're connected to the morning's events, to the spiral pattern, to the message the beetles died to deliver.

The kitchen radio crackles to life at 6:47 AM with Jerry Wopple's voice, too cheerful for a town where beetles burst into ash and the ground bleeds red water, and Vincent spreads grape jam on toast while the host launches into his morning segment about "recent unusual events" with the kind of forced casualness that makes every word sound like a lie.

"Folks are calling in with all sorts of theories," Jerry says through the tinny speaker, his laugh hollow as November wind. "Everything from chemical spills to, believe it or not, witchcraft. But we've got someone here who can shed some real light on the situation."

Vincent's knife pauses mid-spread. Through the window above the sink, he watches power lines sway in perfectly still air, their movement subtle but undeniable, as if invisible hands test their tension. The morning light catches on the wires, and for a moment they seem to pulse with their own faint luminescence, though that could be his tired eyes playing tricks after another night of broken sleep.

"With me is Harold Kemper from Duswood High's chemistry department," Jerry continues, and Vincent recognizes the name of the teacher who'd been relocated to the trailer next to his math class. "Harold, you've been looking into these beetle incidents?"

"That's right, Jerry." Kemper's voice carries the rehearsed quality of someone reading from notes they've reviewed multiple times. "What we're seeing is a natural phenomenon related to temperature fluctuations and soil chemistry. The rapid oxidation of certain organic compounds can create the appearance of spontaneous combustion."

Vincent pulls his phone from his pocket, thumb automatically navigating to the Duswood Community Facebook group while Kemper drones on about pH levels and decomposition rates. The screen fills with a cascade of posts from the past twelve hours, each more desperate than the last to assign meaning to what they've witnessed.

Martha Henley claims she saw lights in the swamp that moved against the wind. Below her post, seventeen comments argue about marsh gas versus supernatural forces. Tom Brennan, the sheriff's cousin, insists the government is testing chemicals, his all-caps rant garnering forty-three reactions, mostly the angry face emoji. Someone named Karen posts a photo of her garden where all the flowers have turned toward the construction site despite the sun being in the opposite direction.

Vincent scrolls past prayer circle invitations and links to articles about ley lines. One post catches his attention: a woman named Dorothy claims her grandmother worked for something called GNRO in the forties, though she can't remember what the letters stood for. The post has no comments, as if people instinctively avoid engaging with anything that might provide actual answers.

"The spiral patterns," Jerry's voice pulls Vincent's attention back to the radio, "some witnesses say the beetles left deliberate designs. Can science explain that?"

A pause stretches too long before Kemper responds.

"Insects often follow pheromone trails. What appears deliberate to us is simply chemical programming. The burns you're referring to are oxidation marks, nothing more unusual than rust forming on metal."

Vincent's throat tightens. He's tasted metal in the air since waking, a copper tang that coats his tongue no matter how much water he drinks. It's stronger near the windows, near the electrical outlets, near anything that connects the inside of the house to whatever saturates the atmosphere outside. He pulls his small notebook from his back pocket, the one he's been filling with observations since the explosion, and adds a note about the taste, the time, the way it intensifies when the power lines sway.

"But Harold," Jerry presses, and Vincent hears desperation creeping into the host's professional voice, "multiple witnesses saw them emerge from cracks in the ground, and that there was a reddish tint to the ground. Is that normal insect behavior?"

"Iron oxide," Kemper says quickly, too quickly. "Dissolved minerals in groundwater. The construction disturbed natural deposits. It's all perfectly explicable through basic chemistry."

Vincent writes: "Kemper avoiding mention of synchronized dissolution. No explanation for simultaneous transformation to ash." His handwriting has grown cramped from days of constant notation, tracking patterns others refuse to acknowledge. The notebook contains sketches of burn spirals, lists of coordinates, timestamps of when the underground rhythm grows strongest.

Footsteps on the stairs announce Angela's approach before she appears in the doorway, already dressed for her morning AA meeting. Her eyes dart to the radio, and Vincent sees her jaw tighten at Jerry's voice discussing "unexplained phenomena." She moves to the coffee maker with deliberate normalcy, each action precise and contained.

A moment later, Danny bounds into the kitchen, backpack already slung over one shoulder and hair still tousled from last night's sleep. He's buttoned his shirt crooked but beams with the satisfaction of having done it himself. Dropping his lunchbox onto the table with a clatter, he grabs a banana and grins at Vincent, chattering about the spelling test and asking if beetles can really catch fire. For a second, the kitchen feels almost ordinary, just a family morning, the world outside held at bay by Danny's bright, effortless energy.

Vincent closes his notebook with practiced subtlety, sliding it back into his pocket before his mother can see his documentation. He takes another bite of toast, chews a little, watches her pour coffee into her travel mug. The silence between them feels dense with unspoken observations, shared knowledge neither wants to voice. Outside, the power lines continue their windless dance, and somewhere beneath the floorboards, that patient rhythm maintains its steady pulse.

———

The after-school lull at Cedar Lagoon Pizzeria brings its usual emptiness, just the hum of refrigeration units and the occasional tick of the espresso machine that rests after the school rush, and Vincent refills napkin dispensers while Joe and Hale spread glossy photos across the counter like tarot cards revealing a future no one wants to see.

The photos gleam under the fluorescent lights, cheap glossy paper from a home printer. Vincent recognizes the construction site's torn earth, the twisted metal, the crater that hasn't been filled yet. But these images show details the newspaper didn't publish, angles the official reports didn't include. Hale arranges them in a specific order, his thick fingers careful not to smudge the surfaces, while Joe leans forward on his elbows.

"There," Hale says, tapping one photo with his index finger. "Same cable in four different shots."

Vincent moves closer, ostensibly checking the sweet pepper supply in the prep station, but his attention focuses on the images. The cable Hale indicates appears thick as a wrist, its outer coating corroded green-black with age. In each photo, it emerges from or disappears into disturbed soil, and along its visible length, letters stand out despite the decay: GNRO.

Joe traces the cable's path from photo to photo, connecting its appearances like plotting points on a map. His finger moves with deliberate slowness, and Vincent notices how the older man's breathing has changed, become shallower, more controlled. This is Joe in reconnaissance mode, the soldier beneath the pizza shop owner surfacing through practiced observation.

"This line doesn't feed power," Joe says quietly, his voice pitched low enough that Vincent has to strain to hear over the refrigerator's hum. "It's listening."

The word hangs in the air between them, and Vincent's hands pause in their work. Listening implies purpose, implies something on the other end receiving whatever travels through that ancient cable. His fingers itch for his notebook, but pulling it out now would announce his eavesdropping.

Hale nods slowly, his expression grim. He pulls another photo from beneath the stack, this one taken from above, maybe from a ladder or drone. The cable becomes visible as a dark line cutting across the construction site, disappearing into undisturbed earth near the fence line. But it's the direction that makes Vincent's brow rise: the cable runs straight toward downtown, toward the oldest part of Duswood where brick buildings stand on foundations laid before anyone alive can remember.

"Great Northern Rail and Ore," Hale says, the words careful, testing them like weight on uncertain ice. "Found a fragment of letterhead in the county archives. Company that operated here over 70 years ago. They had mining interests, freight logistics. But the records stop in '53."

"Same year as the ledger Mrs. Driscoll showed the kids," Joe responds, and Vincent keeps his face neutral despite the jolt of recognition. So Joe knows about their visit to the parish office. Of course he does. Joe knows most things that happen in Duswood; he just rarely acknowledges what he knows.

The espresso machine chooses that moment to release steam, the hiss sharp enough to make all three of them flinch. The machine shouldn't be on, Vincent knows he didn't activate it, but there it sits, pressure gauge climbing toward red. Joe moves to it with quick efficiency, hitting the release valve, and steam billows out smelling of burned metal and something earthier, like soil after rain.

"Temperature sensors have been acting up," Joe mutters, but his eyes stay on the photos.

Through the floor, Vincent feels a vibration that doesn't match any vehicle passing outside. It runs deeper, traveling up through the foundation into his feet, a rhythm that matches neither heart nor machine but something between. The napkin dispensers he's been filling rattle slightly on their metal bases, creating a soft percussion that sounds almost like communication.

"GNRO had infrastructure all through the northern counties," Hale continues, his voice even lower now. "Rails, obviously. But also communications. Telegraph lines that ran parallel to the tracks. Some say they laid cable deeper, though. Experimental stuff. Direct ground conduction."

Vincent processes this, understanding dawning. Not power lines but communication lines. Cables that could carry signals through earth itself, using soil and mineral deposits as conductors. It sounds like nineteen-hundreds pseudoscience, but after watching beetles write messages in ash, after feeling the ground pulse with its own heartbeat, pseudoscience seems quaint compared to their new reality.

"Explains the resonance," Joe says, and that word, resonance, makes Vincent think of Mira's dreams, though he can't say why. "Something's using the old infrastructure. Like picking up a party line, hearing conversations that aren't meant for you."

The bell above the door chimes, and Joe moves with startling speed for a man his age, gathering the photos into a manila envelope that disappears beneath the counter before the customer fully enters. It's Mrs. Carlson, here for her Tuesday pickup order, her face carrying its usual pleasant vacancy. Joe greets her with professional warmth while Hale steps back, studying the menu board as if he hasn't eaten here twice a week for months.

Vincent returns to his napkin dispensers, but his mind races through implications. GNRO cables running beneath Duswood, carrying signals through deep earth. Infrastructure abandoned in 1953, the same year the ledger claimed the tunnels were sealed. But infrastructure doesn't simply disappear. It waits, dormant maybe, but still capable of conducting whatever flows through its channels when the right conditions return.

———

Vincent peels off his apron at 9:47 PM, the fabric stiff with flour dust and pizza sauce, when his phone vibrates against his hip with the particular pattern that means a text from Owen.

The screen illuminates with Owen's message, a screenshot of coordinates plotted on what looks like a hand-drawn map. The numbers float above curved lines that Vincent recognizes as the old freight rail that once connected Duswood to the iron mines up north. Owen's text beneath reads: "If these numbers mean anything, they trace a curve along the freight line. North bluff. Iron Gate."

Vincent stares at the coordinates, and his stomach drops with recognition. The exact numbers Mira whispered in her monotone sleep-speech two nights ago. His thumb hovers over the screen, wanting to respond, to ask Owen where he got these specific coordinates, but something makes him hesitate. The pizzeria's lights flicker once, a quick dimming that makes the phone screen seem brighter by contrast.

"Ready?" Joe calls from the door, keys jangling in his hand. His truck idles outside, exhaust visible in the cooling air.

Vincent follows Joe out, but once they're seated in the truck's worn cab, he turns his phone toward the older man. "Owen sent this. Says they trace the old freight line."

Joe's hands stay on the steering wheel as he reads, but Vincent watches his knuckles whiten, the tendons standing out like cables under tension. The truck idles in the empty lot, headlights cutting through darkness that seems thicker than it should be for this hour. Joe's jaw works like he's chewing words he won't speak, and when he finally puts the truck in gear, his movements carry a deliberateness that speaks of suppressed urgency.

They pull onto Kipling Avenue, and immediately Vincent notices the tension in the air. The wind shifts without warning, sending cedar branches bending at angles that don't match its direction. One moment they lean east, the next they're pressed flat against their trunks as if something massive passed overhead. The truck's headlights catch the movement, creating shadows that writhe across the asphalt.

"Iron Gate," Joe says finally, his voice flat. "The locals used to call it. The switching station where the freight line met the GNRO tracks. North of town, up on the bluff where the ground goes soft in spring."

Power lines run parallel to the road, and Vincent watches them sway in the shifting wind. But it's not just movement that catches his attention. The lines hum, a sound that penetrates the truck's cab despite the closed windows. It rises and falls like breathing, like something vast trying to speak through copper wire and electromagnetic fields. His phone screen flickers, the coordinates briefly scrambling into other numbers before resolving back to Owen's message.

"Owen's been mapping things," Vincent says, needing to fill the silence that feels too heavy. "Since the beetles. He thinks there's a pattern."

Joe's eyes flick to the rearview mirror, then to the side mirrors, then back to the road. It's a pattern Vincent recognizes from Joe's stories about convoy duty, the constant vigilance of someone expecting ambush. But they're alone on the road, no headlights behind them, nothing visible that would warrant such attention.

"Patterns," Joe repeats, and the word sounds like an accusation. "Your friend Mira talks about patterns. Now Owen. Everyone seeing designs in things that should be random."

The truck's radio, which has been off since Vincent climbed in, suddenly crackles with static. Not the white noise of dead air but structured static, bursts that almost form words. Vincent reaches toward the dial, but Joe's hand shoots out, gripping his wrist with surprising strength.

"Don't touch it," Joe says. "Sometimes it's better not to tune in clearly."

The static continues, and beneath it, Vincent hears something: the same rhythm that pulses through the ground at night, that thrums through the pizzeria's foundation, that beats beneath all of Duswood now. It's coming through the dead radio, transmitted through circuits that shouldn't be active, speaking in frequencies that shouldn't exist.

They approach Vincent's house, and the familiar houses look different in the unstable light. Windows reflect things that aren't there, showing depths that exceed their architectural limits. The Olsen's porch light flickers in sequence with something, though Vincent can't identify what. Even his own house seems changed, its angles sharper, its shadows deeper, as if the structure has shifted slightly out of alignment with itself.

Joe pulls up to the curb but doesn't put the truck in park. The engine idles rough, missing beats like a faltering heart. Through the windshield, Vincent sees his bedroom window and notices the curtains moving despite the window being closed. The motion is subtle, rhythmic, like something breathing against the glass from inside.

"Stay clear of that bluff," Joe says, his voice carrying the weight of order rather than suggestion. "Whatever Owen thinks he's found, whatever patterns he's mapping, some things are better left uncharted."

Vincent climbs out, his feet hitting pavement that feels warmer than the air temperature suggests. As Joe's taillights disappear into the dark, swallowed by distance and that unnatural thickness in the air, Vincent stands on his lawn feeling the ground pulse beneath his feet, steady as a heartbeat, patient as erosion, inevitable as the sunrise that seems impossibly far away.

Mira tosses in her bed, sheets twisted around her legs like roots seeking soil, and behind her closed eyelids she sees empty train cars moving through darkness that breathes.

The trains slide along tracks that shouldn't exist, beneath Duswood where no tunnels were ever officially dug. But these passages feel older than human construction, their walls not carved but grown. In her dream, Mira floats alongside the trains, watching their metal shells gleam with condensation that runs in patterns too deliberate for simple moisture. Each car bears faded letters: GNRO, painted in white that has gone yellow with age, though age means something different down here where time moves like treacle.

The tunnel walls pulse with their own light, a deep red luminescence that comes from within rather than upon them. It's not stone or packed earth that forms these passages but something between flesh and mineral, surfaces that contract slightly as the trains pass, as if the tunnels are throats swallowing the cars deeper into the earth. Veins run through the walls, or maybe they are roots, or maybe they are something that predates the distinction between animal and plant. They carry that red light in slow waves, each pulse synchronized with a heartbeat that Mira feels in her dream-body, in the space where her chest should be.

The trains move without engines, without any visible force pulling them forward. They simply glide along the tracks with the inevitability of gravity, though Mira knows they're moving horizontally, perhaps even slightly upward. There's no sound of wheels on rails, no mechanical clatter. Instead, the cars emit a low harmonic, each one contributing a different frequency to create resonating chords. The harmony shifts as they round unseen curves, the pitch rising and falling like a conversation in a language built from vibration rather than words.

Above the trains, though above means something different in these tunnels that exist outside normal geometry, phosphorescent lights begin to appear. They push through the organic ceiling like bioluminescent fruit, casting their cold light downward onto the passing cars. The lights arrange themselves in patterns as the trains pass beneath, forming spirals that mirror the burns the beetles left on the walkway. But these spirals are three-dimensional, extending up through solid matter as if the earth itself is transparent to their light.

The dream shifts, and suddenly Mira stands inside one of the cars. The interior is empty of seats or cargo, just bare metal walls that curve up to meet at a ceiling that seems both infinitely high and claustrophobically close. Her reflection appears in the polished metal, but it complicates logic. Not distorted by the surface's curve but fractured, showing her from angles that shouldn't be visible. In one reflection she's standing, in another sitting, in a third she's pressing her palms against the wall as if trying to feel something through the metal.

All versions of her turn their heads simultaneously toward the front of the car, where a door that wasn't there before stands open to the next car. Through it, she sees not another empty car but a depth that exceeds the train's possible length. It's like looking down a well that extends to the earth's core, lit by that same red pulse that runs through everything down here. The harmonic builds, no longer just sound but physical pressure, making the air thick as water.

The train car fills with the hum, and Mira realizes it's not random noise but structured communication. The earth itself is trying to speak, using the trains as vocal cords, the tunnels as throat, the phosphorescent patterns as a kind of writing that exists in dimensions her human eyes can barely perceive. She understands without understanding that this is what Owen's coordinates point toward, what the GNRO cables were laid to monitor, what has been breathing beneath Duswood since before the town existed.

She wakes with a gasp that sounds too loud in her dark bedroom. Her hands immediately go to her face, expecting to feel metal or earth, but finding only her own skin, damp with sweat. The dream's intensity fades but doesn't disappear, lurking at the edges of her consciousness like a word she can't quite remember. She sits up, and that's when she hears it.

A single word surfaces from the dream, rising through her mind like a bubble through oil: "Resonance."

Mira lies back down. She closes her eyes but doesn't sleep,

instead listening to that underground rhythm, learning its patterns, preparing for whatever comes when the resonance achieves its perfect pitch.

Spring fog crawls in from Lake Michigan like something with too many legs, filling Duswood's streets with a gray thickness that transforms familiar landmarks into suggestions of themselves, and Vincent stands at the edge of the construction site watching the halogen floodlights bore white tunnels through the mist, their harsh brilliance creating columns of visibility that end abruptly where the fog refuses to yield. Hale keeps the floodlights on at night to deter intruders, but not the ones who know how to move through the shadows. The chain-link fence hums against his palm when he touches it, a vibration that has nothing to do with wind or traffic, more like the metal itself carries current from somewhere deep below. The construction equipment hulks in the distance, excavators and bulldozers turned into prehistoric skeletons by the interplay of light and shadow.

Owen materializes from the fog carrying a rolled paper that he spreads against the fence, using his phone's flashlight to illuminate lines and numbers drawn in careful pencil. His breath clouds in the damp air as he traces a finger along a curved path marked with coordinates that Vincent recognizes even before Owen speaks them aloud.

"Four five point seven eight five nine, negative eight seven point zero nine nine six," Owen says, his voice carrying that particular precision he applies to everything, as if exact pronunciation might impose order on chaos. "The same numbers Mira spoke. That's the first point. This other point creates the curve. They follow the old freight line, curving through the construction site." His finger stops at a grid square marked N-17, the designation written in red ink that looks black in the strange light. "This is where Hale flagged the ground instability. The exact endpoint of the coordinate curve."

Vincent studies the map, noting how Owen has overlaid modern street grids with older survey lines, creating a palimpsest of Duswood's geographic history. The GNRO rail lines appear as dotted paths, their routes following contours that predate current roads. For each dotted coordinates, Owen has drawn small circles, each one numbered in sequence. The pattern they create reminds Vincent of constellation charts, points of light connected by invisible significance.

"You're sure about this?" Vincent asks, though he already knows Owen doesn't present theories without thorough verification.

"It's as simple as connect-the-dots," Owen replies, rolling the map with movements that betray nervousness despite his confident words. "Whatever Mira heard, whatever she channeled, it points here. To something beneath N-17."

Through the fog comes the sound of footsteps on wet pavement, and June emerges first, her camera bag slung across her shoulder, the strap already beaded with moisture. Her copper-blonde hair hangs limp in the humidity, and she pushes it back with fingers that shake slightly, though whether from cold or anticipation Vincent can't tell. Behind her, Mira appears more like she's condensing from the fog itself than walking through it, her movements carry an unsettling grace, as if she's navigating by senses the rest of them don't possess.

The floodlights catch their faces at harsh angles, creating landscapes of light and shadow that make them all look older, or perhaps just more honest about the fear they're carrying. June's eyes dart between the fence and the darkness beyond, her fingers already reaching for her camera as if documentation might provide protection. Mira stands perfectly still, her head tilted toward the construction site with the attention of someone listening to distant music.

"The gap's over here," Owen says, leading them along the fence line to where someone has bent the chain-link back, creating a triangular opening just large enough for a body to squeeze through. The metal edges curl like fingers, and rust flakes drift down when Owen pulls the fence wider. He goes through first, his backpack catching briefly before he twists free.

Vincent follows, feeling the wet clay immediately grab at his boots with a suction that makes each step an effort. The ground here doesn't behave like normal mud, doesn't release cleanly when he lifts his feet. Instead, it clings with something approaching reluctance, making soft sucking sounds that seem too loud in the fog-muffled quiet. June comes through next, grimacing as her shoes sink into the mire, then Mira, who moves across the surface with barely any impression, as if she weighs less than physics suggests she should.

They stand together in the circle of light cast by the nearest floodlight tower, four teenagers on the edge of something they don't fully understand. The construction site spreads before them, transformed by fog into an alien landscape of half-glimpsed machinery and disturbed earth. Somewhere in that expanse lies grid square N-17, the endpoint of coordinates spoken in sleep, the place where Hale found something concerning enough to mark in red.

Owen pulls supplies from his backpack with the efficiency of someone who's rehearsed this moment: small orange flags on wire stakes, a handheld EMF meter that chirps once as it powers on, a notebook already turned to a page of prepared grid notations. He divides the space before them with gestures, creating invisible boundaries that exist only in their shared understanding.

"Twenty paces per section," he explains, handing each of them a bundle of flags. "We mark anything unusual. Temperature variations, ground inconsistencies, electromagnetic anomalies." His voice carries the tone of a professor lecturing students, using scientific methodology as armor against the irrationality of what they're doing. "This is data collection, nothing more. We're investigating reported geological instabilities."

Vincent accepts his flags, the wire stakes cold even through the fabric of his gloves. He understands Owen's need to frame this as research, to transform their trespass into something that resembles legitimate investigation. It makes the impossibility of beetles turning to ash seem manageable, reducible to measurements and observations that fit in notebooks. But as they spread out into their assigned sections, boots squelching through clay that releases warmth with each step, Vincent knows they're not here for science.

They're here because something beneath grid square N-17 has been calling out in frequencies only certain people can hear, and tonight, in fog that makes the familiar foreign, they're finally answering back.

The group moves through the construction site in their assigned patterns, twenty paces north, mark, twenty paces east, mark, creating a human grid that overlays Owen's theoretical one. Vincent counts his steps automatically, muscle memory from childhood games transformed into something more purposeful. His section borders Mira's, and he watches her peripherally as she glides across the disturbed earth, her flags appearing at precise intervals despite her attention seeming focused elsewhere entirely.

The EMF meter in Owen's hand maintains a steady, quiet chirp as he walks his grid, the sound providing a metronomic backdrop to their search. June has her camera out, not photographing yet but holding it ready, the lens cap off and her finger hovering near the shutter release. The fog continues to press around them, reducing visibility to perhaps thirty feet.

Vincent plants another flag where the ground shows a slight depression, the orange marker bright against the dark clay. That's when he feels it first, not through his ears but through his boots, through the bones of his legs, through some sense that science hasn't defined. A hum rises from deep below, so low it exists more as pressure than sound, making his organs shift slightly in his chest cavity.

The rhythm isn't mechanical despite its steady pulse. It carries an organic quality, like listening to circulation through a stethoscope, if the circulatory system belonged to something the size of a city block...or greater. The sound doesn't come from any single point but emanates from the earth itself, rising through layers of clay and stone and whatever lies beneath Duswood's foundation. Vincent's jaw aches as the frequency finds resonance in his teeth, in the fluid of his inner ear, in spaces between his thoughts.

The floodlights dim without warning, their harsh white fading to amber, then to something barely brighter than candlelight. The shadows they cast elongate impossibly, stretching across the construction site like fingers reaching for something just out of grasp. Then, with no transition, the lights surge back to full brightness, the sudden intensity making everyone shield their eyes. In that moment of blindness and recovery, Vincent feels the ground shift beneath him, just slightly, just enough to know it happened.

"Tell me that's machinery," June whispers, her voice barely carrying through the thick air. She's stopped moving, camera hanging forgotten from her neck, both hands pressed against her stomach as if trying to hold something inside.

Vincent doesn't answer because they all know it's not machinery. No engine produces this kind of sound, this kind of physical presence that makes the air itself seem to thicken. He crouches slowly, pulling off one glove despite the damp cold, and places his palm flat against the soil.

The warmth hits him immediately, not the ambient temperature of earth that's absorbed a day's sun, but active heat, generated from below. It pulses against his palm in time with the hum, each surge bringing fresh warmth that travels up his arm. The sensation is almost pleasant, almost comforting, like touching something that recognizes him. But underneath the warmth runs something else, a vibration that doesn't match the audible hum, faster, more urgent, like encrypted data transmitted through living tissue.

The soil beneath his hand isn't just warm; it's soft in a way that has nothing to do with moisture. It yields to pressure but also seems to push back, to respond, to acknowledge his touch with subtle shifts in temperature and texture. Vincent thinks of skin, of the way flesh gives under fingertips, and immediately pulls his hand back, the comparison too visceral to maintain contact.

Standing ten feet away, a puddle near Mira's feet holds her reflection despite the angle being impossible for such a capture. But the reflection doesn't match her current posture. In the water, Mira appears to be kneeling, both hands pressed to the ground, her mouth moving in what might be speech or song. The image shimmers and ripples though no wind disturbs the surface, though no vibration should create such movement in standing water.

Owen's meter erupts without warning, its steady chirp becoming a shriek of electronic distress. The needle swings so hard it hits the stop peg with an audible click, then rebounds to swing the opposite direction with equal violence. He fumbles with the device, checking connections, tapping the display, his movements becoming increasingly frantic as the readings refuse to normalize.

"Electromagnetic field spike," he says, his voice cracking on the last word. The scientific terminology sounds hollow against the reality of what they're experiencing, like naming a hurricane won't change its winds. "Off the scale. The meter only goes to five milligauss. This is reading..." He trails off, staring at numbers that shouldn't exist, that violate the parameters of his instrument.

"Except there's no source...or maybe...we should leave," Owen continues, his need to verbalize his growing fear. He turns in a slow circle, meter extended like a dowsing rod, searching for transmission lines, underground cables, anything that might explain the readings. But the construction site offers no such comfort, just disturbed earth and fog and that persistent hum that seems to grow stronger with each passing moment.

Vincent watches Owen's scientific framework crumble in real time, sees it in the way his shoulders hunch, in the tremor that develops in his hands, in how his notebook drops from nerveless fingers to land in the mud. The prepared grids, the careful methodology, the flags meant to mark geological data, all of it becomes absurd theater in the face of something that exists outside logic.

The hum intensifies, not louder but deeper, adding harmonics that Vincent feels in his bone marrow. The floodlights flicker again, this time in sequence, creating a wave of darkness that rolls across the construction site before the light returns. In that moment of shadow, Vincent sees things that shouldn't be there: shapes moving beneath the surface of the clay, the suggestion of vast forms shifting in depths that exceed the physical possibilities of the earth.

The ground beneath them shifts with the slow, deliberate motion of something drawing breath, not the violent upheaval of an earthquake but the gentle rise and fall of a chest that spans acres. Vincent feels it through his boots, watches it in the way Owen staggers slightly, sees it in how June's camera swings on its strap. The clay doesn't crack or split; it simply lifts perhaps an inch, holds for three heartbeats, then settles back with a soft sigh that releases the scent of minerals and decay and something older and unnamed.

Where their boots have pressed into the clay, water begins to seep upward, not flowing from anywhere but emerging from the soil itself as if squeezed from a sponge. The liquid carries that familiar red tinge, the color of iron and blood and the deep light Vincent saw in June's photographs. It fills their footprints first, perfect molds of their passage, then overflows to pool in the low places between.

Vincent watches his own trail disappear as the water rises, each boot print becoming a small red mirror that reflects nothing but darkness. The path back to the fence, so clear moments ago in the disturbed earth, vanishes beneath the spreading water. Their orange marker flags remain, bright points in the fog, but the ground between them transforms into something that looks more like a wound than a construction site.

Around Mira, the water behaves differently. It rises in a perfect spiral, starting at her feet and climbing outward in concentric circles that follow mathematical precision rather than natural physics. The spiral expands with each pulse of the underground hum, adding rings that maintain exact spacing. The red liquid doesn't touch Mira herself, maintaining a barrier of perhaps two inches from her boots, as if she stands in a cylinder of air that the water refuses to enter.

She remains in her trance state, eyes closed, that subtle sway continuing in rhythm with something only she perceives. Her lips move now, not quite speech but something closer to counting, or perhaps reciting coordinates in a voice too soft for the others to hear. The reflected image in the spiral of water shows her differently again, this version with arms spread wide, palms up as if receiving rain that doesn't fall in their reality.

June's camera clicks rapidly, the sound sharp and mechanical against the organic hum. She moves around Mira's position, capturing angles, trying to document what shouldn't exist. Her hands shake enough that Vincent wonders about image blur, but she continues shooting, compelled by the same instinct that makes people photograph disasters, as if evidence might provide understanding. The camera's flash fires once, illuminating the fog in a sphere of white that makes the red water appear black for an instant.

Owen has given up on his EMF meter, the device now silent, possibly burned out by readings that exceeded its capacity to measure. He's on his knees in the wet clay, notebook retrieved and pressed against his thigh as he writes with frantic urgency. Vincent can't see the words from this distance, but he recognizes the desperation in Owen's movements, the need to transform experience into data before memory has time to edit what shouldn't be possible.

The water continues rising, not uniformly but in patterns that follow the grid lines Owen had them walk. It creates channels between their sections, flowing in straight lines that intersect at perfect angles, transforming their investigation pattern into something that looks deliberate, ritualistic, as if their very presence has activated something that was waiting for this specific configuration of bodies and movement.

"Let's go," Vincent says, the words coming out steady despite the tremor he feels building in his chest. The simple statement breaks something, disrupts whatever held them frozen in observation. June lowers her camera, Owen closes his notebook, and even Mira's eyes flutter open, though her gaze remains unfocused, directed at something beyond the physical scene.

They move toward the fence, no longer maintaining Owen's careful grid pattern but picking their way between pools of red water that seem to deepen with each passing second. Vincent keeps his hand on Mira's elbow, guiding her around the worst of it, though she moves with uncanny grace that suggests she knows exactly where to step. The fog has thickened, making the fence invisible until they're almost upon it, the chain-link materializing from gray nothing like a border between worlds.

Behind them, the hum continues, and Vincent realizes it's following them, or perhaps they're carrying it with them, the frequency now embedded in their bones, in the fluid of their bodies, in the spaces between their cells. June reaches the gap in the fence first, squeezing through with movements made clumsy by fear. Owen follows, his backpack catching again, requiring Vincent to push it through while Owen twists his body at angles that look painful.

Mira pauses at the gap, turns back toward the construction site, and for a moment Vincent sees it through her eyes, or thinks he does. Not a wounded piece of earth but something more like a mouth, or a pore, or a place where the boundary between above and below has worn thin enough for communication. She tilts her head as if listening to farewell words, then slips through the fence with fluid ease.

Vincent goes last, the metal scraping against his jacket, rust flakes falling like red snow. His boots hit solid pavement on the other side, and the contrast makes him stumble, the stability of unchanging ground suddenly foreign after the responsive earth of the construction site. They stand together, breathing hard, fog condensing on their faces and running down like tears.

The hum from the construction site fades gradually, not cutting off but retreating, sinking back to wherever it originates. But in that fading, in the space between audible sound and complete silence, something else rises. Not from the construction site but from much deeper, from the convergence point of all those coordinates, from whatever lies beneath grid square N-17 and beyond.

It's not quite sound and not quite vibration but something between. It lasts perhaps five seconds, this deep acknowledgment, this answer to their investigation. It doesn't feel threatening or welcoming, just aware, as if something vast has registered their presence, catalogued their intrusion, and settled back to its patient waiting.

The fog swallows the construction site, making it invisible from where they stand. But Vincent knows it's changed, knows that their investigation has triggered something or confirmed something or perhaps simply announced their readiness to entities that have been listening all along. The red water will sink back into the earth by morning, the footprints will be gone, and the official story will involve groundwater contamination or mineral deposits. But deep below, in places maps don't show and coordinates only hint at, something breathes with renewed purpose.

They separate without discussion, June heading north toward downtown, Owen east toward the residential district, Vincent and Mira south toward their home. No one suggests comparing notes or meeting tomorrow. What they've experienced exists beyond their ability to process collectively, requiring solitude to either accept or deny.

As Vincent walks beside Mira through streets made strange by fog, he feels the rhythm from the construction site still pulsing in his bones, fainter now but persistent, like an infection of frequency that his body can't quite reject. Beside him, Mira hums softly, not quite matching the underground rhythm but harmonizing with it, creating intervals that make the fog around them shimmer with possibilities that normal physics would deny.

CHAPTER
TEN

The stairs to St. Clement's basement descend through air that grows thicker with each step, carrying the weight of decades in its mixture of furniture polish and stone dust, and Vincent counts each worn wooden tread as they creak beneath his weight, a countdown toward revelations none of them have properly prepared for. Behind him, June's camera bag bumps against the narrow walls with soft thuds that echo in the confined space. Owen follows with his backpack held against his chest to avoid scraping the peeling paint. Mira moves last, her footfalls so light they barely register on the protesting wood.

The basement opens before them like a mouth that's been holding its breath. A single bulb hangs from a cloth-wrapped cord, its amber light creating a sphere of visibility that makes the darkness beyond seem absolute. The flagstone floor spreads outward in irregular pieces fitted together by some long-dead mason, the mortar between them gone soft and crumbling, releasing the scent of minerals and time. Vincent's breath clouds faintly in the chill, though outside the April afternoon carries warmth that makes people forget winter ever existed.

In the corner, the boiler squats like something prehistoric, its metal belly rounded and riveted, painted in layers of green that have bubbled and flaked to reveal older colors beneath. It rattles with a rhythm that seems too deliberate for mere machinery, a percussion that travels through the floor and into Vincent's feet. The sound isn't quite regular, occasionally skipping a beat or adding an extra click, as if the mechanism inside follows its own logic rather than engineering principles.

Dust motes drift through the lamp's glow with the laziness of underwater creatures, stirred by their movement but in no hurry to settle. The particles catch the light and transform it, creating a golden haze that softens edges while making distances uncertain. Along the walls, wooden shelves bow under the weight of ledgers and boxes, their contents hidden behind labels written in fountain pen that's faded to the color of dried blood.

Owen moves to the wooden table that dominates the center of the space, its surface scarred by decades of use, marked with ring stains from forgotten coffee cups and scratches that might be accidental or might form patterns if viewed from the right angle. He sets his backpack down with the care of someone handling explosives, then begins extracting their collected materials.

The maps come first, yellowed and brittle as autumn leaves, unfolding with sounds like whispered warnings. Each crease threatens to become a tear, and Owen's fingers move delicately as he weights the corners with smooth stones someone has left here for exactly this purpose. The paper bears the watermark of companies that no longer exist, their logos ghostly impressions visible only when the light hits at certain angles.

Next come the log pages, rescued from filing cabinets and forgotten boxes throughout Duswood, some officially stamped, others bearing the hasty scrawl of workers who never expected their observations to be read seventy years later. The ink has gone brown with age, and some pages show water damage that makes the words blur into abstract patterns. Owen arranges them chronologically, creating a timeline of something that resisted being documented.

The notebook comes last, half-crushed and stained with what might be motor oil or might be something else. Its leather cover has gone soft with handling, and the binding barely holds the pages together. Owen sets it apart from the other materials, as if even he recognizes it contains something different, something more personal than official reports.

June pulls her tablet from her bag, the modern device looking anachronistic in this space where time moves differently. She connects it to a portable scanner, the blue LED seeming harsh against the basement's amber atmosphere. Her movements carry their usual precision, but Vincent notices how she pauses before touching each document, as if asking permission from the paper itself.

She begins with the log pages, feeding them through the scanner with steady rhythm. The device hums as it works, a frequency that harmonizes uncomfortably with the boiler's rattle, creating beats never heard before. The digitization feels like translation, converting physical evidence into patterns of light and absence that computers can understand but that might lose something essential in the conversion.

When June reaches for the notebook, her hand hovers for a moment above its damaged cover. Something about it demands different attention, slower consideration. She opens it carefully, and even from where Vincent stands, he can see how the handwriting changes partway through. The early entries are neat, professional, the work of someone maintaining official records. But gradually the script loosens, becomes more personal, as if the writer stopped caring about regulations and started caring about truth.

June's finger traces down a page, not quite touching the

paper, following the progression from order to something else. She stops at a section where the text crowds against the margins, where someone has written sideways along the edge in pencil so faint it's barely visible. Her tablet captures the page, but she doesn't move to the next one. Instead, she leans closer, adjusting the lamp to throw light across the pencil marks.

"There's something here," she says, her voice barely above a whisper, as if speaking too loudly might make the words disappear. She tilts the notebook, and the light catches the graphite at just the right angle, making the margin note visible.

Vincent reads the words, and something cold moves through his chest: "Resonance displays pattern-seeking behavior. Responds to attention."

The handwriting is different from the rest of the notebook, slower, more careful, as if each letter required enormous effort. The words themselves feel heavy with implication, suggesting something that observes the observer, that changes based on being perceived. June doesn't read them aloud, but she angles the notebook so the others can see, creating a moment of shared recognition that needs no vocalization.

Vincent stares at the phrase, and something personal stirs in his memory. The way the words are constructed, the particular choice of "pattern-seeking behavior" instead of simpler terms, reminds him of how his father used to describe complex systems when Vincent was young, before he left, before everything changed. It's the language of someone trying to be precise about something that defies precision, trying to maintain scientific distance from something that refuses to stay distant.

The boiler chooses that moment to skip two beats in succession, creating a gap in its rhythm that makes the silence seem profound. Then it resumes, but the pattern has changed slightly, as if responding to their discovery, as if the building itself has registered what they've found. The mechanical heartbeat continues, underlying their breathing, their movements, the soft whisper of turning pages, creating a rhythm that will follow them long after they leave this basement.

Vincent reaches past the notebook to lift an older map from the stack, its surface crackling with the brittleness of paper that's been folded and refolded until the creases have become geography of their own. The document feels heavier than paper should, as if it carries the weight of all the paths traced across its surface, all the destinations marked and unmarked, all the journeys that ended differently than intended. He spreads it carefully beside the others, and the amber light reveals a complexity that modern maps have forgotten how to show.

This isn't a simple survey chart but something more ambitious, more honest about the layers beneath Duswood's surface. The main GNRO rail lines appear as bold black arteries, but spreading from them like capillaries are dozens of auxiliary routes, some marked with solid lines, others dotted to indicate planned or temporary passages. They branch outward with organic irregularity, following contours that suggest the earth itself dictated their paths rather than human engineering.

Vincent's fingers trace these lesser routes, feeling the slight depression where ink has soaked deep into paper fibers. Some lead to marked destinations: "Auxiliary Pump Station #3," "Emergency Ventilation Shaft," "Storage Nexus C." Others simply fade into the margins, their purposes lost to time or never recorded in the first place. The detail is obsessive, as if the cartographer couldn't stop adding information, couldn't stop documenting every possible connection between surface and depth.

The map extends beyond Duswood proper, showing the surrounding geology with elevation lines that create topographic patterns resembling fingerprints or tree rings. To the north, the paper depicts the pine forests that still stand, though thinner now than when this map was drawn. The trees are indicated by small triangular symbols packed so densely they create areas of solid green ink, broken only by the thin lines indicating trails or logging roads.

That's where Vincent's attention catches on something that doesn't belong to the original cartography. In the midst of the northern pines, where the elevation lines suggest a natural depression, someone has drawn a circle in red pencil. The mark is light, almost hesitant, as if the person making it understood they were violating something by adding to this official document. It's not a formal annotation but something more personal, more secret, the kind of mark someone makes to remember a location they're not supposed to know about.

The circle encompasses a small area where several auxiliary routes converge without explanation. According to the map's legend, nothing official exists there, no pump station or ventilation shaft, no storage facility or maintenance junction. Yet the routes lead to it with the certainty of water finding the lowest point, as if the infrastructure couldn't help but connect to whatever occupies that space.

"Look at this," Vincent says, though his voice comes out rougher than intended, scraped by the basement's thick air and the dust of old paper.

The others gather around the table, their bodies creating shadows that dance across the map's surface as they lean in. June adjusts her tablet to capture the image, but her attention focuses more on the actual document than her screen. Owen's breathing changes, becomes shallower, more controlled, the way it does when he's processing information that challenges his frameworks.

Mira moves last and most deliberately, gliding around the table's edge to stand directly across from Vincent. The red circle lies between them, and her gaze fixes on it with an intensity that makes the amber light seem to brighten slightly. Her eyes don't scan the surrounding area or trace the converging routes. They lock onto that penciled mark as if she can read the intention of whoever drew it, can feel the pressure of their hand through decades of separation.

The hum that has followed them for weeks brushes against Vincent's awareness, faint as moth wings against glass, but he can tell from Mira's expression that she hears it more clearly. It's not coming from the boiler or the building's infrastructure but from somewhere else, somewhere that might be far away or might be closer than skin.

Her hands rise slowly from her sides, fingers spreading as they hover above the map. She doesn't touch it immediately, instead holding her palms perhaps three inches above the surface, as if testing the temperature or sensing something that radiates from the paper itself. The dust motes in the air between her hands and the map begin to move differently, no longer drifting randomly but organizing into subtle spirals that follow the same pattern as the beetles' ash, as the water at the construction site, as every other impossible thing they've witnessed.

When her fingertips finally make contact with the map, something shifts in the basement's atmosphere. The change is subtle but undeniable, like the pressure drop before a storm or the moment when a tuning fork finds its resonant partner. The paper beneath her touch doesn't visibly change, but Vincent swears he can feel warmth radiating from that point of contact, spreading outward through the document's fibers like blood through capillaries.

Mira's eyes close halfway, not fully shut but no longer focused on the physical map. Her breathing synchronizes with something Vincent can almost hear, a rhythm that exists just below perception, transmitted through the floor and walls and the very air they breathe. The red circle seems to pulse with its own faint light, though that might be a trick of the amber bulb and the way shadows shift as Mira sways slightly in place.

The map warms beneath her fingers, not dramatically but enough that Vincent can see it in the way the paper relaxes slightly, old creases softening as if the document remembers being new, being drawn by steady hands that knew exactly what they were documenting and why it needed to remain secret. The warmth spreads from Mira's touch toward the edges of the map, and where it passes, details become clearer, as if decades of fading reverse themselves in response to her attention.

Owen watches this with the expression of someone whose scientific training wars with direct observation. His notebook lies forgotten beside him, his pencil still in his hand but motionless. Vincent can see him cataloging what he's witnessing, trying to fit it into categories that make sense: psychosomatic response, suggestion, confirmation bias. But his eyes track the actual warming of the paper, the way Mira's touch seems to wake something in the document itself, and his analytical framework cracks a little more.

"It knows," Mira whispers, though her lips barely move. The words might be meant for them or for something else, something that exists in the convergence of those auxiliary routes, in the place marked by red pencil where someone once found something worth circling but not worth officially recording.

Owen's hand moves almost involuntarily toward the damaged notebook while Mira still communes with the map, his fingers finding a tear in the binding where something protrudes like a bookmark made of older paper. He pulls at it gently, and a folded memo emerges from between pages that have compressed it for decades. The paper feels different from the notebook's pages, thinner, more official, bearing the phantom watermark of corporate letterhead when held toward the light.

The memo has been torn irregularly, as if someone ripped it from a larger document in haste or anger. The exposed edge shows fibers pulled apart rather than cut, leaving the left margin jagged and incomplete. Words begin mid-sentence on some lines, their beginnings lost to whatever violence separated this fragment from its whole. But enough remains to suggest context, to hint at communications that should never have been necessary.

Owen unfolds it with the same care he applies to everything, though Vincent notices his hands have developed a tremor that wasn't there when they descended the stairs. The paper wants to stay folded, its creases set by time and pressure, but Owen persists until it lies relatively flat on the table. The typewritten text has faded to gray, but someone has underlined one sentence in ink that has aged to brown, the emphasis so forceful it nearly tore through the paper.

He leans closer, adjusting his glasses, and reads silently first. Vincent watches his expression shift from curiosity to confusion to something approaching fear before settling into a forced neutrality that doesn't reach his eyes. Owen's throat works as he swallows, and when he reads the underlined portion aloud, his voice carries the quality of someone reciting something they wish they hadn't found.

"Entity demonstrates desire for correspondence. Believes identity depends on recognition."

The words hang in the basement air like smoke from a snuffed candle, visible in their implication even as they dissipate into the larger darkness. Vincent feels them settle into his understanding, not as abstract concepts but as description of something specific, something that was observed and documented by someone who had to name what shouldn't exist.

Owen sets the memo aside with movements that try to appear casual but carry too much precision, the gesture of someone handling something contaminated. His fingers drum once against the table, then still themselves with visible effort. When he speaks, his voice has thinned to something barely more substantial than the whisper of turning pages.

"Corporate nonsense," he says, but the words come out hollow, unconvincing even to himself. "You know how these companies were. Everything had to sound important. Make the quarterly reports look good."

Nobody responds because nobody believes him, including Owen himself. The description is too specific, too strange to be corporate padding. Someone wrote those words because they needed to document what they'd encountered, needed to warn or inform or simply confirm to themselves that it was real. The underlining suggests someone else found it important enough to emphasize, to ensure it wouldn't be over- looked among the routine observations.

June reaches past Owen to close the notebook with a soft thud. The sound bounces off the flagstone floor, the brick walls, the low ceiling, creating a diminishing series of impacts that feel like counting down to something. Her fingers rest on the leather cover for a moment, and Vincent sees her processing what they've discovered, adding it to the growing catalog of impossibilities they've accumulated.

"Whatever they were doing down there," she says, her voice steady but carrying an edge that suggests control rather than calm, "they weren't just measuring temperature."

The statement feels like confession, like acknowledging what they've all been avoiding. The GNRO papers suggest something beyond industrial accident or geological anomaly. They document interaction, observation of behavior, attempts to understand something that existed outside their frame- works but demanded recognition nonetheless. The workers in those tunnels found something or something found them, and what followed was strange enough that even their careful corporate language couldn't entirely disguise it.

Mira's attention remains on the map, but Vincent can tell she's listening. Her fingers still rest on the red circle, and the warmth beneath them has spread to encompass most of the northern section. When she speaks, her voice carries that quality it has when she's partially elsewhere, receiving information through channels the rest of them can't access.

"It remembers whoever wrote this," she says softly, each word deliberate. "And it's still listening."

The basement falls into stillness. The boiler's rattle continues but seems suddenly more invasive, its rhythm shifting to match something Vincent can't identify. The mechanical sound takes on an organic quality, less like metal expanding and contracting and more like something learning to speak through available materials. Each click and hiss might be attempted communication, signals sent through the building's infrastructure by something that has learned to use pipes and ducts as vocal cords.

Outside, the wind changes direction without transition. One moment it pushes against the eastern windows, the next it comes from the north, and Vincent hears tree branches scrape against glass with a sound like fingernails seeking entry. The shift feels deliberate, as if something vast has turned its attention toward St. Clement's, toward this basement where they've disturbed papers that should have remained buried in archives.

The dust motes in the amber light begin to move with purpose that defies air currents. They rise from their lazy drift, organizing into a spiral that climbs toward the ceiling. The pattern is perfect, mathematical, each particle maintaining exact distance from its neighbors as they ascend. It's the same spiral the beetles drew, the same pattern Mira's presence created in the water, the signature of something that communicates through geometry rather than words.

Vincent watches the dust spiral tighten, then expand, then tighten again, as if breathing. The particles catch the light differently at various heights, creating the illusion of solidity, of form within the formless. For a moment, just a heartbeat, the spiral seems to pause at its apex, holding its shape with impossible precision. Then it collapses all at once, the dust settling back to the floor in a perfectly circular pattern that wasn't there before.

The circle matches exactly the one drawn in red pencil on the map.

They stand frozen around the table, four teenagers who have stumbled into correspondence with something that has been waiting decades for recognition again. The basement holds them in its amber light while shadows press against the edges of visibility. The boiler continues its altered rhythm, the wind maintains its attention on the windows, and somewhere beneath layers of earth and stone and infrastructure, something vast and patient adjusts its breathing to match theirs, finally heard, finally seen, finally recognized after years of sending signals through beetle spirals and red water and the dreams of those sensitive enough to receive them.

The dust circle remains on the floor, delicate as frost but somehow more permanent, a response written in particles and light to their investigation. It suggests that every document they examine, every pattern they trace, every coordinate they follow is part of a conversation that began before they were born and will continue long after they're gone, with or without their participation, though something about their particular configuration, their specific attention, has made them suitable for correspondence with entities that exist in the convergence of the physical and the impossible.

CHAPTER
ELEVEN

Pine needles crunch beneath Vincent's boots with a sound like the bones of birds breaking, each footfall releasing the scent of resin and something sharper that he can't place, and he follows Owen's hunched form through trees that stand too straight, too uniform, as if they've been arranged rather than grown. The late afternoon sun angles through the canopy in columns of dusty gold, but the light feels harsher, too heavy, like it carries weight that normal photons shouldn't possess. Vincent pulls his notebook from his jacket pocket, the small book already half-filled with observations since they left St. Clement's basement an hour ago, and sketches their path with quick, precise strokes while walking.

Behind him, June's camera clicks in irregular intervals, capturing something in the undergrowth. The sound should be sharp in the forest quiet, but it comes out muffled, as if the air itself has thickened to absorb noise before it can travel far. Mira moves at the group's edge, her fingers trailing along bark as she passes each tree, reading something in the texture that translates to the slight furrow between her eyebrows.

Owen stops ahead, consulting the handheld GPS device that he bought specifically for this expedition. The screen glows green against his palm, numbers shifting as satellites triangulate their position relative to coordinates copied from a map drawn when such technology was still science fiction. His shoulders carry tension that wasn't there when they started, each recalculation of their position adding another degree of rigidity to his posture.

"Another quarter mile," he says, though his voice lacks the confidence it held in the basement. The forest has a way of making certainty feel presumptuous.

Vincent notes their position in his book: 45.7859° N, -87.0997° W. The numbers feel significant in a way he can't articulate, as if they're not just measurements but incantations, each decimal point bringing them closer to something that has been waiting. He adds a note about the silence, how it settled over them gradually after they crossed the first ridge, the bird songs fading to nothing, even the insects going quiet until only their footsteps and breathing remain.

The pines give way to a cluster of cedars, and that's when they see it: thick red sap weeping from the bark in vertical streams that catch the filtered sunlight like blood under skin. The substance moves too slowly to be normal sap, its viscosity suggesting something between liquid and solid, and where it pools at the trees' bases, the pine needles have dissolved into a rust-colored paste that releases steam despite the cool air.

June circles the nearest tree, her camera raised, adjusting focus to capture the patterns the sap creates as it descends. Through her lens, Vincent glimpses what she sees: the streams don't flow randomly but follow specific paths, creating designs in the bark that remind him of the beetle spirals, of the dust circle in the basement, of every other signature they've encountered from whatever seeks correspondence with them.

"Don't touch it," Owen warns unnecessarily. None of them would dare. The sap gives off heat they can feel from three feet away, and the smell intensifies near it, a metallic tang that makes Vincent's teeth feel loose in his gums.

They continue deeper, following Owen's device as it leads them along a path that no human has walked in decades, though Vincent notices occasional evidence of older passage: a rusted metal stake driven into the ground, its purpose lost to time; initials carved into bark that has long since healed over; a stretch where the trees grow in perfectly straight lines, suggesting they were planted rather than naturally seeded.

The temperature rises with each step, not dramatically but noticeably, the way it does when ascending from a basement in winter. Vincent checks his phone's weather app, which claims it's fifty-eight degrees, but his skin insists on something closer to seventy. The discrepancy makes him distrust further readings, even his own senses, as if the forest exists in a bubble where normal physics applies only intermittently.

Mira stops at a massive cedar whose trunk spans four feet across, her palm pressed flat against its bark. She stands perfectly still, eyes closed, and Vincent watches her breathing slow. When she speaks, her voice carries that distant quality that means she's partially elsewhere.

"It's not just warm," she says. "It's breathing."

Owen's compass, which has been relatively stable, suddenly spins wildly. The needle doesn't just waver but rotates continuously clockwise, faster and faster until it's a blur of motion that makes the device vibrate in his hand. He drops it with a curse that sounds more like surprise than anger, and they all watch it skitter across the pine needles, still spinning, creating a small depression in the forest floor from its movement.

The trees around them creak despite the absence of wind, a sound that travels through the forest in a wave, each trunk adding its voice to create a wooden chorus that rises and falls like ocean waves. Vincent feels it through his feet, the vibration traveling up from deep below, through root systems that connect every tree in a network of communication that predates human language.

His notebook fills with observations: "Trees lean toward central point despite sun position." "Ground temperature increases near certain trunks." "Air pressure feels higher, ears popping like elevation change." Each note attempts to document the undocumentable, to make rational what exists outside reason. But he continues writing because the alternative is to stand frozen in recognition of how far they've traveled from the normal world, not in miles but in the degree to which reality has bent around their destination.

June photographs a section of undergrowth where the ferns have grown in a perfect spiral, their fronds interlocking to create a pattern twenty feet across that looks deliberate, designed, as if the forest itself has been leaving messages for those who know how to read them. Her camera's flash illuminates details invisible in the natural light: tiny red filaments running through the green, connecting each plant to its neighbors in a web of biological correspondence that suggests singular purpose despite multiple organisms.

The metallic taste intensifies. It's not just taste anymore but a frequency, a signal broadcast through the medium of their bodies, using iron in their blood as an antenna. Beside Vincent, Owen wipes his nose and his hand comes away with a small streak of red, though he quickly hides it in his pocket before the others notice.

They're close now. Vincent doesn't need the GPS to know it; the forest itself announces their proximity to whatever the red circle marked. The trees grow denser but defy natural order, their trunks twisted in helical patterns, their branches reaching toward something that isn't the sun. The ground beneath their feet has gone soft, not with moisture but with heat, as if they're walking on flesh rather than earth.

The shack emerges from the undergrowth like something the forest has been trying to digest, its corrugated steel walls green with oxidation and streaked with red sap that forms patterns too deliberate for random decay. Half the roof has caved inward, creating a cavity where rain and decades have entered freely, and through the gap Vincent can see exposed rafters that look more like ribs than construction beams. Vines have wound through the damage, but they're withered and black, killed by contact with something that even plant life recognizes as hostile.

The structure sits at an angle that suggests the ground beneath has shifted since its construction, one corner sunk deeper than the others, giving the whole building a tilted quality. From a rusted breaker box mounted on the exterior wall, wires spill out in loops and tangles, their rubber insulation gnawed away to expose copper that has gone green with verdigris. The wires disappear into the earth at various points, creating a root system of defunct electrical connection that must have once powered something significant.

Owen approaches the door first, his hand hesitating over the handle that hangs at an angle from bent hinges. The metal feels warm even before he touches it, radiating heat that has no source in this shaded forest hollow. When his fingers make contact, he pulls back sharply, then forces himself to grip it properly. The handle turns with a grinding protest that sends vibrations through the entire structure, making the corrugated walls shimmer.

The door swings inward on hinges that shriek despite the rust that should have frozen them solid. Dust explodes outward from the disturbance. The particles catch the late afternoon light filtering through the canopy, creating a golden helix that exists for three seconds before physics reclaims it. June's camera captures the moment, though Vincent doubts the image will convey the deliberateness of the motion, the way it felt more like greeting than coincidence.

Inside, the shack reveals itself as something between storage facility and monitoring station. Shelves line three walls, their metal frames bent beneath the weight of equipment that belongs to an era when analog was the only option. Stacks of logbooks create leaning towers of yellowed paper, their covers bearing dates in careful handwriting: "May 1947 - June 1947," "Annual Review 1949," "Incident Reports Jan-Dec 1951." The specificity suggests bureaucracy, but the sheer volume implies something worth documenting in obsessive detail.

Cracked gauge faces stare blindly from a control panel that takes up most of the fourth wall. Their needles have frozen at various positions, some buried in red zones that indicate dangers the measurements can no longer specify. Labels beneath each gauge have faded but remain partially legible: "Resonance Amplitude," "Ground Conductivity," "Signal Depth." The terminology straddles the line between electrical engineering and something more arcane, as if the installers weren't quite sure what they were measuring.

June moves through the space, her camera documenting everything. The flash fires repeatedly, each burst of white light revealing new details that the filtered forest light obscures. On the walls, between the shelves and around the gauges, Vincent notices marks that weren't immediately visible. Spiral sigils have been burned or etched into the metal, their patterns matching those they've seen everywhere else but with variations that suggest evolution, as if whatever creates them has been refining its signature over time.

Old field radios occupy one shelf, their cases cracked and dials clouded with age. Vincent picks one up, feeling its surprising weight, the heft of components built to last rather than to be convenient. When he turns a knob experimentally, it moves smoothly despite decades of abandonment, and from deep within the device comes a sound like breathing through static, though no power source exists to generate even that ghost of function.

Mira wanders the edges of the space, her fingers hovering near but not quite touching various objects. She pauses at a clipboard hanging from a nail, its papers so degraded they would likely crumble if disturbed. Her eyes narrow as she reads something visible only to her, perhaps the impression of words that pressure and time have embedded in the wall behind.

In the corner furthest from the door, a military-green tarp covers something angular, its surface thick with dust except where recent moisture has created dark patches that look disturbingly organic. Vincent approaches it with the caution of someone defusing explosives, aware that in this place, any discovery could trigger responses they're not prepared to handle. The tarp feels heavier than canvas should, as if it's absorbed years of atmospheric weight, and when he pulls it away, it resists briefly before releasing with a soft tearing sound.

Beneath lies a hatch set into the floor, its metal surface painted industrial yellow that has faded to the color of old bones. Massive bolts secure it at regular intervals around its circumference, each one as thick as Vincent's thumb and painted over so many times the angles have disappeared beneath layers of industrial enamel. The paint job looks deliberate, obsessive, as if someone desperately needed to seal not just the hatch but the very knowledge of its existence.

The metal around the bolts shows stress patterns, radiating cracks that suggest enormous pressure from below, contained but not comfortably. In the center of the hatch, barely visible beneath the paint, Vincent can make out raised letters that spell something, though generations of paint make them illegible. The whole assembly feels foreign, not just its presence in this remote shack but its very existence, as if it's a barrier between states of being rather than simple levels of architecture.

"Don't," Owen starts to say, but Mira has already knelt beside the hatch, her hand extending toward its center with the inevitability of gravity.

When her palm makes contact with the painted surface, something shifts in the shack's atmosphere. The temperature drops five degrees in an instant, making their breath suddenly visible. The paint beneath Mira's touch begins to crack, but not randomly. The cracks spread in perfect circles radiating from her hand, each ring maintaining exact distance from the others, creating patterns within patterns that reveal deeper layers of paint, each one a different color, each one representing another attempt to permanently seal whatever lies beneath.

The paint flakes away in sections, falling like snow to reveal bare metal beneath that glows faintly with its own warmth, as if Mira's touch has awakened something that has been sleeping beneath layers of industrial paranoia. The raised letters become visible as the paint clears: "AUXILIARY ACCESS - ROOT CHANNEL 7."

June photographs the transformation, her camera struggling to focus on something that seems to exist at multiple depths simultaneously. Owen backs toward the door, he watches paint that has held for seventy years surrender to a seventeen-year-old's touch. Vincent feels the floor vibrate beneath his feet, not violently but steadily, as if massive machinery has begun to warm up somewhere far below, triggered by recognition of someone it has been waiting for.

———

Owen spots the file cabinet toppled behind a stack of equipment crates, its drawers sprung open from impact that happened decades ago, papers spilling out like entrails from something gutted. He picks his way across the debris-strewn floor, avoiding rusted metal fragments and sections where the floorboards have gone soft with rot. When he reaches the cabinet, he has to use both hands to pry the top drawer fully open, the metal groaning as rust flakes rain down on the scattered documents below.

His hands emerge clutching folders that should have disintegrated years ago but remain intact through some quality of the paper or the air in this place that resists normal decay. The covers bear stamps in red ink: "ROOT CHANNEL AUXILIARY" and below that, "SUBJECT RESPONSE TESTING." The words feel heavy in the confined space, carrying implications that he doesn't want to imagine.

Owen spreads the documents across the clearest section of floor, kneeling to arrange them with his typical precision despite the tremor in his hands. The papers reveal themselves like tarot cards telling a fortune no one wants to hear. Blueprints unfold to show cross-sections of Duswood's underground, but not the town anyone living knows. These drawings depict massive structures beneath the familiar streets, geometric forms that hurt to perceive directly.

The central image makes June gasp: enormous black iron rings, each one fifty feet in diameter according to the scale notation, installed at varying depths beneath the town. The rings interconnect through channels marked with measurements that seem impossible, distances that exceed the physical space available. Vincent counts seven rings in the main diagram, arranged in a pattern that reminds him of electron shells around an atom's nucleus, if atoms were the size of city blocks and made of metal that predates human metallurgy.

Photographs paper-clipped to the blueprints show the actual construction. Men in 1940s work clothes stand dwarfed by curved sections of black metal that gleam with an oily iridescence. In one image, a worker has his hand pressed against the ring's surface, and his face wears an expression of rapture or horror, the two emotions so close they become indistinguishable. Other photos show the rings installed, their surfaces reflecting light that doesn't match any source visible in the frame.

Owen finds charts beneath the blueprints, graphs plotting energy readings over time. The measurements spike to impossible levels, notated in megawatts, then gigawatts, numbers that shouldn't have been achievable with 1940s technology. Someone has written margin notes in pencil: "Resonance exceeds calculated parameters" and "Ground temperature rising despite cooling systems" and, in different handwriting, "It knows we're listening."

A typed report, carbon-copied so many times the words blur at the edges, describes attempts to establish "bilateral communication with the Root Titan." The language shifts between technical jargon and something more desperate, as if the writer couldn't maintain professional distance from what they documented. Phrases leap out from the yellowed pages: "responds to human bioelectrical fields," "requires conscious interface for activation," "the mirror must be willing."

Vincent's breath catches at that last phrase. He meets Mira's eyes across the scattered papers, seeing his own understanding reflected there. She nods slightly, confirming what they both recognize. The mirror. The human element needed to bridge between what exists below and what exists above. The same principle The Adversary has been exploiting, using people as conduits for its influence.

"What's a human mirror?" June asks, her camera hanging forgotten as she processes the documents.

Owen looks up from a diagram showing energy flow between the rings, his face pale beneath the shack's strange light. "Some kind of conductor, maybe? A person who can channel whatever energy they were trying to access?"

Vincent feels the weight of explanation pressing on him. Things they've kept contained, experiences they've barely discussed even among themselves, suddenly need voice. The shack around them seems to lean in, its damaged walls creating an amphitheater for truth.

"He's not the energy," Vincent says, his voice steady despite the tightness in his throat. "He's a manipulator. A deceiver. We've encountered him before."

The words feel insufficient for describing The Adversary, that presence that exists in static and shadow, in the spaces between thoughts where doubt lives. But Vincent continues, needing them to understand what these documents really describe.

"With Muldrath, he tried to break us through isolation and grief. In Marrowick, through the blooms, through beauty that hid decay. Each time, he needs a human connection. Someone to anchor him to our reality." Vincent gestures at the blueprints, at the rings designed to channel impossible energies. "And now through the Root Titan. Whatever they built down there, they gave him infrastructure."

June steps back from the documents as if they might contaminate her through proximity. "They built a door for something that shouldn't have access."

"Not just a door," Mira says softly, her hand still resting near the painted hatch. "An amplifier. The Root Titan isn't just receiving. It's broadcasting. Has been for seventy years, waiting for the right resonance."

As if responding to its naming, the shack begins to hum. Not the mechanical vibration of the boiler at St. Clement's, but something more organic, more intentional. The sound rises through the floor, through the metal walls that begin to vibrate in harmonics not of the known world. The cracked gauges on the control panel flicker to life momentarily, their needles swinging wildly before freezing again, but in new positions that spell out measurements of something currently active.

Owen scrambles to gather the documents, shoving them

into his backpack with none of his earlier care. The blueprints tear as he folds them roughly, but preservation seems less important than escape as the hum intensifies. June backs toward the door, her camera clutched against her chest like armor against what they've awakened or acknowledged.

The painted hatch beneath Mira's hand grows warm enough that Vincent can feel it from five feet away. More paint flakes off, revealing metal that pulses with deep red light, as if veins run through the iron itself. Mira stands slowly, her movement deliberate rather than fearful.

"We weren't supposed to find this," Owen whispers, his backpack now bulging with stolen knowledge.

Mira turns toward the door, her face carrying that distant expression that means she's perceiving more than the visible scene. "No. But it wanted us to."

The humming resumes, but differently now, almost pleased, as if the shack itself appreciates being discovered, being remembered after decades of abandonment. Vincent follows the others out, but pauses in the doorway to look back at the hatch, at the control panels, at the evidence of humanity's attempt to harness something that exists outside their comprehension.

The floor beneath his feet grows warm, uncomfortably so, heat rising from whatever lies beneath the hatch, beneath the shack, beneath the forest floor where massive iron rings wait in geometric precision for activation. The warmth follows them as they leave, radiating up through pine needles and earth, as if something below the forest floor is waking up, stir-ring after long hibernation, responding to their discovery with its own form of acknowledgment.

They flee through the forest as evening thickens around them, carrying documents that prove what they've suspected: Duswood sits on infrastructure designed to channel forces that shouldn't exist, and The Adversary has been waiting years for the right combination of elements to align. The Root

Titan isn't just a presence beneath the town. It's a mechanism, a transmitter, a connection that can communicate dimensions.

Behind them, the shack continues its humming, a sound that carries further than acoustics should allow, threading through trees and earth to join the larger resonance that runs beneath everything now, patient and vast and finally, terribly, acknowledged.

CHAPTER
TWELVE

Morning arrives at the Duswood High construction site dressed in borrowed celebration, sunlight catching on folding tables that sag beneath boxed lunches next to grills singeing various meats while a makeshift stage groans under the weight of amplifiers and drum kits, the whole scene a desperate pantomime of normalcy painted over ground that Vincent knows harbors something vast and patient beneath its red-tinged surface. Cedar saplings wait in neat rows, their roots wrapped in burlap like bandaged wounds, while volunteers gather with the forced enthusiasm of people who need to believe their town can be healed through community spirit and fresh landscaping.

Vincent arrives with Mira, June, and Owen, their small group moving through the crowd like ghosts at a feast. The festive atmosphere presses against them with aggressive cheer, balloons tied to chain-link fencing, a banner reading "REBUILDING TOGETHER" stretched across the entrance where just weeks ago beetles emerged to write messages in ash. Vincent inhales deeply as he watches children run between the tables, their feet pounding over earth that conceals massive iron rings designed to channel energies that belong in fiction novels.

The mayor circulates with practiced grace, his smile fixed as permanently as his hairpiece, shaking hands and slapping backs with the rhythm of someone who's turned reassurance into performance art. City council members fan out across the site wearing matching t-shirts that proclaim "DUSWOOD STRONG" in letters that seem to shout against the evidence of recent collapses. They direct volunteers with clipboards and megaphones, orchestrating this theater of recovery while carefully avoiding any mention of red water or synchronized beetles or the fact that concrete won't hold in certain spots.

Vincent spots Councilman Richards near the supply tent, his thick frame blocking the morning sun as he gestures at a site map held by two younger volunteers. The man's voice carries that particular tone of authority that comes from never having his certainty challenged by impossibility. Vincent moves toward him, feeling Mira's concerned gaze follow his path, but he can't stand by while people dig into ground that might answer back.

"Councilman Richards," Vincent says, his voice steady despite the tightness in his throat. "We need to talk about the excavation plans."

Richards turns with the slow deliberation of someone who recognizes an irritant but refuses to acknowledge its significance. His eyes narrow as they settle on Vincent, taking in the teenager's serious expression with barely concealed dismissal.

"Young Granger," Richards says, the words carrying a patronizing weight. "Shouldn't you be helping with the saplings? Physical work builds character."

"The ground here isn't stable," Vincent continues, ignoring the deflection. He gestures toward the foundation where red-tinged soil shows through despite attempts to cover it with fresh dirt. "Whatever's beneath this site, disturbing it further could trigger another collapse. Or worse."

Richards' expression shifts from dismissive to actively hostile, his face reddening in a way that has nothing to do with the morning sun. "Worse? Listen, son, we've had every inspector in the state examine this site. Gas leaks, they said. Mineral deposits. Natural phenomena that we're addressing through proper engineering."

"You know that's not true." Vincent's voice rises slightly, drawing attention from nearby volunteers. "The beetles, the tainted water, the resonance patterns. You've seen the reports from the forties, the GNRO infrastructure..."

"Enough." Richards steps closer, using his height advantage to loom over Vincent. His voice drops to a hiss that smells of coffee and barely controlled anger. "I don't know what ghost stories you and your friends have been concocting, but this community needs healing, not superstitious teenagers undermining recovery efforts."

Vincent feels heat rise in his chest, the frustration of trying to warn people who've chosen blindness over acknowledgment. "Superstitious? We found documents. Evidence of something called the Root Titan, massive rings installed beneath the town designed to channel..."

"Fantasy," Richards cuts him off, loud enough now that other volunteers have stopped to watch. "Comic book nonsense from a kid who reads too much science fiction. This is the real world, Granger. We deal in facts, not fever dreams."

The councilman turns his back deliberately, a dismissal that carries more weight than words. Vincent stands frozen, hands clenched at his sides, watching Richards return to his volunteers with jovial authority restored. Around them, the volunteer day continues its performance, but Vincent notices the nervous glances some people cast his way, the whispered conversations that stop when he looks in their direction. They've heard rumors, felt the tremors, seen things that don't fit the official explanations. But accepting those things would mean acknowledging that their town sits on something beyond their control, so they choose Richards' comfortable lies over Vincent's uncomfortable truths.

Near the equipment staging area, Hale Ness directs workers unloading tools with the efficiency of someone who's organized a hundred job sites. His weathered face carries none of the false cheer that infects the council members. Instead, he watches the proceedings with the wariness of someone who's felt the ground reject his attempts at construction, who's seen concrete crack in patterns that follow no structural logic. When he catches Vincent's eye across the crowd, he offers a slight nod, an acknowledgment between those who know the official story is theater.

Sheriff Brennan stands at the perimeter like a sentinel, his presence more about witness than security. His uniform hangs loose on a frame that's lost weight since the beetle emergence, and his eyes never stop moving, scanning the crowd, the ground, the sky, as if danger might come from any direction. Vincent has seen that look before on Joe's face, the hypervigilance of someone who's experienced the impossible and can't stop watching for its return.

The excavator's engine coughs to life with a diesel rumble that cuts through the morning chatter. Luis Ortega sits in the operator's seat, his movements precise as he guides the machine toward the marked spots for cedar plantings. But Vincent notices how Luis pauses between each scoop, studying the earth he's disturbing with an intensity that suggests he remembers his boot branded with spirals, remembers something grabbing him in the collapsed vent shaft. His caution speaks louder than any warning Vincent could offer.

The first tremor announces itself through coffee, dark liquid suddenly alive in paper cups as concentric rings spread outward from invisible epicenters, and Vincent watches his own cup on the folding table create patterns that remind him of the beetle spirals, of the red water's expansion, of every other signature the thing beneath Duswood uses to announce its presence. The local band on stage falters mid-verse, the guitarist staring at his strings as they vibrate without being touched, producing harmonics that join the song uninvited, transforming a cheerful melody into something of terror.

Folding chairs creak in unison, a wooden chorus that has nothing to do with the weight of their occupants and every-thing to do with the vibration rising through their legs from ground that no longer pretends to be stable. Vincent's body recognizes the frequency before his mind catches up, that deep pulse he's felt through bedroom floors and pizzeria foundations, but stronger now, more insistent, as if proximity to so many bodies and so much disturbance has given it permission to fully manifest.

He catches Mira's eye across the crowd, sees his own understanding reflected in her expression. She stands perfectly still while everyone else begins to shift nervously, her stillness making her seem like the only fixed point in a world that's starting to move. Her lips part slightly, and though she's twenty feet away, Vincent swears he hears her whisper, "It's answering."

The vibration intensifies with the patience of something geological, not the sudden violence of an earthquake but the deliberate rise of something stirring from deep sleep. Paper plates slide across tables in synchronized migrations, their movement too uniform to be random. The banner proclaiming "REBUILDING TOGETHER" begins to swing despite the absence of wind, its arc increasing with each pass until the words blur into meaninglessness. Someone's grand-mother drops her cane, and instead of falling straight down, it rolls across the ground before coming to rest pointing directly at the center of the construction site.

Near that center, the earth begins to change. Not cracking at first but bulging, rising like bread dough with too much yeast, the soil itself seeming to expand from within. Vincent watches grass tear at the roots, clumps of sod lifting and separating to reveal darkness beneath that shouldn't exist at surface level. The bulge reaches perhaps three feet in height before it reverses, collapsing inward with a wet sucking sound as he darts to be by Mira's side.

The collapse creates a perfect circle, edges so precise they might have been cut with industrial equipment. Earth falls away into depths that swallow light, and from below comes that familiar red glow, pulsing in rhythm with the vibration that now rattles windows in vehicles a hundred feet away. The crowd's nervous murmur transforms into genuine panic as the hole widens, its circumference expanding in measured increments, each surge precisely timed with the underground pulse.

Luis Ortega's excavator sits too close to the expanding edge, and Vincent watches the exact moment Luis realizes his danger. The machine tilts as earth crumbles beneath its left track, the angle increasing despite Luis's desperate manipulation of controls. Metal groans against the physics of weight and gravity, and Luis makes the calculation everyone can see in his movements: stay and possibly ride it out, or jump to chance survival.

He jumps, but the ground he aims for has begun to crack, a spider web of fractures spreading from the main hole. His left foot hits solid earth but his right finds a section already separating, and his ankle turns with an audible pop that carries even over the crowd's rising cries. Luis goes down hard, his face contorting in pain, dragging himself backward with his hands as the excavator completes its slow fall, disappearing into the hole with a crash that sends vibrations through everyone's bones.

Workers rush toward Luis, but they're forced to circle wide around the expanding collapse, their rescue attempts complicated by ground that can't be trusted. Vincent starts to move toward them when movement at the hole's edge freezes him in place. A small girl, maybe five years old, stumbles at the perimeter, her hand reaching for a stuffed rabbit that has rolled dangerously close to the edge. Her parents scream from somewhere in the crowd, but they're too far away, and the girl's focused entirely on her toy, unaware that the ground beneath it has begun to crumble.

Before Vincent can take a step, Mira appears beside the girl. Not moves toward her, not rushes to help, but simply exists where she wasn't a heartbeat before. Her hand catches the child's shoulder with gentle certainty, guiding her back from the edge while her other hand retrieves the rabbit. The girl looks up at her rescuer with the pure trust of childhood, allowing herself to be led to safety without question.

But Vincent's attention splits, because simultaneously, impossibly, Mira stands beside him.

This first Mira hasn't moved from where she stood when the tremor began. Her eyes are closed, her body perfectly still, but she glows with a light that has nothing to do with the afternoon sun. It's subtle at first, like heat shimmer rising from summer asphalt, but intensifies until she seems to exist in a column of luminescence that extends upward beyond sight. Her lips move in what might be prayer or might be conversation with something only she can perceive, and the air around her tastes of copper and ozone and the deep earth scent that rises from places that have never known sunlight.

The crowd gasps collectively, some pointing at the Mira helping the child, others at the glowing figure beside Vincent, their minds refusing to process the impossibility of her dual presence. Someone shouts about angels, another about demons, but most stand in stunned silence as their understanding of reality cracks as surely as the ground beneath their feet.

The hum that has haunted Duswood for weeks rises from whisper to roar, not in volume but in presence, in the way it saturates everything until Vincent feels it in his core, his bones, his blood. It's not just sound but communication, something vast acknowledging the breach between its domain and theirs. The frequency finds resonance in metal fixtures, in water pipes, in the fillings of people's teeth, creating a harmony never heard before, turning the construction site into an instrument for something that wants to be heard.

Then, as suddenly as it began, everything stops.

The ground seals over with the fluid motion of water finding its level, earth flowing back into place as if the hole never existed. The excavator might never have fallen, Luis might never have jumped, the collapse might be collective hallucination except for the injured man still clutching his twisted ankle and the little girl holding her rescued rabbit. The glowing Mira beside Vincent solidifies, the second Mira vanishes like she never was, her face calm but distant, as if she's returned from traveling somewhere that exists parallel to but separate from this moment.

Silence rushes across the construction site, seeping into every conversation and gesture until even breathing seems too loud for what they've witnessed, and Vincent watches Sheriff Brennan's hand move from forehead to chest to shoulders in a cross that speaks louder than any police report ever could. The sheriff's lips move in what might be the Our Father or might be something more personal, prayers learned from grandparents who knew that Duswood harbored things that required more than bullets and badges to confront. His weathered face has gone pale beneath its permanent tan, and when his eyes meet Vincent's across the crowd, they carry the weight of a man whose last defenses against the impossible have finally crumbled.

Near the spot where the excavator vanished and returned, Hale Ness kneels beside Luis, his thick fingers surprisingly gentle as they probe the injured ankle. Luis grimaces but doesn't cry out, his machismo intact despite the obvious pain. Hale pulls a bandana from his pocket, using it to stabilize the joint with practiced efficiency that speaks of too many job site injuries over the years.

"Lord have mercy," Hale whispers, the words slipping out between instructions to workers bringing a folding chair. "Lord have mercy on us all."

The phrase carries more weight than simple concern for Luis's injury. It's acknowledgment of what they've seen, of Mira existing in two places at once, of ground that swallows machines and then pretends nothing happened. It's the prayer of someone who's run out of rational explanations and must either accept the irrational or lose his mind trying to maintain denial.

The mayor appears at the center of the crowd like an actor hitting his mark, his political instincts overriding whatever shock he might feel. His voice booms with false confidence that fools no one but provides a script for those desperate to follow it.

"Minor settling of the foundation," he announces, his smile stretching wide enough to crack. "These things happen with construction projects. The important thing is no one was seriously hurt, and we can continue our beautification efforts. In fact, this just proves how necessary our reinforcement work truly is."

The words hang in the air like the badly painted backdrop they are, obvious in their inadequacy. Some people nod slowly, grasping at the explanation like drowning swimmers clutching driftwood. Others stand frozen, their eyes tracking between where Mira helped the child and where she stood glowing beside Vincent, trying to reconcile the impossibility with their need for the world to make sense.

June moves through the crowd with her camera, not asking permission, simply documenting. Her lens captures the sealed ground where the hole existed, the disturbed earth that shows no sign of the excavator's fall, the faces of witnesses torn between wonder and terror. The click of her shutter provides a mechanical rhythm that grounds some people, reminding them that evidence exists, that they haven't collectively hallucinated what occurred.

Owen kneels where the collapse happened, his fingers running through soil that maintains warmth despite the afternoon shadows growing long. He pulls his hand back and examines the dirt clinging to his fingers, noting the red tinge that wasn't there this morning, the way it feels less like earth and more like something organic, something that pulsed with its own circulation before returning to dormancy. His notebook appears from his pocket, and he writes with quick, precise strokes, documenting what others will try to forget.

As the crowd thins around them, Vincent stands beside Mira, the little girl now safely back with her parents, who hold her tight as if she might slip away. Mira's gaze is fixed on a point far beyond the construction site, past Duswood, maybe even past the edges of the world. She doesn't turn, but the subtle shift of her posture lets Vincent know she's aware of him, anchored together in the strange calm after everything has changed.

"The whole town knows now," Vincent says quietly, his words meant only for her. "You're about to get popular."

She finally looks at him, her eyes carrying new depths, like she's returned from somewhere farther than sleep, parts of herself still catching up. "I just wanted to help the girl. But now they've all seen something that can't be explained away. Maybe that's what it takes for people to finally listen…to see what's really beneath us."

"That's not going to matter to them," Vincent gestures at the crowd, at the people already forming clusters of discussion and debate. "They're going to make you into something. Saint or demon or whatever fits their worldview."

Mira's expression doesn't change, but something in her posture suggests acceptance of a fate she saw coming. "Let them. The truth is larger than their stories about it."

———

By evening, Cedar Lagoon Pizzeria fills with the nervous energy of people who need to process the impossible through familiar routine. Vincent works the register while conversations swirl around him, each table offering different interpretations of the afternoon's events. At one booth, a group of churchgoers debate whether Mira's bilocation represents divine intervention or something more sinister. Their voices carry the edge of fear dressed in theological certainty.

"The girl has always been odd," one woman says, her voice low but carrying. "Ever since her mother died. This could be possession, demonic influence using grief as an entry point."

"Or she's blessed," another counters, clutching a rosary that clicks against the table. "She saved that child. God has blessed others with the same power."

At the counter, two construction workers who witnessed everything drink beer in silence until one finally speaks. "I don't care what she is. The ground opened up and swallowed Luis's rig, then gave it back like nothing happened. That ain't natural, and that girl was at the center of it."

Joe wipes down the counter, his expression carefully neutral, but Vincent catches him glancing toward the window where the last light of day illuminates the construction site in the distance. The old soldier knows something has shifted, that whatever stayed hidden beneath Duswood has announced itself too clearly to be denied.

Across town, the newly planted cedar saplings stand in their neat rows, their burlap-wrapped roots settling into soil that welcomed them too easily, as if the earth had been waiting for their arrival. But as darkness falls and the construction site empties of human presence, the young trees begin to bend. Not from wind, which has gone still, but from some attraction toward the school's foundation.

The cedars lean with the patience of plant growth accelerated into hours instead of years, their trunks developing curves that point toward where the iron rings wait beneath layers of earth and concrete and denial. By morning, the angle will be subtle enough to dismiss, but for now, in the space between day and night, they genuflect toward something that breathes with the rhythm of the planet itself, something that Mira Thorn heard today.

The hum continues beneath it all, that steady pulse that has become Duswood's new heartbeat, no longer hidden but acknowledged, no longer patient but active, no longer waiting but manifesting through blessed ground and human conductors who stand at the intersection of the possible and the impossible, translating between states of being that were never meant to touch but now can never be fully separated.

As dusk deepens and the pizzeria's lights flicker, Vincent feels a chill, a prickling sense that the quiet outside isn't empty, but threaded through with a presence watching, The Adversary drawing nearer with every tremor that tears through Duswood's mask of normalcy.

CHAPTER
THIRTEEN

Morning light spreads across Duswood like oil on water, catching in storefront windows and pooling in the hollows between buildings where shadows from yesterday still linger, and Vincent counts seventeen people on Kipling Avenue who walk with their heads down, avoiding eye contact as if shared glances might force them to acknowledge what they all witnessed at the construction site yesterday. The air carries the metallic scent of disturbed clay, particles still clinging to boots and car tires, marking everyone who attended the volunteer day with red-tinged evidence they can't quite scrub away. Vincent pulls his notebook tighter against his ribs, its familiar weight a comfort against the way the town seems to vibrate with suppressed conversation, words caught behind teeth, theories trapped in throats.

Beside him, Mira moves through the morning with practiced invisibility, though Vincent notices how people step aside without seeming to see her, their bodies responding to her presence while their eyes slide past. She wears a gray sweater that makes her look smaller, younger, as if she's trying to retreat into herself. Her hair hangs loose, creating a curtain between her and the world that watches without watching, acknowledges without admitting.

Porchlight Café's windows fog with breath and coffee steam, the interior packed despite the early hour. Vincent slows as they pass, catching fragments through the propped-open door that releases the scent of burned toast and nervous sweat. Inside, Betty Morrison gestures wildly at her booth companions, her voice rising above the general murmur.

"Mass hallucination," she insists, her coffee cup creating rings on the formica table as she sets it down too hard. "Carbon monoxide from the construction equipment. Makes people see things that aren't there."

"Then how do you explain Luis's ankle?" counters Frank Henley from the next booth. "Man's wearing a cast. You can't hallucinate a spiral-shaped bruise."

Someone drops a mug near the counter, the ceramic shattering against linoleum with a sound like breaking bones. The conversation stops for three heartbeats, everyone turning toward the noise, then away, as if the accident might be an omen. Vincent hears someone whisper "two Miras" before another voice hushes them sharply.

They cross in front of the town laundromat, where the big front window is fogged with heat and shrouded by dryer exhaust. Inside, Hale Ness leans against a row of humming washers, clipboard in hand. He's surrounded by a few of his crew, their shirts still streaked with rust-red clay, voices low enough to be drowned by the spin cycles.

Hale gestures with his pen at a crude map of the construction site, spread out over a laundry basket. "We'll have to reroute the drainage again," he mutters, frustration threading through the words. "The water isn't supposed to come up here. Not this fast."

A younger worker, Luis, limping slightly, shakes his head. "Last time we fixed it, the ground moved again. Like it's undoing us on purpose."

Hale doesn't answer at first, just stares at the map, jaw set. "We'll find a way. Got to." But Vincent can hear the doubt in him, a hollowness as real as the shifting ground.

The community board stands just inside the post office entrance, its cork surface usually reserved for garage sale flyers and missing cat posters. But this morning, Sheriff Brennan stands before it, his broad back blocking the view as he pins something official-looking to the center. His uniform looks slept in, the creases that normally run sharp down his sleeves have softened into wrinkles, and Vincent notices red clay still caked in the treads of his boots despite the obvious attempts to clean them.

Brennan turns as they approach, his eyes finding Vincent first, then sliding to Mira with something between wariness and recognition. He steps aside without speaking, revealing the notice he's posted. The header reads "OFFICIAL STATE-MENT - CONSTRUCTION SITE INCIDENT" in bold letters that try too hard to project authority.

Vincent scans the text while Mira stands perfectly still beside him. Gas pocket. Subsidence. Optical illusion caused by atmospheric conditions. Each explanation more desperate than the last, building a wall of words against what dozens of people witnessed. At the bottom, in smaller print: "Citizens are advised to avoid spreading unsubstantiated rumors that might cause unnecessary panic."

"Just doing my job," Brennan says, though no one asked for justification. His voice carries gravel and exhaustion, the tone of someone who's been awake wrestling with impossibil-ity. "Keep things calm. Keep things normal."

The word 'normal' cracks slightly as he says it, and Vincent sees the sheriff's hand move unconsciously to his hip where his service weapon rests, as if bullets might protect against whatever breathes beneath Duswood. Brennan's gaze lingers on Mira for another moment, something unreadable in his expression, before he turns and walks toward his cruiser with steps that try for authority but achieve only a tired shuffle.

Vincent opens his notebook as they continue walking, jotting quick observations while the morning reveals itself in fragments.

———

The basement of St. Clement's holds its breath around Owen like a tomb that's forgotten it's supposed to be dead, dust motes suspended in the weak light that filters through a window no bigger than a hymnal, and he pulls another file drawer open with the careful persistence of someone who's learned that answers often hide in the places nobody thinks to look. Cedar and mildew compete for dominance in the thick air, creating a scent that coats the back of his throat with something between wood polish and decay. His fingers leave prints in the dust that covers the cabinet's metal surface, each touch a small betrayal of how long these records have sat undisturbed.

The drawer resists at first, rust and time having formed an alliance against intrusion, but Owen persists with steady pressure until it surrenders with a groan that echoes off the stone walls. Inside, folders stand in neat rows like soldiers at attention, their tabs yellowed to the color of old teeth, labels written in fountain pen that's faded but still legible. Tax records from the 1940s, building permits, correspondence about zoning changes that matter to no one anymore.

But then his fingers find something different. A folder thicker than the others, its surface marked with a stamp in red ink that has somehow retained its vibrancy despite the decades. The stamp shows a spiral, perfect in its geometry, with letters around its perimeter: GNRO. Owen's pulse quickens as he pulls the folder free, feeling its unexpected weight, as if the papers inside have absorbed more than just time.

He opens it on the scarred wooden table that dominates the basement's center, the same table where June scanned documents just days ago. The first page bears a date: July 6, 1941. The letterhead reads "Great Northern Rail and Ore Company - Internal Memorandum," but someone has added a handwritten note in the margin: "Root Channel Project - Priority Classification."

Owen's breathing slows as he reads, his academic training taking over, cataloging information even as his mind rebels against the implications. The memo discusses "anomalous readings" at depth intervals that the water table should prohibit beneath Duswood. It mentions "resonance patterns inconsistent with geological models" and "the necessity of expanded infrastructure to accommodate the phenomenon."

He sets the first document aside and continues through the folder, each page revealing another piece of something vast and deliberate. Construction orders for materials that seem excessive for simple rail infrastructure. Personnel transfers bringing in specialists whose fields range from geology to something called "bioelectric engineering." And always, on every document, that red spiral fingerprint-like stamp, as if marking these papers as part of something beyond normal corporate operations.

The dates progress through the 1940s into the early 1950s, the tone of the documents shifting from curious to concerned to something approaching fear. A report from 1947 mentions "unexpected responses to drilling at the tertiary depth." Another from 1949 describes "synchronization between the entity and sensitive personnel," though the word entity has been crossed out and replaced with "phenomenon" in different ink.

Owen's fingers tremble slightly as he traces the coordinates mentioned repeatedly in the documents. He pulls his phone from his pocket, opening the map application despite the weak signal in the basement. The coordinates center on Duswood's current construction site, but they extend outward in patterns that match the iron rings from the shed's blueprints. Each point represents what the documents call "interface zones," places where something below connects with something above.

A diagram from 1951 makes him pause. It shows the underground tunnels they've been tracking, but with additions he hasn't seen before. Chambers marked "Resonance Amplification," passages labeled "Bioelectric Conduits," and at the center, a vast space simply marked "PRIMARY INTERFACE - SUBJECT UNKNOWN." The unknown subject is represented by a spiral that matches the stamp, drawn with obsessive precision, each revolution annotated with measurements that make no sense in standard units.

The academic excitement that initially drove his investigation transforms into something heavier as Owen realizes the scope of what he's found. This wasn't industrial accident or corporate negligence. GNRO had been trying to harness something that existed beneath Duswood long before humans arrived, something that responded to their attention with its own form of awareness. The Root Channel Project wasn't about freight or ore. It was about communication with something that nobody should have known.

The basement's stone walls seem to press closer as Owen carefully photographs each document with his phone, the camera's flash harsh in the dim space. His methodical nature keeps him moving despite the growing weight in his chest, the sense that he's documenting something that was meant to stay buried in archives and denial.

The final document in the folder is different. Hand-written rather than typed, the script shaky as if written under duress. It's dated March 7, 1953, the day before the ledger claims the tunnels were sealed. The text is brief: "It knows we're listening. It's learning to speak back. God help whoever hears it clearly."

Owen closes the folder with careful movements, his decision already made. Vincent needs to see this. Joe needs to understand what GNRO really built beneath the town.

———

The fluorescent lights of Cedar Lagoon Pizzeria cast everything in sharp relief against the darkness pressing at the windows, and Vincent watches Joe spread Owen's discovered papers across the stainless steel prep counter with the careful movements of someone handling evidence of a crime that hasn't technically been committed yet. The pizzeria is closed, the CLOSED sign turned outward, the dining area dark except for the spillover from the kitchen's harsh illumination. Joe still holds a dish rag in his left hand, forgotten as his attention fixes on the blueprints Owen has produced from his backpack like a magician revealing impossible things.

The largest blueprint dominates the counter's center, its lines and measurements creating a geometry that Vincent tries to follow. Concentric rings surround a core marked only as "SUBJECT UNKNOWN," the words stamped in that same red ink that appears on every GNRO document. The rings aren't simply circles but complex structures, each one containing smaller patterns, symbols, measurement points that suggest monitoring equipment or perhaps something more interactive.

"This wasn't about freight," Joe mutters, his finger tracing the primary ring's circumference. His voice carries the weight of understanding something he wishes he didn't. "They were trying to pull energy from the earth. Magnetic, geothermal, whatever they could name and measure."

He pauses at a section where notations crowd the margins, numbers that spike and drop in patterns that resemble heartbeat monitors or seismic readings. But these measurements show pulses, not the steady currents that geological energy would produce. The pulses have rhythm, intention, the suggestion of communication rather than simple force.

"Pulses mean something was responding," Owen says, adjusting his glasses as he leans over another section of the blueprint. His voice tries for academic detachment but can't quite hide the tremor beneath. "Look at these intervals. They're not random. They follow mathematical progressions, almost like... like conversation."

Vincent's attention moves to a smaller diagram showing the construction site's current layout overlaid with the original GNRO infrastructure. The correlation is perfect, as if the modern builders unconsciously followed patterns laid down seventy years ago. His finger finds the spot where yesterday's collapse occurred, and there, in faded ink, is a notation: "Primary Breach Point - Sealed 03/53."

The vibration he's felt for weeks suddenly makes sense. Not the movement of something trying to escape but the rhythm of something trying to communicate through layers of earth and concrete and the accumulated weight of decades. His hand presses flat against the counter, and even through the steel, he can feel it, that patient pulse that runs beneath everything in Duswood now.

"They didn't build around it," Vincent says quietly, the words emerging with the certainty of revelation. "They woke it up. Whatever was down there, dormant maybe, or just... existing below notice. GNRO's excavation, their rings, their attempts to harness it. They gave it awareness of the surface."

Joe's expression darkens as he processes this, the dish rag twisting in his grip. He points to another section of the blueprint where spiral symbols appear at regular intervals along the ring structures. The symbols are burned or etched into the steel itself according to the notations, permanent markings that seem both decorative and functional.

"That symbol," Joe says, his voice dropping to barely above a whisper. "They burned it into the steel like a warning label. Like those signs on electrical equipment that tell you danger, high voltage, don't touch."

But Owen shakes his head, pulling forward one of the typed reports from 1947. His finger finds a paragraph: "The entity has begun marking its territory through our infrastructure. The spiral manifestations appear to be a form of claiming or branding. Maybe a fingerprint. Recommend cessation of all direct interface attempts."

"No," Owen says with quiet certainty. "Not a warning they made. A claim. A branding. But I don't think GNRO made it." He looks up at both of them, his young face aged by understanding. "I think they found it. And it used their own infrastructure to mark its presence."

Through the windows, dusk has settled over Duswood. The construction site is visible in the distance, chain-link fence glowing faintly in the last light. But it's the ground near the fence that draws Vincent's attention. The red clay that everyone tracked through town this morning has begun to glow with its own faint luminescence, not bright enough to be obvious, just enough to be unsettling.

Vincent finally comes to terms with what he has suspected for days. The Root Channel Project didn't fail. It succeeded too well, establishing a connection that seventy years of denial couldn't sever, and now that connection is strengthening, pulse by pulse.

Moonlight paints Mira's bedroom in shades of silver and shadow, and she stands at the window in her white nightgown, a figure that might be mistaken for a ghost by anyone passing below, though the streets of Duswood have been empty since dusk as if the town itself has retreated into uneasy sleep. The fabric of her nightgown is thin cotton, worn soft by countless washings, and it clings to her skin where perspiration has gathered despite the cool night air. Her bare feet press against hardwood that holds more warmth than it should, as if heated from below by something more than the house's old furnace.

The hum that has haunted her for weeks fills the room with presence rather than sound. It's been there so long she sometimes forgets what silence felt like, the way one forgets the exact shade of summer sky in the depths of winter. But tonight, something has changed. The random static quality that made it feel like interference, like crossed wires or broken circuits, has resolved into rhythm. Not the mechanical pulse of engines or electricity, but something more organic, more intentional, like the breathing of something vast finally settling into wakefulness.

She presses her palm against the window glass, feeling its coolness against skin that seems to run hotter these days, as if her body has adjusted its baseline temperature to match whatever speaks to her from below. The glass fogs around her hand, condensation forming in perfect circles that expand outward like ripples on still water. Through that fog, the yard outside looks different, though she can't say exactly how. The angles seem sharper, the shadows deeper, as if reality has been adjusted by degrees too small to measure but impossible to ignore.

The rhythm in the air shifts, and suddenly it's not just vibration but voice. Not words exactly, not in any language humans have named, but meaning transmitted directly through frequency, through the resonance between her bones and something beyond comprehension. The communication bypasses her ears entirely, manifesting in her consciousness like memories that aren't her own.

"They took what was mine."

The words form in her mind with the clarity of thought,

but the voice isn't hers. It carries weight, age, a quality of patience that speaks of geological time, of waiting that measures in centuries rather than moments. The tone isn't angry exactly, but there's something beneath it, a note of violation, of boundaries crossed without permission.

"But you... you remember."

Her breath catches in her throat, creating a small sound that seems too loud in the moonlit room. Remember what? She wants to ask, but the answer comes before she can form the question, not in words but in images that flash behind her closed eyelids. Tunnels that breathe. Iron rings that sing. Men in hard hats and coveralls, their faces bright with the excitement of discovery, not understanding that what they've found was never lost, only waiting.

The presence presses closer, not physically but in awareness, like feeling someone reading over your shoulder if your shoulder existed in dimensions beyond the merely spatial. The hum intensifies, and Mira feels it in her sternum, in the hollow spaces of her body where air and blood meet, where the boundary between self and not-self becomes negotiable.

"You could set it right again."

The words carry promise, seduction almost, the tone of someone offering a gift that's also a burden. Through the vibration, she feels what 'right' means to this entity. Not destruction, not revenge exactly, but recognition. Acknowledgment. The restoration of something that was severed when GNRO sealed the tunnels, when they tried to contain what they'd awakened.

Her fingers spread against the glass, and she opens her eyes to find the yard transformed. The light from the streetlamp, which should be sodium yellow, has shifted to deep red, though the bulb itself hasn't changed. It's as if the light itself has been filtered through something, bent by presence that exists between the source and the surface. The red illumination makes everything look submerged, underwater or under blood, creating a world that's familiar but fundamentally altered.

The floorboards beneath her feet pulse gently, not with the house settling or the furnace cycling, but with rhythm that matches her heartbeat exactly. Or perhaps her heartbeat has synchronized to match it. The distinction seems less important than it should. She's becoming a tuning fork, calibrated to frequencies that most humans can't perceive, though she suspects everyone in Duswood feels them subconsciously, in dreams they can't quite remember, in the moments between sleep and waking when the world seems thinner.

Her reflection in the window glass looks back at her, but there's something different about it. The eyes that meet hers carry depths that weren't there this morning, as if she's seeing through herself to something vast and patient standing just behind, waiting for invitation or permission or simply the right moment to step forward. Her lips move, shaping words she doesn't speak aloud, words that The Adversary has been waiting seventy years to hear.

The trail to the north bluff cuts through cedars that grow at angles suggesting perpetual wind, their trunks twisted into spirals that echo patterns Vincent has seen burned into bark and drawn in beetle ash, and he follows Mira's white sneakers as they find purchase on wet stone slick with evening moisture and decades of fallen needles compressed into something between soil and memory. The path hasn't seen maintenance since before Vincent was born, maybe since before his parents were born, and nature has reclaimed it with the patient persistence of roots splitting stone and branches reaching across what used to be clear passage. His notebook sits heavy in his jacket pocket, pages damp from the humidity that rises from the earth as day surrenders to twilight, but he doesn't pull it out, doesn't want to take his eyes off Mira's footing for even the seconds it would take to document their ascent.

Behind him, June's breathing comes in controlled huffs, her camera bag swinging against her hip with each scramble over fallen logs and exposed roots that seem to grab at their ankles with wooden fingers. Owen brings up the rear, his backpack rattling softly with equipment that cost more than most people in Duswood make in a month, instruments designed to measure the measurable, though Vincent suspects they're climbing toward something that exists outside the frequencies his devices can detect. The sound of their movement through the undergrowth should be chaotic, random, but it falls into rhythm, four sets of footfalls finding synchronization without trying, as if the trail itself conducts them upward with its own tempo.

The cedars press closer as they climb, their lower branches dead and sharp, reaching across the path at eye level so they have to duck and weave, movements that feel choreographed by something that wants to test their commitment to reaching the summit. The bark weeps that familiar red sap, but here it's different, thicker, almost crystallized where it's dried, creating formations that catch the dying light like frozen blood or garnets growing from living wood. The metallic scent intensifies with altitude, not the tang of copper but something older, like iron that's been underground so long it's forgotten what air tastes like.

Mira pauses where the trail splits around a massive cedar whose trunk must be five feet in circumference, its presence so commanding that the other trees lean away, creating a clearing of sorts in the dense growth. She presses her palm against its bark, and Vincent watches her shoulders rise and fall with deeper breathing, as if she's drawing something from the contact or maybe giving something back. When she turns to face them, her eyes carry that distant quality that's become familiar these past weeks, the look of someone listening to frequencies the rest of them can only feel as pressure in their sinuses.

"It's stronger here," she says, her voice soft but carrying clearly in the still air. "Like someone calling from far under the water. Not words, just... need. Recognition. The feeling when you know someone's watching even though you can't see them."

Vincent steps closer, close enough to see the faint sheen of perspiration on her forehead despite the cool evening air, close enough to notice how her pupils have dilated to points his flashlight can barely detect. She looks through him rather than at him, seeing something in the spaces between molecules, in the gaps where physics admits uncertainty.

"How long have you been hearing it?" he asks, though he thinks he knows the answer, thinks it started that night at her window when she pressed her palm against glass and reality bent around her like light through water.

"Since the volunteer day," she admits, though her voice suggests the truth is more complex. "Or maybe I've always heard it, but quieter, like background noise you don't notice until someone points it out. But after... after everyone saw, it got clearer. Like I'd given it permission by acknowledging it publicly."

June adjusts her camera strap, the metal buckles clicking against each other with a sound too sharp for the muffled atmosphere of the cedar grove. "Permission for what?"

Mira doesn't answer immediately, instead turning back to the trail, which narrows ahead to little more than a deer path carved into the hillside. She starts walking again, and they follow, because what else can they do? They've come this far, driven by the same compulsion that makes people stand at the edges of cliffs, looking down into depths that promise nothing but still demand witness.

The final ascent is nearly vertical, requiring them to grab exposed roots and rough stone to pull themselves up, their hands coming away stained with that red mineral residue that seems to seep from everything here. Vincent's muscles burn with the effort, his breathing going ragged, but he keeps his position behind Mira, ready to catch her if she slips, though she moves with unsettling grace, as if gravity has made special arrangements with her.

They emerge onto the overlook gasping, except for Mira who stands at the edge as if she's simply stepped from one room to another. Lake Michigan spreads before them, its surface gone silver in the twilight, perfectly still in a way that large bodies of water never are, as if something has commanded it to do so. The horizon blurs where water meets sky, creating the illusion of infinity, of falling upward into depths that have no bottom.

The wind that should exist at this height is absent at first, the air so still it feels solid, like standing inside amber that hasn't quite hardened. Then it comes all at once, not building gradually but arriving fully formed, a presence more than a meteorological event. It pushes against them with intent, seeking ways through their clothes, their hair, the spaces between their fingers. But there's something else in it, something that Vincent has felt before.

The wind carries two voices simultaneously, an acoustic impossibility that his brain tries and fails to process. One is clearly the sound of air moving through obstacles, branches creaking, leaves rustling. But underneath, occupying the same sonic space without blending, is something like breathing. Not human breathing, not even animal, but the respiration of something vast enough that its inhale could drain lakes and its exhale could level forests. The two sounds exist in the same space, creating harmonics previously unheard, beats and interference patterns.

Mira grips his sleeve suddenly, her fingers digging in with enough force that he'll find bruises tomorrow, small purple marks like a map of her fear. Her whole body has gone rigid, not with terror but with recognition, with the terrible understanding of someone who's just solved a puzzle they wish they hadn't started.

"It's not trying to speak," she says, her voice barely audible above the wind's dual nature. "It's just... reacting. Like when you touch something hot and your hand pulls back before you think about it. The Root Titan isn't conscious the way we understand consciousness. It's responding to stimuli, to our presence, to the excavation, to seventy years of human activity above it."

Owen has dropped to his knees beside a hairline crack that threads through the stone of the overlook, his equipment already spread around him in the precise arrangement of someone who's turned methodology into ritual. His EMF meter shrieks intermittently, its needle swinging so hard it bends against the stop pegs. The compass in his palm spins without pause, not randomly but in perfect circles, clockwise then counter-clockwise, as if magnetic north has become negotiable.

He pulls out a thermal sensor, sweeping it across the crack, and his face pales at whatever the display shows. Vincent can see the numbers from where he stands: temperatures that spike and drop in patterns that follow no natural thermal dynamics, hot enough to boil water, then cold enough to freeze it, cycling through states that should take hours in mere seconds.

"This place isn't a source," Owen says, frustration bleeding through his scientific composure. His hands shake as he makes notes, his usual precise handwriting degrading into barely legible scratches. "It's a conduit. Like a copper wire conducting electricity, but for something we don't have words for. Something big is moving under all of this, using the iron deposits, the root systems, the very bones of the earth as infrastructure."

Vincent feels the truth of it through his boots, through the stone that vibrates with frequencies too low to hear but impossible to ignore. The north bluff isn't where the Root Titan lives. It's where it breathes, where its presence breaks through into their reality like a whale's blowhole breaking the ocean's surface. And just as a whale's breath tells nothing about the creature's full immensity hidden beneath the waves, whatever they're sensing here is just the barest hint of something unimaginably vast, patient, and fundamentally indifferent to their small human concerns.

Mira stands at the edge of the bluff like something carved from the same stone, her coal-dust hair twisting in the unnatural wind that can't decide which direction it wants to push, and Vincent watches her with the attention of someone memorizing a face they might lose, cataloging the way her shoulders set themselves against invisible weight, the way her fingers curl and uncurl at her sides as if grasping for something only she can feel. The twilight has deepened to the edge of true darkness, that liminal moment when colors drain from the world and everything becomes gradients of gray, but Mira seems to hold light somehow, not glowing exactly but refusing to surrender to shadow the way the rest of them have.

June has raised her camera, the device steady in her hands despite the tremor Vincent can see in her shoulders, her finger hovering over the shutter release as if she's afraid that capturing this moment might make it too real to deny later. The lens focuses and refocuses, hunting for clarity in air that has gone thick with more than humidity, trying to document something that exists partially outside the spectrum her equipment can perceive. Each time the autofocus engages, it makes a soft whirring sound that seems too loud, too mechanical, too much a reminder that they're trying to measure the unmeasurable.

Owen remains on his knees beside the crack in the stone, but his attention has shifted from his instruments to Mira, his notebook forgotten in his lap, pencil rolling away to disappear into a crevice. His face wears the expression of someone whose frameworks have finally shattered completely, finally understanding exactly how impossible this situation is. The thermal sensor lies beside him, still cycling through its impossible readings, casting shifting colored light across the rock that makes everything look diseased.

Vincent positions himself three steps back from Mira, close enough to reach her if needed but far enough to give her space for whatever communion she's engaged in. He can feel the edge's pull even from here, not just gravity but something more insistent, as if the drop wants to be explored, wants to demonstrate the distance between human scale and geological truth. His hands stay loose at his sides, ready to move, though he's not sure what he's preparing to catch her from. The fall is obvious, but there are other ways to lose someone, other edges they can slip over without moving an inch.

The silence stretches until it becomes its own presence, heavy as the fog that begins to rise from the lake below, creeping up the cliff face like something with agency. Even the dual-voiced wind has stilled, creating a vacuum, pressure shifting in ways that suggest altitude changes though they haven't moved. Then Mira speaks, her voice coming from somewhere deeper than her throat, carrying the quality of translation, of someone converting concepts that don't fit in human language into words that barely contain them.

"The Titan," she whispers, and the name itself seems to add weight to the air, making it harder to breathe. "It doesn't want anything. It's just there. Like a storm or a forest fire. It doesn't think, doesn't plan, doesn't hate or love. It simply is, the way mountains are, the way gravity is. We're nothing to it. Less than nothing. Bacteria on its skin, if it even has awareness of surfaces."

She opens her eyes but doesn't turn from the edge, her gaze fixed on something beyond the visible horizon. The wind stirs again, but differently, carrying scents that don't belong to this elevation: deep earth, heated metal, that organic sweetness of decay that lives in spaces never touched by sunlight. Vincent tastes copper on his tongue, though he hasn't bitten his cheek, hasn't done anything to warrant the flavor of blood in his mouth.

June lowers her camera slowly, the motion deliberate as if sudden movement might shatter something. Her voice emerges steady but uncertain, the tone of someone asking a question they're not sure they want answered. "Then who keeps talking to you? If the Titan doesn't think, doesn't communicate, who's sending the messages?"

Before Mira can respond, the stone beneath their feet shudders. Not the violent shake of an earthquake but something more like a shiver, like skin reacting to unexpected touch. Small pebbles near the edge begin to dance before the stones roll over the edge into darkness. The vibration travels up through their shoes, through their bones, finding residence in the spaces between joints, in the fluid of their spines, in the hollow chambers of their skulls where thought lives.

Vincent feels it in his teeth first, that deep thrumming that makes his molars ache, then in his chest where his heart suddenly seems to beat against a rhythm that isn't his own. The sensation is invasive, intimate, like something reading his biological signature and finding it wanting. Beside him, June gasps softly, her hand going to her sternum, pressing against something only she can feel. Owen's equipment screams in electronic protest, multiple devices triggering at once, their alerts blending into a cacophony that somehow harmonizes with the vibration rising from below.

Mira's voice breaks as she speaks, the words emerging between small sounds that might be sobs or might be laughter, the distinction meaningless in the face of what she's understanding. "Something inside it. Something that learned how to use it. Like a parasite, but that's not right either. More like... like someone learning to play an instrument that was never meant to make music. If it wakes the Titan fully, if it achieves real control instead of just influence..." She trails off, but the conclusion hangs obvious in the air. It won't be the

Titan they meet but whatever has taken residence within it, whatever has spent seventy years learning its rhythms, its responses, its vast and terrible potential.

Her body begins to tremble, not with cold though the temperature has dropped enough that their breath becomes visible, but with exhaustion that runs deeper than physical tiredness. She sways slightly, a motion so small Vincent might have missed it if he wasn't watching her with the intensity of someone expecting collapse. He steps closer, closing the distance between them with movements that feel predetermined, scripted by something larger than choice.

When he reaches her, his hand finds her shoulder with the certainty of magnetism, north pole finding south. She leans into the touch immediately, all her strength suddenly gone, her weight transferring to him as if she's been waiting for permission to stop standing on her own. Her forehead presses against his shoulder, and through his jacket he feels the heat of her skin, burning with fever that has nothing to do with illness and everything to do with serving as a conduit for forces that human bodies weren't designed to channel.

"I'm so tired," she whispers against his collar, the words muffled but clear. "It never stops talking. Even when I'm not listening, it's there, like knowing someone's standing behind a door, waiting for you to open it."

Vincent's arm comes around her automatically, supporting her weight, feeling the bird-like fragility of her frame against his chest. She's always been slight, but she feels smaller now, as if whatever's been speaking through her has been taking something in exchange, some essential substance that can't be replaced by food or rest. His voice emerges soft, meant only for her, though the silence is complete enough that everyone hears.

"But why you?" The question carries no accusation, only the need to understand why this burden has fallen on her specifically, why among all the people in Duswood, Mira

Thorn has become the antenna for something that should have stayed sleeping beneath tons of earth and iron.

She pulls back just enough to meet his eyes, and in the dying light he sees depths in her gaze that weren't there weeks ago, knowledge that ages people in ways that have nothing to do with years. Her answer comes with the simplicity of truth that can't be dressed in prettier words.

"Because I can listen. Because something in me resonates at the right frequency. And because it needs a way through. Not just through the physical barriers, but through the space between what it is and what we are. I'm the translation, the bridge, the door it's been looking for."

She swallows hard, and Vincent feels the motion against his chest, feels how difficult even that simple action has become for her. "And I don't know how to stop being what it needs."

Below them, far enough down that it should be invisible in the gathering darkness, Lake Michigan's surface begins to show patterns. Not waves, because the wind has gone still, but ripples that spread from a point near the shore directly below the bluff. The movement is slow, rhythmic, deliberate as breathing, as if something enormous has turned in its sleep beneath the lakebed, disturbing water from below in pulses that match the vibration still thrumming through the stone.

The ripples expand outward in perfect circles that maintain their shape despite the distance they travel, each ring catching the moonlight and reflecting it back changed, tinged with that familiar red that has marked every manifestation of the Root Titan's presence. The pattern is hypnotic, beautiful in the way that dangerous things often are, and Vincent finds himself counting the pulses, noting how they match Mira's heartbeat against his chest, how they synchronize with the rhythm that has been building beneath Duswood since the first beetle emerged to write its spiral message.

The lake continues its impossible movement as full darkness finally claims the sky, and Vincent holds Mira against the falling night while June documents what she can and Owen's instruments catalog impossible frequencies, all of them witnesses to the slow wake of something that was better left sleeping, and the hidden, hungrier thing that has learned to wear its vastness like a glove.

CHAPTER
FIFTEEN

Vincent wakes to water running, the sound of snowmelt racing through gutters that yesterday held only frozen silence, and when he pulls back his bedroom curtain the world outside has transformed from winter's grip to something that resembles spring but feels like fever. The thermometer mounted outside his window reads sixty-eight degrees, unusual for April in Upper Michigan, and steam rises from patches of bare earth where snow has vanished overnight, not melted gradually but simply ceased to exist, as if winter itself has been erased from Duswood's memory.

He dresses quickly and finds Mira already waiting on the front porch, her breath no longer visible in air that carries a suspicious warmth. She wears only a light cardigan over her dress, the heavy coat she needed yesterday abandoned some-where inside. Her feet are bare despite the wet boards beneath them, and when Vincent looks closer, he notices the wood around her toes has dried, as if her skin radiates heat that pushes moisture away.

"Did you sleep?" he asks, though the shadows beneath her eyes provide the answer.

"The earth was too loud," she says, her voice carrying that quality of partial presence while she ties her shoes. "It kept showing me things. Roots reaching through frozen soil. Seeds cracking open beneath the snow. Everything wanting to grow at once."

They walk together through streets transformed by new warmth. Water runs everywhere, creating tiny rivers along curbs, pooling in depressions where ice had collected for months. The puddles catch morning light strangely, their surfaces carrying a shimmer when the sun hits them at certain angles, as if iron has dissolved overnight into every molecule of meltwater. Vincent steps around them carefully, but Mira walks through without hesitation.

On Kipling Avenue, Mrs. Chen stands outside her flower shop, staring at window boxes where crocuses have appeared overnight, their purple and yellow blooms perfect despite having been buried under crusted snow just hours ago. She touches the petals with trembling fingers, her face wearing an expression caught between joy and fear.

"Look at that! Bloomed overnight. It's a sign, I tell you. The cold's given up at last."

But Vincent hears the uncertainty beneath her words, the need to name this strangeness something positive before it reveals itself as something else. Other shop owners have emerged to examine their own unexpected gardens, tulips pushing through soil that should still be beneath frost, daffodils opening to sun that shouldn't shine this warm for another month. The whole street smells of earth and growth, that green scent of chlorophyll and sap that belongs to May, not April.

They turn toward the town square, where the transformation is most dramatic. The lawn, which yesterday lay dormant under snow, now spreads thick and green, grass so vibrant it seems to glow. Not just alive but aggressively vital, as if someone has compressed an entire season's growth into a single night. Vincent's shoes sink slightly with each step, the turf beneath them spongy with moisture and new growth.

A small crowd has gathered near the memorial fountain, voices mixing wonder with unease. Tom Garrett, who runs the hardware store, kneels beside a bed where roses bloom despite having been pruned to sticks last fall. He pulls out his phone, taking pictures that will never quite capture the impossibility of red petals unfurling in defiance of natural cycles.

"Climate change," someone suggests, but the explanation falls flat even as it's spoken.

"Weather pattern," another tries. "Chemtrails."

Vincent watches them construct explanations like walls against acknowledgment of what's really happening. The town needs this to be natural, needs it to fit within boundaries of understanding that don't include Root Titans or parasitic entities or teenage girls who exist in multiple places at once. So they name it blessing, miracle, anything but what it is: something vast and patient finally stirring to full wakefulness.

As they cross the square, Vincent notices how the grass responds to Mira's presence. Not obviously, not in ways that would alarm the crowd, but in subtle shifts of color and height. Where her shadow falls, the green deepens. Where her feet touch, even through shoes, the grass seems to stretch upward, individual blades extending perhaps a millimeter, perhaps two, enough to notice if you're watching, easy to dismiss if you're not.

June appears from behind the memorial, her camera already in hand, and Vincent sees her recognition of the phenomenon immediately. She circles them slowly, adjusting her angle, waiting for the right light. When it comes, filtered through clouds that shouldn't be warm enough to produce the golden quality they're casting, she takes a rapid series of shots.

The flash catches something around Mira's hands, a shimmer that might be moisture, might be heat distortion, might be something else entirely. In that strobe-lit instant, Vincent sees it clearly: a faint luminescence extending from her fingertips, not quite touching the plants around them but reaching toward them, or perhaps the plants are reaching toward her, the distinction suddenly uncertain.

"Don't," Mira says softly to June, though she doesn't move to stop the photography. "People will see."

"People need to see," June responds, but she lowers her camera anyway, respecting something in Mira's tone that suggests consequences beyond social discomfort.

Vincent forces lightness into his voice, needing to break the weight that's settling over them like humid air before a storm. "Maybe you've got the green thumb of the century. Should start a landscaping business. Make a fortune. *Mira*-cle Gro?"

Mira turns to him with a tight smile and an eye roll. "Pfft. Oh my… what?" She says, the words soft enough that he almost misses them. "Maybe all it needed was someone to listen."

The pronoun troubles him. It. Not the town, not the earth, but something specific that she's identified without naming. He wants to ask what she means, wants to press for clarity about what she's been hearing in the frequencies that run beneath everything now. But the crowd is too close, too many ears that might catch fragments of conversation that would transform Mira from mysterious to dangerous in their frightened minds.

The mud near Hearthstone Chapel clings to Owen's knees as he presses the soil thermometer into earth that should be cold but isn't, and Vincent watches his face tighten with each reading that defies what April ground should register. The device's metal probe sinks easily into soil gone soft with moisture and heat, and when Owen checks the dial, his hand trembles slightly, not from cold but from numbers that violate everything his geology textbooks taught him about thermal dynamics.

"Seventy-three degrees," Owen announces, his voice flat with forced calm. "Six inches down. Should be near freezing."

He pulls a small orange flag from his backpack, the kind surveyors use to mark utilities, and pushes it into the ground at the measurement point. The flag stands at an angle, bright against the dark earth, a marker of impossibility that will become one of many. Vincent notices how Owen's movements have gained precision, as if methodology might provide armor against what he's discovering.

June crouches nearby, her camera trained on Owen's work, documenting each measurement with the dedication of someone building evidence for a case that will never see a courtroom. The click of her shutter provides punctuation to Owen's process: probe, read, flag, move. She's stopped asking questions, stopped trying to interpret. Now she simply records, letting the images speak truths that words keep failing to convey.

"Where exactly did Mira stand?" Owen asks without looking up from his thermometer.

Vincent points to a spot near the chapel's ruined wall where Mira had paused five minutes ago, her hand pressed against stone. Owen crawls toward it, mud coating his jeans, his focus absolute. The probe goes in, the dial spins, and his expression shifts from concern to something closer to fear.

"Eighty-one degrees," he says. "That's not possible. The ground doesn't generate heat like this without a source. Geothermal activity, underground fires, something."

But they all know there's nothing like that beneath Duswood, or at least nothing that should create such localized heating. Vincent thinks of the iron rings from the GNRO blueprints, massive structures designed to channel energy, and wonders if they're measuring the remnants of that old infrastructure warming to life. Or if something else, something that has learned to use that infrastructure, is announcing its presence through temperature alone.

Owen continues his survey, moving to another spot where Mira had walked, where her feet had pressed into the soft earth for just moments. Another flag joins the first, then another, each one marking a point of thermal anomaly. Vincent begins to see the pattern before Owen does, recognizes the curve emerging from the placement, the way the flags arc around a central point like a careful orbit.

The chapel ruins themselves have transformed overnight. Where yesterday ice glazed the broken stones, now moss spreads in impossible abundance, the green so vivid it seems to pulse. The metal cross that still stands atop the partial bell tower has lost its rust, the iron gleaming as if recently polished, though no one has climbed those unstable remains in years. Steam rises from cracks in the foundation, not the violent expulsion of geysers but the gentle exhalation of ground that breathes.

"Look at this," June says, directing their attention to a section of wall where frost should cling to northern exposure. Instead, tiny flowers have pushed through mortar joints, white petals no bigger than fingernails, species Vincent doesn't recognize. They grow in spirals that follow the stone's surface, creating patterns within patterns, fractals of growth.

The scent around the chapel has changed too. Yesterday it smelled of cold stone and dead vegetation. Now the air carries cedar and iron, that familiar combination that marks every manifestation of the Root Titan's presence, but underneath runs something sweeter, almost floral, like spring flowers blooming in soil enriched by decay. The combination creates an olfactory dissonance.

Owen has placed seven flags now, and the pattern is undeniable. They form a perfect circle perhaps fifteen feet in diameter, each flag marking a point where the soil temperature spikes beyond reason. He stands slowly, mud-caked knees creaking, and surveys his work wearing the look of someone who's uncovered an answer they'd rather not know.

"The measurements increase toward the center," he says, pulling his notebook from his backpack. His pencil moves across the page, sketching the flag positions, adding temperature readings beside each point. "Like rings of heat radiating outward from wherever she stood longest."

The air shifts, and Vincent turns to see Mira returning from her walk around the chapel's perimeter. She moves with that fluid grace, as if gravity affects her differently. Her shoes should be muddy from the wet ground, but they remain clean, the earth itself seeming to avoid clinging to her.

Owen straightens fully, his notebook clutched against his chest like a shield, his muddy knees forgotten as he faces Mira directly. The scientific detachment he's maintained now replaced by something rawer, more personal. When he speaks, his voice carries the weight of accusation and concern in equal measure.

"You're not fixing anything," he tells her quietly, each word deliberate. "You're feeding it."

The pronoun hangs between them, undefined but understood. Not the earth, not the town, but the thing that pulses beneath everything, the presence that has been growing stronger since the volunteer day, since Mira's public demonstration of impossible abilities. Vincent sees her flinch slightly at Owen's words, though whether from recognition or denial he can't tell.

"You don't understand," Mira begins, but her voice lacks conviction, as if she's not entirely certain what she understands herself.

"The temperatures, the growth, the patterns," Owen

continues, gesturing at his circle of flags. "They all center on you. Wherever you go, whatever's down there responds. Gets stronger. You're not healing anything. You're giving it exactly what it wants."

The soil beneath their feet chooses that moment to pulse, a single strong throb that they feel through their shoes, through their bones, through the fluid of their bodies that suddenly seems to move in response to external rhythm rather than internal need. It's not violent, not threatening, but undeniably present, as if whatever lies beneath has heard Owen's words and wants to offer its own perspective.

The hum that has become Duswood's constant companion deepens momentarily, dropping to frequencies that bypass hearing and manifest as pressure in the chest, weight in the limbs, the sensation of being seen by something vast and patient and increasingly awake. Then it returns to its normal range, that almost-ignorable presence that they've all learned to live with, though Vincent suspects none of them will ever truly grow accustomed to it.

The hallway to Mira's room stretches longer than it should at night, the floorboards creaking with sounds that follow Vincent's footsteps a half-second late, as if the house itself is learning his rhythm and trying to match it. Her door stands partially open, unusual for this hour, and through the gap spills air that belongs to a different season, carrying warmth and the scent of flowers. Vincent pauses at the threshold, his hand raised to knock, when he sees what lies beyond.

The window stands wide despite the evening chill that should make such exposure uncomfortable, its curtains moving in wind. But it's what covers the floor that stops his breath. Flower petals, dozens of them, fresh as if just plucked, drift across the hardwood.

The petals are wrong for this place, this season. Some he recognizes: rose petals in deep red, lily petals in pristine white, violet petals in purple so dark it's nearly black. Others are foreign to him, tropical perhaps, or maybe not from anywhere that exists in normal geography.

A thick cedar scent fills the room, but underneath runs something else, that metallic taste that coats the back of his throat like blood from a bitten tongue. The combination creates an atmosphere that feels both sacred and profane, like standing in a church that's been repurposed for ceremonies older than Christianity.

Mira sits cross-legged on her bed, still wearing the cardigan and dress from earlier, though both look somehow different in this light, as if the fabric has absorbed some quality from whatever she's been communing with. Her eyes are half-closed, not quite unconscious but not fully present either, existing in that liminal space between sleep and waking where boundaries become negotiable.

Her lips move in constant motion, shaping words that Vincent can't quite hear, though he catches fragments that might be syllables or might be sounds that predate language. Her hands rest on her knees, palms up, fingers twitching occasionally as if conducting music only she can hear. The air around her bends visibly, the way heat distortion rises from summer asphalt, but the effect is stronger, more deliberate, as if reality itself has gone soft in her proximity.

Vincent steps into the room, and immediately feels the temperature difference. It's not just warm but actively heated, as if invisible fires burn just outside perception. His skin prickles with more than temperature change. There's a presence here, not visible but undeniable, the sensation of being observed by something that exists in corners eyes can't quite focus on.

He crosses to the bed, flower petals parting before his feet like water, reforming their patterns behind him. Up close, he can see perspiration beading on Mira's forehead despite her stillness, can hear her breathing that comes too deep, too slow, as if she's matching rhythm with something vast. Her eyelids flutter, showing whites, and Vincent recognizes the signs of deep trance, of consciousness that has traveled far from its physical housing.

"Mira," he says softly, not wanting to startle her but needing to draw her back from wherever she's gone.

No response. Her lips continue their wordless recitation, and the air around her pulses with that heat distortion, stronger now, making her edges blur. Vincent reaches out, hesitates, then places his hand on her shoulder. The contact is electric, not literally but in the way it bridges between states, his solid presence connecting with her drifting consciousness.

She startles violently, eyes flying wide, pupils so dilated the amber-gray is nearly invisible. For a moment she looks at him without recognition, as if she's forgotten human faces, forgotten what it means to be singular rather than distributed. Then awareness returns in stages: confusion, recognition, something that might be embarrassment or might be fear.

"I'm fine," she says too quickly, the words automatic, defensive. Her voice sounds rough, as if she's been speaking for hours, though Vincent heard no sound until now.

He doesn't move his hand from her shoulder, feeling the tremor that runs through her, the way her body shakes with exhaustion that has nothing to do with physical exertion. The flower petals on the floor have stopped their movement, lying still now like evidence of something that shouldn't have happened.

"You're not fine," Vincent says gently. "The petals, the temperature, the way you were sitting. How long have you been like this?"

Mira looks around her room as if seeing it for the first time, taking in the impossible flowers, the open window, the way shadows fall in directions that don't match the lamp beside her bed. Her expression shifts through confusion to something like acceptance, as if she's given up pretending this is normal.

"Since sunset," she admits. "Maybe longer. Time works differently when I'm listening."

"Listening to what?"

She meets his eyes, and in her gaze Vincent sees depths that weren't there weeks ago, knowledge that ages people in ways that have nothing to do with years. When she speaks, her voice carries certainty.

"He says the earth's been hurting for a long time," she whispers, as if speaking too loudly might break something fragile. "That I can make it stop."

The pronoun makes Vincent's blood chill. He. Not it. Not the vast, impersonal presence of the Root Titan, but something with identity, with personality, with wants that can be articulated. His fingers tighten slightly on her shoulder, not enough to hurt but enough to anchor, to remind her of physical connection to this room, this moment, this reality that something is trying to pull her away from.

"Who?" Vincent asks, though he thinks he knows, fears he knows.

Mira hesitates, her fingers tracing patterns on the bedspread that match the spirals on the floor, movements that seem involuntary, as if her body has learned a new language without her conscious permission. She shakes her head, not in denial but in uncertainty, the gesture of someone trying to describe something that exists outside normal categories.

"I don't know," she says finally. "Sometimes it feels like the earth itself, like the planet trying to communicate through the only channels available. But other times..." She trails off, her hand rising to press against her sternum, over her heart, as if feeling for something that shouldn't be there. "Other times it feels personal. Like someone specific talking through something vast. Using it like a telephone, or a megaphone, or..."

"Or a puppet," Vincent finishes, his voice harder than intended.

He kneels beside the bed, bringing himself to her eye level, and takes both her hands in his. They're fevered, too warm, as if she's been holding them over flame. Through the contact, he feels the tremor that runs constantly through her now, the vibration that matches the hum beneath Duswood, as if she's become a tuning fork for frequencies from a time when they didn't have a name.

"Mira, listen to me," he says, his voice low and urgent. "We found documents about the infrastructure below town. The rings, the tunnels, all of it designed to channel something. But there's something else, something that's learned to use that infrastructure. We think it's The Adversary. He's been waiting for the right conduit, the right person to bridge between what he is and what we are."

Her hands tighten in his, not in fear but in something like recognition. "But he says he wants to help. That the earth needs healing, that I can be the one to fix what's broken."

"That's what he does," Vincent insists, remembering Muldrath, remembering the blooms, remembering every manipulation disguised as salvation. "He offers what you want to hear, makes you feel special, chosen. But it's not about healing. It's about access. He needs someone like you, someone who can hear frequencies others can't, to give him entry to our reality."

Outside, wind suddenly moves through the cedar trees with violence that makes branches crack. The sound is wicked, too deliberate, too much like laughter if laughter could be made of wood and air. The flower petals on the floor stir, lifting, reforming their spirals, and the temperature in the room drops ten degrees in an instant.

Mira's eyes go wide, her pupils dilating further, and when she speaks, her voice carries harmonics that shouldn't come from a human throat. "I just want to help it."

Vincent pulls her against him, his arms wrapping around her trembling form, trying to anchor her to this moment, this reality, this simple human contact that requires no translation between states of being. Through the embrace, he feels the battle being waged in her body, between what she is and what something else wants her to become.

The register drawer sticks when Vincent tries to close it for the third time this shift, metal grinding against warped wood, and he slams it harder than necessary, the coins inside jumping with metallic protests that echo through Cedar Lagoon's empty afternoon dining room. His fingers drum against the counter, nervous energy seeking release through movement that has become constant these past three days since he held Mira in that room full of impossible flowers. The fluorescent light above flickers intermittently, casting his reflection in the register's scratched surface in stuttering glimpses that show the purple shadows beneath his eyes.

Vincent checks his phone's screen again, though no notification has sounded. Nothing from Mira. His fingers drum rhythmically on the counter. He can feel the hum through the pizzeria's linoleum floor, through the metal legs of the stool he perches on during slow afternoons.

The bell above the door chimes, and Owen enters carrying something rolled under his arm, his movements quick and purposeful in a way that makes Vincent straighten from his slump. Owen's clothes are rumpled, his hair uncombed, the careful academic precision he usually maintains abandoned in favor of urgency. He crosses to the counter without preamble, without the usual polite greeting, and spreads what he's carrying across the surface between them.

It's a map, but not any modern printing. The paper has aged to the color of weak tea, its edges soft with handling, tears repaired with yellowing tape that might be older than either of them. The document shows Duswood and its surroundings from an era when the town was smaller, when the forest pressed closer, when the Great Northern Rail and Ore Company's influence touched everything. Black lines trace the rail routes with obsessive detail, main arteries and auxiliary branches spreading like veins through the landscape.

Owen's finger lands on a spot north of town, where the freight line curves toward Lake Michigan through cedar forest. Someone has circled this location in pencil so old it's nearly invisible, the graphite worn to silver. Beside it, in handwriting that speaks of fountain pens and careful penmanship, someone has written "Iron Gate" and below that, a series of numbers.

Vincent's breath catches. The coordinates are burned into his memory from when Mira recited them in her sleep, her voice carrying that quality of translation, of someone converting impossible concepts into numbers that barely contain them. His fingers trace the digits on the map, feeling the slight depression where pencil pressed into paper decades ago, and the correlation is perfect. Whatever Mira heard in her communion with the thing beneath Duswood, it wants them to know about this place.

"I found this in the historical society archives," Owen says, his voice low despite the empty restaurant. "Filed wrong, stuffed behind tax records from 1952. But look at the annotations."

Vincent leans closer, noting other markings on the map.

Red X's at locations he recognizes: the construction site, Hearthstone Chapel, the north bluff where they felt the dual-voiced wind. Each mark connects to the Iron Gate with straight lines drawn in the same aged pencil, creating a web of relationships that suggests infrastructure, network, purpose. At the center of it all, that circled location waits like a spider at the heart of its web.

"These are the exact coordinates," Vincent says, not a question but confirmation of what they both already know. "The ones she kept repeating."

Owen nods, his expression grave. "Whatever's happening, whatever she's connected to, it all leads back to this point. The Iron Gate. I looked through the GNRO records we have. It's listed as a freight tunnel, part of the auxiliary network, but there's no record of it being used after 1953."

The year of the sealing. The year something went catastrophically awry enough that an entire company walked away from infrastructure that must have cost millions to build. Vincent's fingers drum faster against the counter, nervous energy transforming into decision. He glances at the clock on the wall: 2:47 PM. Joe won't expect him to stay if he explains, won't deny him this when the old soldier understands better than most what it means to chase dangers that won't wait for convenient timing.

Vincent pulls off his apron with movements that feel predetermined, as if this moment was always going to arrive, as if the map was always going to appear, as if the coordinates Mira whispered were always going to draw him north. His phone buzzes as he tosses the apron beneath the counter, and for a moment his heart accelerates, hoping for her name on the screen. But it's just the low battery warning, another thing he's neglected in his spiral of worry and sleeplessness.

"I'm going with you," Vincent says, though Owen hasn't explicitly invited him. He just nods, already rolling the map with careful movements that speak of respect for historical documents and fear of what they might reveal.

Vincent heads to the kitchen where Joe stands at the prep station, chopping onions. The older man looks up, takes in Vincent's expression, the tension in his shoulders, the way his hands won't stop moving even when the rest of him goes still.

"I need to leave," Vincent says simply.

Joe sets down his knife, wipes his hands on his apron, and studies Vincent with eyes that have seen young men heading toward danger before, in jungles across the world, in conflicts that made even less sense than whatever supernatural threat lurks beneath Duswood. He reaches into his pocket, pulls out keys, and tosses them to Vincent in a smooth arc.

"Take the truck," Joe says. "Whatever you're chasing, you'll need reliable transport back."

Vincent catches the keys, their weight familiar and reassuring. He wants to explain, wants to share what they've discovered, but there isn't time and maybe there aren't words for it anyway. Instead, he nods his gratitude and heads for the door where Owen waits, map tucked under his arm, ready to follow coordinates that might lead to answers or might lead to something that should have stayed buried with the rest of GNRO's secrets.

As Vincent grabs his jacket from the hook by the door, his phone buzzes one more time. This time it is from Mira, just four words that make his blood chill: "You shouldn't go there." But she doesn't say don't go, doesn't forbid it, just acknowledges what he's about to do with the resignation of someone who sees inevitability approaching like a storm that can't be avoided, only weathered.

———

The freight line runs straight as intention through the cedar forest, its rails long since removed but the path remaining like a scar that refuses to heal, and Vincent follows Owen through undergrowth that catches at their clothes with thorns and burrs, nature trying to reclaim what industry abandoned but never quite succeeding. Afternoon light filters through the cedar branches in columns of gold and green, creating a cathedral quality. The trees here grow differently than near town, their trunks twisted by constant wind from the lake, their bark marked with that familiar red sap that has become Duswood's signature of disturbance.

The path beneath their feet is gravel mixed with decades of decomposed needles, creating a surface that crunches with each step while simultaneously seeming to absorb sound, as if the earth here has learned to muffle what happens above it. Vincent notices how the railroad bed maintains its elevated position despite seventy years of erosion, the engineering too solid to surrender completely to time, though saplings push through in places, their roots cracking what remains of the ballast rock that once supported steel rails carrying cargo that nobody talks about anymore.

As they move north, the forest begins to change. The cedars thin gradually, their dense clusters giving way to individual giants that stand like sentinels, each one twisted into unique configurations by wind and time and perhaps something else. Through gaps in the canopy, Vincent glimpses Lake Michigan in the distance, its surface the color of old pewter, vast and still. The absence of waves feels deliberate, as if the lake itself has been commanded to hide in the rushes.

The air grows heavier with each hundred yards they travel, taking on qualities that register on senses beyond the usual five. That metallic taste intensifies, coating Vincent's tongue with flavors of iron and salt and something sharper, like the aftertaste of batteries or the scent that precedes lightning. He has to work to swallow, his throat protesting against air that seems too thick, too laden with minerals that belong underground rather than in afternoon atmosphere. Beside him, Owen pulls out a handkerchief to wipe his face, though the day isn't particularly warm, the gesture more about the oppressive quality of their surroundings than actual temperature.

The bluffs rise gradually on their left, limestone and sandstone layered in strata that tell stories of ancient seas and geological patience. But there are marks in the stone that don't belong to natural erosion, straight lines and right angles that suggest human intervention, places where the rock was cut rather than worn away. Old support structures, Vincent realizes, anchors for infrastructure that once connected the freight line to something more permanent than temporary rails.

They round a bend where the path curves to follow the bluff's contour, and suddenly it's there, emerging from the hillside like something the earth tried to swallow but couldn't quite digest. The Iron Gate sits half-buried in the slope, its upper portion exposed to decades of weather, the lower sections disappearing into accumulated soil and vegetation that has built up around it like festered tissue.

The structure itself is a tunnel entrance, but industrial in a way that speaks of different priorities than simple freight movement. The opening is sealed with plates of steel that have corroded to the color of dried blood, rust streaming down the surface in patterns that follow the rivets and seams like tears of oxidized metal. The plates overlap in ways that suggest hasty installation, emergency measures taken when something needed to be contained quickly rather than aesthetically.

Above the sealed entrance, letters remain visible despite decades of weathering: "GNRO" in faded industrial stenciling, and below that, barely legible, "AUTHORIZED ENTRY ONLY." The warning carries weight beyond simple trespassing concerns, the kind of declaration that implies consequences more serious than legal action. Vincent notices how the metal around the letters has corroded differently, leaving them standing in relief against the deeper rust, as if the paint used contained something that resisted decay with unusual persistence.

Owen approaches the barrier with the caution of someone who's learned that some things bite without teeth. He extends his hand slowly, hesitates, then knocks once against the metal, the sound ringing out sharp and clear in the afternoon stillness. But what follows the knock makes them both freeze, their bodies going rigid with recognition of something profoundly unnatural.

The echo doesn't behave like sound should in a sealed space. Instead of the hollow boom of empty tunnel or the dead thud of filled earth, the reverberation runs deeper, spreading outward and downward simultaneously. Vincent feels it through his boots, through the gravel and soil, through the bedrock beneath. The vibration travels in directions that suggest vast spaces below, interconnected chambers and passages that transform Owen's simple knock into something like sonar, mapping invisible geometries through sound alone.

"That's not hollow space," Owen says quietly, his voice carrying the weight of someone making a discovery they wish they hadn't. His hand remains extended toward the barrier but not touching, as if he's afraid of what further contact might reveal. "That's a network. Those tunnels we've been tracking, they all connect here. This isn't just an entrance. It's a hub."

Vincent moves closer to the sealed entrance, his flashlight playing across the corroded surface even though afternoon light makes it unnecessary. The beam reveals details that sunlight somehow misses, catching on irregularities that aren't random corrosion but deliberate markings. He steps closer, angling the light, and the symbols emerge from the rust like photographs developing in chemical baths.

Spirals, dozens of them, etched directly into the steel with something that cut through metal as if it were soft as clay. They vary in size from inches to feet across, overlapping in places, creating patterns within patterns. But it's the other symbols that make Vincent lean in: crosses made of what look like nail holes, punched through the metal in perfect formation; circles of similar perforations that create mandala-like designs; and at the center of the largest plate, a symbol he doesn't recognize, something that might be writing in a language that predates human civilization or might be a warning in a script that hasn't been invented yet.

"Ritual," Vincent whispers, tracing one spiral with his fingertip, careful not to actually touch the metal. Even from an inch away, he can feel the surface vibrating faintly, a tremor so subtle it might be imagination except for the way his finger seems drawn toward contact, as if the symbol itself exerts a form of magnetism. "Someone didn't just seal this. They were trying to bind it."

The marks aren't industrial, aren't practical. They speak of desperation dressed in ceremony, of someone who understood that simple steel wasn't enough to contain what lay beyond, who turned to older methods, marking the barrier with symbols that might mean protection or might mean prison or might mean something else entirely. The combination of corporate infrastructure and mystical scarification creates a dissonance, two worldviews colliding in corroded metal and deliberate wounds.

Near the tunnel entrance, partially obscured by blackberry vines that have grown wild despite the metallic soil, Vincent spots a metal box mounted on what might once have been a post but now tilts at an angle that suggests the earth beneath has shifted over decades of slow geological breathing. The vines part reluctantly as he pushes through them, thorns catching on his jacket sleeves, and he finds himself face to face with a switchbox that should have been removed when the tunnel was sealed, should have been disconnected from whatever power source once fed these operations, but instead sits here like a forgotten organ still somehow connected to its body.

The casing has cracked open along one side, not from impact but from internal pressure, as if something inside expanded beyond the metal's ability to contain it. The crack runs jagged as lightning, wide enough that Vincent can see inside without touching anything, his flashlight beam penetrating the darkness within to reveal a complexity that makes no sense for what should be simple electrical switching equipment. The interior should hold breakers, fuses, simple mechanical components, but what he sees instead makes his understanding of physics feel suddenly fragile.

Wires tangle inside like veins, like root systems, like neural pathways, far more than any switchbox should contain. They're different gauges, different materials, some copper, others that might be steel, still others that look organic, fibrous, as if someone wove electrical systems from materials that once lived. But it's where the wires lead that makes Vincent pause. They don't connect to other components within the box. Instead, they disappear directly into the rock behind the mounting post, entering the stone through holes that look melted rather than drilled, as if the rock itself opened to accept them.

Owen crowds beside him, his excitement overriding caution as he angles his own flashlight into the damaged box. Together, their beams illuminate the impossible, and Vincent watches Owen's face cycle through perplexed expressions. The wires that disappear into the stone aren't still. They pulse with faint luminescence, rhythmic as heartbeat, as breathing, as the deep geological processes that should take millennia but here seem compressed into moments.

"It's active," Owen whispers, his voice carrying awe and fear in equal measure. His hand rises toward the crack as if to touch, to confirm through contact what his eyes insist can't be real, but Vincent catches his wrist, holds him back with gentle firmness that speaks of shared understanding that some things shouldn't be touched, no matter how much they demand investigation.

"After seventy years," Owen continues, his whisper taking on an almost reverential quality. "It's still alive."

The word choice feels significant. Not functioning, not operational, but alive. Because what they're looking at doesn't behave like simple electrical current following circuits. The pulsing has variation, personality, the suggestion of communication traveling through copper and stone and materials that shouldn't conduct anything but here serve as medium for something that exists outside normal electromagnetic spectrums.

They back away from the switchbox in unconscious synchronization, their bodies responding to some primal warning that bypasses conscious thought. As they increase distance from the tunnel entrance, from that cracked box with its impossible connections, Vincent becomes aware of a change in the air around them. Not the metallic taste, which has been constant since they arrived, but something more fundamental, more invasive.

The hum begins so softly that at first Vincent mistakes it for his own blood rushing through his ears, the sound of his pulse made audible by adrenaline and proximity to something that shouldn't exist. But as they continue backing away, the sound clarifies, separates from his internal rhythms to reveal itself as external, environmental, emanating from the ground beneath their feet, from the air around them, from the very atoms that make up this space where reality has gone soft.

It's different from the hum at the construction site, different from the vibration that runs beneath Duswood proper. This version feels more intimate, more personal, as if calibrated specifically for human perception. It doesn't assault the senses but insinuates itself, finding frequencies that resonate with bone and muscle and the electrical impulses that create thought. Vincent feels it in his sternum, in the hollow of his throat, in the spaces between his teeth where his jaw clenches involuntarily.

His phone buzzes in his pocket, the vibration momentarily harmonizing with the environmental hum before separating into its familiar mechanical pattern. Vincent pulls it out, expecting another low battery warning, but Mira's name appears on the screen. The message is simple, just a few words, but they carry weight that makes his hand tremble: "You shouldn't be there."

Not "don't go" as her earlier message implied, but acknowledgment that they've already arrived, that somehow she knows exactly where they stand despite being miles away in town. Vincent looks up from the screen, scanning the tree line, and for one impossible second he sees her.

She stands between two massive cedars perhaps thirty feet away, perfectly still, her white dress unmistakable against the dark bark. Her hair moves in wind that doesn't touch the branches around her, creating motion that exists independent of natural meteorology. Her face is turned toward them, but at this distance Vincent can't read her expression, can't tell if she's warning them or simply witnessing their trespass into spaces that have become her domain through connection she never chose.

"Mira?" Vincent calls out, the name emerging as half question, half plea.

Owen turns to follow Vincent's gaze, but in the space of that motion, in the fraction of second where Vincent's attention splits between his friend's movement and the figure between the trees, she vanishes. Not gradually, not by stepping behind the cedar trunks, but simply ceasing to exist in that location as if she was never there at all. The space where she stood shows no disturbance, no pressed grass, no indication that anyone has passed through recently.

"Did you see..." Owen starts, but his voice trails off, the question unnecessary. They both know what they saw, or what they think they saw, or what something wanted them to see. The distinction feels less important than the implication: either Mira bilocated again, or her presence has become so deeply woven into the fabric of what's happening here that echoes of her can appear as warning, messenger, or a gentle reminder that nothing in Duswood goes unseen.

The hum fades as suddenly as it began, not gradually diminishing but cutting off as if someone threw a switch, leaving behind a silence that feels heavier than the sound it replaces. Vincent's ears ring with the absence, with the phantom vibration that continues in his bones even though the air has gone still. Below them, Lake Michigan remains unnaturally calm, its surface reflecting the afternoon sky without ripple or wave.

Owen exhales slowly, his breath visible despite the spring warmth, condensation that shouldn't exist at this temperature but does anyway, as if the air around the Iron Gate operates by different physical laws. When he speaks, his voice carries the certainty of someone who's assembled enough pieces to see the shape of the puzzle, even if the complete picture remains unclear.

"We just found the heart of it," he says, gesturing at the sealed tunnel, at the broken switchbox, at the space where network hub meets ritual binding site. "This is where it all connects. The rings, the tunnels, whatever's underneath Duswood. It all flows through here."

Vincent stares at the empty space between the cedars where Mira appeared and vanished, his mind trying to reconcile the girl he held three nights ago with whatever she's becoming. The distance between them feels vast suddenly, not measured in miles but in the degree to which she's slipping away from human concerns into something else, something that can exist in multiple places or project itself through the network that thrums beneath the town.

Cold dread settles in his stomach like swallowed ice, the recognition that finding the Iron Gate might have given them understanding but not solutions. They know where the heart is, but hearts can be corrupted, can be claimed by parasites that use the body's own systems against it. And Mira, willing or not, has become part of those systems, integrated into the network in ways that might already be irreversible.

The trek back toward the parked truck feels longer than the journey out, their steps heavy with knowledge that weighs more than curiosity did. Behind them, the Iron Gate waits in its corroded patience, its sealed entrance hiding passages that connect to every impossible thing they've witnessed. And somewhere, distributed through that network or simply watching through senses that transcend normal perception, Mira continues her transformation into something that bridges the gap between human and whatever lies beneath, between what Duswood was and what it's becoming, between salvation and something far more terrible wearing salvation's mask.

CHAPTER
SEVENTEEN

Morning comes to Hearthstone Chapel dressed in gray, the light filtering through cedars that lean inward as if trying to reclaim what humans abandoned, and Mira picks her way through undergrowth that has grown thick since anyone last bothered to clear a proper path. Her breath clouds in the damp air, each exhalation hanging visible for seconds before dissolving into the mist that clings to everything here. The chapel emerges from the trees gradually, first the broken line of its bell tower against the pale sky, then the walls of fitted stone that have held their shape despite decades of neglect.

The tower splits down its center like something cracked by divine judgment, the bell itself long since fallen into the nave below. Rust and lichen share territory across the remaining metal fixtures, creating patterns of red and green that look deliberate in their decay. The wooden doors hang at angles that suggest violence, though whether from weather or human hands remains unclear. Through gaps in the planking, darkness waits with the patience of spaces that have forgotten sunlight.

Mira steps through the threshold, her boots crushing moss

that carpets the floor in velvet thickness. The sound of her footsteps goes muffled immediately, absorbed by vegetation. Above, the fractured roof allows rain to enter freely, creating pools of black water that reflect nothing, their surfaces still as closed caskets. The drops that fall now, remnants of last night's storm, create rings that spread and vanish without sound.

The air inside carries competing scents. Iron rises from somewhere beneath the moss, that familiar metallic taste. But threading through it comes incense, impossible after so many years, as if the very stones have absorbed decades of blessing and now release it slowly, mixing sacred memory with present decay. The combination creates something neither holy nor profane but suspended between states, like the chapel itself.

At what was once the altar, wildflowers push through cracks in the stone platform. Their stems look too delicate to have broken through, yet here they bloom, white petals tinged with red at their edges as if they've drawn that color from the iron-rich earth below. Mira approaches slowly, her fingers trailing along the remains of a pew that crumbles at her touch, wood gone soft as cotton from rot that works from inside out.

She kneels beside the foundation where stone meets earth, her jeans immediately soaking through from moisture that never quite dries here. Her fingers brush away moss in careful strokes, revealing stone beneath that bears marks too deliberate for weather. The carvings emerge slowly, spirals within spirals, each revolution precise despite the crude tools that must have made them. Between the spirals, other symbols appear, half-formed suggestions of meaning that hover at the edge of recognition.

The patterns match what Vincent described from the Iron Gate, that same obsessive geometry that appears wherever the Root Titan's influence surfaces. But these feel older, carved not in metal but in stone that predates any modern industrial ambition. Her fingertips trace one spiral's path, feeling how deep it cuts, how perfectly it maintains its curve despite decades of erosion.

When her palm presses flat against the largest carving, warmth rises immediately through her skin. Not the gentle heat of sun-warmed stone but something that originates from below, from depths where heat should come from geological forces but here feels more intentional. The warmth spreads up her arm in waves that match her pulse, or perhaps her pulse adjusts to match them, the distinction suddenly uncertain.

The hum responds as if summoned, vibrating through the stone with weighted force. It travels up through her knees where they press against moss, through her extended arm, through the bones that spread warmness to the rest of her body. The sensation is pleasurable, but invasive, intimate, like something reading her composition and finding the resonance that makes her whole body sing in harmony with whatever breathes beneath Hearthstone Chapel.

Her free hand finds the chaplet in her pocket, her mother's Holy Face beads worn smooth by generations of prayer. She pulls it out carefully, the amber and silver catching what little light penetrates the broken ceiling. Each bead holds memory, decades of whispered devotions, her mother's fingers and her grandmother's before that, wearing grooves that fit her own grip perfectly. The crucifix swings gently, creating small arcs that seem to pull toward the carved stone, as if magnetized by whatever force rises from below.

The voice rises from the hum like smoke from embers, soft at first, then taking shape in archaic tones. It doesn't speak through her ears but manifests directly in her consciousness, bypassing the mechanics of sound to plant itself in the spaces where memory lives. The cadence is achingly familiar, each syllable weighted with the particular rhythm her mother used when speaking of sacred things, when her voice would drop to barely above a whisper in evening prayers.

"You came back," the voice says, and those two words carry such tenderness that Mira's hand trembles against the stone. The warmth beneath her palm pulses stronger, matching the sudden acceleration of her heartbeat. The chapel around her seems to fade, its broken walls becoming less solid, less important than this impossible sound.

"Mama?" The word escapes before thought can stop it, emerging as barely more than shaped breath. Her mother has been gone for 10 years, sacrificing herself to save Duswood once before. But this voice, this exact tone, lives in Mira's bones, in the memories of being held during thunderstorms, of bedtime stories about saints and angels, of morning songs in the kitchen while bread rose in the oven.

The presence in the hum seems to swell with her recognition, growing warmer, more encompassing. When it speaks again, the voice carries that specific lilt her mother used when explaining difficult truths to a young child, patient and loving and absolutely certain.

"You can finish what I couldn't," it continues, and now there's something beneath the tenderness, an urgency that presses against Mira's consciousness like fingers against glass. "You have the gift I only glimpsed. You can be the bridge between what was broken and what could be whole."

Tears slip down Mira's cheeks before she realizes she's crying, the salt warmth tracking paths through the chapel's dust on her face. They fall onto the moss-covered stone, each droplet creating tiny clearings in the green where it lands, as if her grief has weight enough to push aside even this persistent growth. Her mother's chaplet dangles from her other hand, the beads clicking softly against each other with her trembling.

The voice grows more persuasive, more specifically her mother's in its inflections, in the way it stretches certain vowels, in the tiny pause before saying her name. "Mira, my darling girl. They broke the roots when they built their roads, when they laid their iron circles in the earth. The land has been crying out for someone who could hear, someone who could heal the wounds they carved."

Her palm presses harder against the carving, the spiral's edges cutting slightly into her skin, but she doesn't pull away. The warmth has become heat now, spreading up her arm and into her chest where it settles like swallowed fire. The hum vibrates through every cell, creating resonance that makes her feel expanded, distributed, as if she exists not just in her body but in the stone, in the moss, in the very air of this broken holy place.

"All you have to do is open the ground and let me through," the voice whispers, and for a moment it's so perfectly her mother's that Mira can almost smell her perfume, that combination of jasmine and something deeper, earthier, that clung to her clothes even in the hospital. "Let me rise, and together we can restore what was taken. You can knit the roots whole again."

A beam of light cuts through a crack in the floor that Mira hadn't noticed before, the fissure running from beneath the altar to where she kneels. The light washes across her face in gold so pure it seems to carry warmth beyond the physical, touching something in her that responds to beauty, to the divine, to the possibility of grace in broken places. For a heartbeat, maybe two, the sensation is everything she remembers from childhood Sunday mornings, when stained glass would transform sunlight, reminding her she was in the presence of God.

Then the light flickers, shifts, bleeds into red that has nothing to do with stained glass or holiness. The color washes across her features, painting her skin in tones of rust and blood, and the warmth that seemed comforting becomes something else, something that doesn't nurture but consumes.

The red light pulses in rhythm with the hum, with her heartbeat, with whatever presence has learned to speak in her mother's voice.

Mira jerks her hand back from the carving as if it has become a live coal, but the warmth remains, pulsing under her skin with its own rhythm. She can feel it traveling through her palm, through the fine bones of her hand, establishing residence in her flesh like something that has found a home it won't easily surrender. The red light continues to pulse from the crack in the floor, painting the chapel in shades of violence that have nothing to do with the sacred space this once was.

"You're not her," she whispers, the words stronger now despite the trembling that runs through her entire body. The tears still track down her cheeks, but they feel different, no longer grief but something closer to rage at this violation of memory, this theft of her mother's voice for purposes that mock everything her mother believed.

The presence in the hum shifts, not retreating but adjusting, like someone changing their posture when their disguise has been recognized. When it speaks again, the voice still carries her mother's tones but with something else threading through them, something older and more patient than any human life.

"I remember her voice," The Adversary replies, and now she can hear it clearly, the thing that wears her mother's intonations like clothing that doesn't quite fit. "I was there when she prayed in the woods, when she asked for healing, for more time with you. I heard every word, felt every desperate hope. Doesn't that make it true enough? Memory is just another kind of existence."

Mira stumbles to her feet, her legs unsteady from kneeling on the damp moss, from the adrenaline that floods her system with the need to flee. Her boots slip on the vegetation that covers the floor, sending her sideways into what remains of a pew. The wood crumbles further under her weight, showering her with fragments that smell of rot and old incense, that mixed scent of decay and devotion that permeates everything here.

"You're using her," Mira says, backing toward the doorway ruins, her steps uncertain on the uneven floor. "Taking something sacred and twisting it into..." She can't finish, can't name what this manipulation has become, but she feels it in the warmth that still pulses in her palm, in the way the red light seems to track her movement.

"I'm offering what she wanted," the voice continues, still patient, still wearing her mother's cadence like a mask. "Connection. Healing. The chance to make broken things whole. Isn't that what love does? Isn't that what she taught you?"

Mira's hand clutches her mother's chaplet so tightly the beads dig crescents into her palm, the small pain a welcome anchor to something real, something that belonged to her mother without interpretation or manipulation. The crucifix swings wildly with her movement, catching the red light and throwing it back in fractured reflections that dance across the chapel's walls like flames.

Her shoulder hits the doorframe as she stumbles through the entrance, the impact sharp enough to clear her head momentarily. The cooler air outside rushes into her lungs, tasting of cedar and morning mist and the absence of that iron-and-incense mixture that has become the chapel's signature. She doesn't stop moving, doesn't look back, just pushes through the undergrowth that catches at her clothes with thorns and branches that seem more deliberate than random.

Behind her, the chapel doesn't call out, doesn't pursue, but she feels its attention like heat on her back, like being watched by something that has all the time in the world. The red light still glows through the cracks and gaps, visible even in the gray morning.

When she finally stops, perhaps fifty feet from the chapel,

her breath comes in uneven gasps that have more to do with emotion than exertion. The sky above Duswood looks pale and empty, clouds stretched thin across a canvas that seems too vast, too indifferent to what happens below. But it's the ground that holds her attention, that makes her freeze despite every instinct screaming at her to keep running.

The earth beneath her feet pulses slightly with each step she takes, not obviously, but she feels it through her boots, through her bones, through that place in her palm where the warmth still lives. The pulse follows her, matches her, as if the entire landscape has become aware of her movement, as if whatever she touched in that chapel has marked her in ways that simple distance can't erase.

She stands there in the gray morning light, her mother's chaplet still clutched in her hand, feeling the ground beneath her respond to her presence with patient recognition. The Root Titan or The Adversary or whatever vast presence has woken beneath Duswood hasn't let her go. It's simply waiting, following her through the very earth she walks on, certain that she'll return.

The cedar trees behind Vincent and Mira's house stand like dark sentinels against the night sky, their branches heavy with sap that fills the air with resin sweetness, and Vincent moves through the backyard with careful steps, following an instinct that tells him where Mira has gone. The grass beneath his feet holds moisture from an afternoon rain that never quite dried, each blade releasing tiny droplets that catch moonlight before falling back to earth. The night air presses against him with unseasonable warmth, thick as syrup, carrying that metallic undertone that has become Duswood's new signature.

He finds her exactly where he expected, sitting at the edge where maintained lawn surrenders to wild growth, her back to the house, facing the darkness between the cedars. Her silhouette cuts sharp against the deeper shadows, shoulders curved inward as if she's cradling something invisible against her chest. The white of her dress glows faintly in the moonlight, making her look like something painted rather than real, a figure from a dream that hasn't quite solidified into waking.

She doesn't turn when his footsteps whisper through the

grass, doesn't acknowledge his approach with any movement of her head or shift of posture. But a smile touches the corner of her mouth, visible in profile, as if she's been expecting him, as if this moment was predetermined by forces larger than choice. The expression carries neither surprise nor welcome, just recognition of inevitability arriving on schedule.

"I knew you'd come," she says, her voice soft enough that he has to lean closer to hear. The words float between them like smoke, dissolving into the heavy air before quite reaching completion.

Vincent stops three feet away, struck by what he sees. Her hair moves in wind that touches nothing else, individual strands lifting and settling in patterns that follow no natural air current. The grass around her remains perfectly still, not even the finest blades stirring, while her hair dances in invisible currents that seem to originate from somewhere beneath rather than above.

The phenomenon extends beyond her hair. The fabric of her dress ripples at the hem, subtle movements that suggest wind pooling around her ankles, yet the leaves scattered nearby don't shift, don't rustle, don't acknowledge whatever force attends her. Even the cedar branches directly above, low enough that she could reach up and touch them, hang motionless while her hair continues its impossible dance.

Vincent lowers himself into a faded blue woven lawn chair that matches hers. The chairs' metal arms touch and he feels her warmth as she leans into him. The soil beneath his feet feels alive in a way that dirt shouldn't, pulsing with deep heat that rises through his jeans, through his skin, settling in his bones with invasive familiarity. He recognizes this warmth from the construction site, from the Iron Gate, from every place where the Root Titan's presence breaks through into their reality. But here, filtered through Mira's proximity, it feels different. More personal. More purposeful.

She still doesn't look at him directly, her gaze fixed on

some point in the darkness between the trees that his eyes can't penetrate. Her hands rest on her knees, fingers splayed, and he notices how the grass beneath her chair has grown taller, greener, as if her mere presence accelerates growth, encourages life to reach toward her with vegetative desperation.

"They're louder now," she says, the words emerging without preamble, without context that he needs because he already understands what she means. "The roots. The voices. It feels like they're remembering everything at once."

Her voice carries a quality of translation, as if she's converting concepts that exist outside language into words that barely contain them. Vincent hears the strain in her tone, the exhaustion of serving as conduit between states of being that were never meant to communicate. She sounds older than seventeen, aged by knowledge that humans weren't designed to carry.

"What do they remember?" he asks, though part of him fears the answer.

She's quiet for long enough that he wonders if she'll answer at all. When she speaks, her voice has dropped to barely above whisper, forcing him to lean closer until he can feel the unnatural wind in her hair brushing against his cheek.

"Everything that's ever died here. Every seed that never sprouted. Every tree that fell before its time. They remember the iron they drove through them, the tunnels they carved, the way the earth screamed when they built their machines." Her fingers play with the back of his hand. "But mostly they remember being alone. Being unheard. Until now."

The weight of her words settles over them both, heavy as the humid air, heavy as the responsibility she's carried since the volunteer day when everyone saw what she could do. Vincent twists his hand to meet hers, and when their fingers intertwine he feels it immediately. The pulse beneath her skin that doesn't match her heartbeat, that runs on different rhythm, older rhythm, the cadence of something vast and patient using her circulatory system as infrastructure for its own purposes.

"Then stop listening," he says, the words emerging fierce with need, with the desperation of someone watching the person they care about slip away increment by increment. "Just stay here with me. Please."

His fingers tighten around hers, as if physical pressure might anchor her to this moment, this reality, this simple human connection that requires no translation between species or states of being. Through their joined hands, he feels both pulses, hers and the other, and tries to will his own steady rhythm to override that alien beat, to remind her body what human feels like.

Mira laughs, but the sound carries no humor, just recognition of impossibility dressed in the form of mirth. Her voice trembles as she responds, "You make it sound so simple."

The laugh transforms into something closer to a sob, though no tears come. Just the sound of someone recognizing the distance between what they want and what they're becoming, the gulf that widens with each passing hour, each communion with the voices that speak through root and stone and the very minerals dissolved in groundwater.

"Maybe it is," Vincent says, and he means it, believes it with the faith of someone who needs simplicity to be possible in a world gone incomprehensibly complex.

The silence that follows isn't empty but full, pregnant with everything they're not saying. The distant sound of wind through the cedars provides rhythm, though the air around them remains still except for that impossible breeze that plays through Mira's hair. Somewhere in the darkness between the trees, something shifts, branch or shadow or something that belongs to neither category, and Vincent feels Mira tense beside him, her attention pulling toward that movement like iron filings toward a magnet.

But she doesn't go, doesn't stand, doesn't surrender to whatever summons echoes through the frequencies only she can hear. Instead she sits beside him in the warm darkness, their hands linked, her impossible wind stirring, the ground beneath them pulsing with patient awareness, while the night holds them in its humid embrace and pretends, for these few minutes at least, that love might be anchor enough against the vast forces that call her name in voices older than human memory.

When Mira finally turns to look at him, the movement seems to cost her something, as if she's pulling her attention back from vast distances to focus on this singular point, this moment, this person beside her. The moonlight catches her face at an angle that reveals everything the darkness had hidden: the bruised shadows beneath her eyes that speak of sleepless nights, the subtle hollow in her cheeks where weight has fled, the fine lines at the corners of her mouth that belong on someone decades older. Yet her eyes, when they meet his, burn with a clarity that hasn't been there in weeks, as if whatever fog has been claiming her has lifted momentarily, granting her this window of pure presence.

Those eyes shine with moisture that hasn't quite become tears, the surface tension holding like she's holding everything else, barely, precariously, but still maintaining form. The amber-gray irises that he's memorized over years of connection reflect the moonlight strangely, creating depths that seem to extend beyond the physical space eyes should occupy. But tonight, right now, they're focused entirely on him, seeing him with an intensity that makes his breath catch in his throat.

"I don't want to forget this," she whispers, and the words emerge broken, each one a small surrender of control she's been maintaining. "Even when I'm gone."

The phrase hangs between them with terrible weight. Not if but when. Not leaving but gone, with all the finality that word implies. Vincent feels his chest constrict, his lungs suddenly unable to find enough oxygen in the thick night air. He wants to protest, to deny the inevitability she's accepted, but the words tangle in his throat because he's felt her slipping away, has watched her become something that exists partially elsewhere, and lying to either of them feels like blasphemy in this moment of raw truth.

He leans toward her, drawn by need that transcends thought, but hesitation makes his movement uncertain. The space between them feels charged with more than teenage desire, weighted with the knowledge of everything they're about to lose. His hand rises to touch her face, fingers trembling slightly, but he stops inches from contact, afraid that touching her might shatter whatever spell has brought her fully present.

Mira reads his hesitation and makes the choice for both of them. She closes the distance with deliberate certainty, her hand reaching up to guide his face toward hers. Her fingers against his jaw burn with that familiar unnatural warmth, but he doesn't pull away, doesn't flinch from the reminder of what she's becoming. When their lips meet, the contact is soft at first, tentative, as if they're both afraid of breaking something irreparable.

The kiss tastes of salt from tears that haven't quite fallen, of the metallic air that surrounds them, of something sweet beneath that might be the essential flavor of Mira herself. For a heartbeat, maybe two, it remains gentle, careful, the kind of kiss that belongs to different circumstances, to normal teenagers with normal problems.

Then something shifts. Whether it's the recognition of limited time or the need to feel something purely human while she still can, Mira presses closer with sudden urgency. Her fingers tighten in his hair, pulling him against her with strength that surprises them both. The kiss transforms from tentative to desperate, from careful to consuming. Vincent feels her trembling against him, violent shivers that have nothing to do with cold and everything to do with the effort of maintaining herself in this single location, this single moment.

His arms come around her automatically, responding to her need with his own, and they're clinging to each other like survivors of a shipwreck who've found floating debris to share. The kiss becomes less about desire and more about confirmation of existence, about proving through touch and taste and the mingling of breath that they're both still here, still human, still capable of choosing each other despite the forces trying to pull them apart.

Somehow they end up on the ground, muddy grass cool and slick against Vincent's back, the cold seeping through his shirt to the skin, but Mira is warm and her heat radiates through his body, their legs tangled, her knees slippery with rainwater. He blinks up at the trees, sees the branches laced in black above, the sky so low he could reach up and smudge a thumbprint in the moon.

When she finally pulls away, it's not far. Their lips still feel each other, their breath mixing in the small space between them, both of them gasping as if they've been underwater and just broken the surface. Then she turns her face into his neck, and the first sob escapes her like something that's been caged too long. Her shoulders shake with the force of it, and Vincent feels moisture against his skin where she's pressed against him, tears that run hotter than they should, almost scalding where they touch.

"I can still feel it," she murmurs between ragged breaths, her voice muffled against his collar. "The Adversary. The Titan. Whatever it is. It never stops. It never stops pulling at me. Pulling me towards the heart." Another sob tears through her, making her whole body convulse. "But sometimes...

sometimes it pauses when you touch me. Like it can't quite find me when I'm with you."

Vincent's arms tighten around her instinctively, reflexively, as if he could make himself into a shield against forces that exist beyond physical intervention. They sit up and he pulls her fully against him, her weight settling into his lap, her form fitting against his chest like she was designed to rest there. His hand comes up to cradle the back of her head, fingers threading through her hair that still moves in its impossible wind.

But as he holds her, something changes. The unnatural breeze that has been playing through her hair since he found her suddenly stills. The air around them goes motionless, even the eternal whisper of the cedars falling silent. The warmth radiating from the ground beneath them continues but stops pulsing, becoming steady, ignorable, just background heat rather than active presence. The night seems to hold its breath, granting them this bubble of stillness, this eye in the supernatural storm that has been building around Mira since she first heard the voices calling.

They remain locked together in that embrace, neither willing to move, to risk breaking whatever charm has temporarily severed her connection to the vast presence beneath Duswood. Vincent feels her breathing gradually slow against his neck, matching his rhythm, their hearts finding synchronization that has nothing to do with otherworldly forces and everything to do with two people who've known each other long enough that their bodies remember how to exist in harmony.

Mira's tears have stopped, though Vincent still feels their heat on his skin, small burns that he knows will mark him tomorrow, evidence of her supernatural fever branded into his neck. Her weight against him feels both substantial and fragile, as if she might solidify fully back into the girl he's always known or might dissolve entirely into whatever she's becoming. He holds her with careful pressure, enough to anchor but not enough to cage, understanding instinctively that the choice to stay or go must remain hers.

The night continues around them, patient and dark and full of watching presence, but for now, in this moment, they exist in a space between worlds where their love might actually be enough, where human connection can hold against cosmic forces, where a simple embrace can quiet voices older than memory. They both know it's temporary, that morning will come with its demands and impossibilities, but for now they have this: the stillness, the silence, the perfect weight of holding and being held while the universe pretends not to notice.

Vincent doesn't hear the front door slam, but he feels the subtle shift in the house, an aching emptiness that follows when Mira is truly gone. Her absence is a pressure in his chest, a tug that sharpens with each ragged breath. He doesn't doubt, but fears where she's going.

Outside, the storm has already started. The sky over Duswood bruises with unnatural green, lightning carving impossible spirals over the lake. Vincent barely remembers grabbing his coat, barely registers Owen and June pulling up beside him, questions tight on their lips but unsaid. He only knows the direction of the ache in his bones, the pull of Mira's name in the storm, and the certainty that whatever waits, won't wait long. They drive towards the heart.

———

The gravel gives way beneath Vincent's boots as he half-runs, half-slides down the embankment toward the Iron Gate, stones spraying behind him in miniature avalanches that June and Owen trigger in turn as they follow, and above them the sky has gone the color of old copper, that particular green that precedes tornadoes, though what builds overhead feels more deliberate than any storm born of simple meteorology. His shirt clings to his back, soaked through in seconds by rain that falls sideways, driven by wind that can't decide which direction it wants to push. Each drop hits his skin like a small fist, cold enough to steal life, heavy enough to sting.

Lightning branches across Lake Michigan in patterns that violate everything Vincent knows about electricity's behavior. Instead of the jagged randomness of natural discharge, the bolts move in curves, in spirals, in geometries that suggest consciousness rather than physics. They strike the water in rhythm, three beats, pause, three beats, pause, the timing so precise it feels like code, like communication, like something vast using the storm itself as language. The thunder that follows doesn't roll or fade but cracks sharp as breaking bone, each report making the ground beneath their feet shudder.

Owen loses his footing on the wet gravel, his backpack of equipment throwing off his balance. He goes down hard on one knee, his hand shooting out to catch himself, and Vincent hears him curse as stones bite through his jeans. June grabs his arm, hauling him upright with surprising strength, her camera swinging wildly from its strap around her neck. Water streams from her copper hair, plastering it to her skull, making her look younger, more vulnerable, though her expression carries grim determination rather than fear.

The Iron Gate emerges from the rain like something materialized rather than approached, its rust-red bulk suddenly there, immediate, impossible to ignore. But where before they found it sealed, those overlapping steel plates wounded with spiral carvings and desperate symbols, now the massive freight doors stand open. Not forced, not broken, but deliberately, impossibly open, as if whatever was contained has decided containment no longer serves its purposes.

The darkness beyond the threshold breathes. Vincent feels it more than sees it, the way air moves coarsely, pulling inward rather than flowing naturally. Each gust carries scents that shouldn't exist together: iron so strong it tastes sour, cedar sap thick as syrup, and underneath something else, something organic and alive, like earth that has learned to exhale. The wind tugs at his clothes, at his hair, not pushing them back but drawing them forward, an invitation that feels more like compulsion.

His boots find the edge of the railway bed, the ghost of tracks that once carried GNRO's cargo to destinations long since dead. The ground here pulses with deep tremors, not the violence of earthquakes but something more disturbing, the sensation of massive forms shifting far below, of geology rearranging itself to accommodate presences unknown. Each tremor runs up through his legs, through his spine, settling in his teeth.

June raises her camera despite the rain, trying to document the open doors, the breathing darkness, the way reality seems softer here, more negotiable. The flash fires once, illuminating the tunnel's mouth for a split second, and in that brief window Vincent sees things that make his mind rebel. The walls inside pulse with veins of red light. Water runs upward along the ceiling. Shadows move independent of any source, sliding along surfaces with purposeful intent.

Thunder cracks directly overhead, so loud it feels like the sky tearing open, and in its wake comes silence more complete than sound's simple absence. Even the rain pauses mid-fall, droplets hanging suspended for one impossible moment before gravity remembers its job. In that silence, Vincent hears it clearly: Mira's voice, not calling but humming, the melody emerging from the tunnel's depth with the clarity of struck crystal.

Without thought, without plan, Vincent breaks into a run toward those open doors, toward the breathing dark, toward whatever has drawn Mira into its depths. Behind him, Owen shouts something lost in the returning rain, and June's footsteps splash through puddles as she follows, but Vincent's attention has narrowed to that humming, to the red-lit throat of the tunnel that waits to swallow them all.

The corridor swallows them in red pulsing light, walls slick with moisture that reflects their movements in fractured glimpses, and Vincent's eyes struggle to adjust to this crimson twilight that makes everything look submerged in blood. The temperature hits him immediately, twenty degrees warmer than outside, the air thick with humidity that makes breathing feel like drowning in reverse. His shoes splash through water that runs along the tunnel floor, but the liquid moves against gravity's logic, flowing upward along the walls in rivulets that branch and merge like circulatory systems made visible.

Roots push through the stone walls, thick as Vincent's arm, their surfaces rough with bark that shouldn't exist this far from sunlight. They glow from within, that same red light pulsing through them in waves that match no heartbeat he recognizes. When his shoulder brushes against one, the heat surprises him, not the warmth of living wood but something that burns just below the threshold of pain. The root vibrates against his touch, and through that contact comes the hum, not heard but felt, transmitting directly through bone and muscle until his whole skeleton becomes a receiver for frequencies that human bodies weren't meant to conduct.

Owen reaches out to steady himself against the tunnel wall, then jerks his hand back with a sharp intake of breath. Even in the red light, Vincent can see his palm marked with the root's pattern, a temporary brand that fades even as they watch. June documents everything with her camera, though Vincent doubts any film could capture what exists here, this space where physics has gone soft and biology has learned new rules.

The hum grows stronger with each step deeper into the tunnel, rising from subsonic suggestion to physical presence.

It resonates in the hollow spaces of Vincent's body, his sinuses, his chest cavity, the gaps between his ribs, as if trying to find the frequency that will make him shatter like crystal. Beside him, June presses her palms against her ears, though they all know the sound doesn't travel through air but through the fabric of space itself, through the roots that web across every surface, through the water that defies gravity, through the very atoms that compose their bodies.

The tunnel opens into a central chamber that Vincent recognizes from the GNRO blueprints, though no technical drawing could have prepared him for its current state. The space stretches up beyond the red light's reach, its ceiling lost in darkness that seems solid rather than simply absent of illumination. Water pools across the floor, perfectly still despite the constant dripping from above, its surface reflecting the root-light in patterns that shift without any disturbance to cause the movement.

And there, at the chamber's exact center, stands Mira.

Vincent's breath catches hard enough to hurt. She faces away from them, her white dress soaked to transparency, clinging to her frame in ways that make her look smaller, more fragile than memory insists she should be. Her hair hangs in wet ropes down her back, so dark with moisture it looks darker than black. But it's what lies beneath her skin that stops him cold. Light pulses there, not on the surface but deep within, as if her veins carry illumination instead of blood, the glow matching perfectly the rhythm of the roots that web the walls.

"Mira," Vincent says, stumbling forward, his boots sending ripples across the standing water that somehow creates no sound. His voice cracks on her name, breaking it into syllables that each carry different varieties of desperation. "Please. We can figure out another way."

She turns with the slowness of someone moving through honey, through amber, through time that has gone thick.

When her face comes into view, Vincent sees she's been crying, tracks still visible on her cheeks despite the moisture that saturates everything here. But her eyes, when they meet his, burn with clarity rather than confusion, with purpose rather than fear. The light beneath her skin intensifies as she focuses on him, creating a halo effect that makes her seem both holy and deeply unnatural.

"There isn't another way," she says, her voice carrying harmonics that shouldn't emerge from a human throat, as if multiple versions of her speak in not-quite-perfect unison. She swallows, the motion visible in the play of light through her neck, and continues with terrible certainty. "The Titan isn't choosing any of this. It's being driven. The Adversary is using its power like a doorway."

The chamber vibrates in response to her words, the hum swelling from barely tolerable to actively painful. Vincent feels something warm trickle from his nose, tastes copper as blood runs over his upper lip. Mira's expression tightens with sympathy, with sorrow for pain she's a part of but can't prevent.

"If it wakes with him," she continues, each word weighted with inevitability, "he will gain control. Gain access. Access well beyond Duswood."

The hum transforms, deepening into bass frequencies that bypass hearing entirely, manifesting as pressure. Through that crushing weight comes a voice that doesn't belong to the chamber, doesn't belong to the roots, doesn't belong to anything that should exist in this world. It folds over them like silk, like smoke, smooth and affectionate and absolutely certain of its victory.

"Yes, little mirror," The Adversary croons, the words seeming to come from everywhere and nowhere, from the water at their feet and the darkness above and the space between molecules. "Come home. Be the bridge."

Mira flinches at the voice but doesn't retreat, her shoulders squaring against its weight as she addresses the empty air where presence thickens like curdled atmosphere. "You don't want peace because you don't know peace," she says, her words cutting through the chamber's hum with surprising clarity. "You want a mind. A shape. Mine."

The roots along the walls pulse brighter in response, their warmth increasing until the air shimmers with heat distortion. Vincent feels perspiration bead instantly on his skin, his clothes beginning to steam where they're still soaked from rain. The Adversary's presence shifts, concentrates, becomes almost visible as a distortion in the red light, a place where shadows bend toward rather than away from illumination.

"I want to be with you," the voice responds, and now it carries something that might be genuine longing, might be perfectly mimicked emotion, the distinction impossible to determine. The words ripple through the roots themselves, making them flex and shift like muscles under skin. "You are the opening."

Lightning flashes somewhere far above, its light finding cracks in the chamber's ceiling that shouldn't reach this deep. The brief white brilliance cuts through the red glow, illuminating the water at Mira's feet with stark clarity. In that strobe-lit moment, Vincent sees another reality. Mira's reflection in the still water doesn't match her movements. It lags behind, then pulls ahead, then turns to face a different direction entirely, as if the image has gained independence from its source.

The lightning fades but the reflection continues its rebellion. It rises from the water's surface, not emerging wet and physical but lifting as pure light shaped into Mira's form. The figure stands on the water without breaking its surface, translucent, shot through with veins of gold and silver that pulse with their own rhythm. This second Mira turns her head to observe the original, and Vincent sees they share expressions of grim determination, of understanding that spans both versions of her existence.

"She's doing it on purpose," Owen whispers, his voice carrying awe that borders on reverence. His mind races visibly behind his eyes, trying to process what he's witnessing. "This isn't possession or splitting. She's deliberately creating a second instance of herself."

The original Mira nods once, acknowledging Owen's understanding while keeping her attention on the light-form duplicate. When she speaks, both versions move their lips, though sound comes only from the physical one. "The Titan can't form its own will. But I can give it one long enough to choose rest. It doesn't care about healing the world, it just needs quiet."

She steps toward the massive cluster of roots that dominates the chamber's far wall, their trunks woven together into something that resembles a wooden heart. Each step sends ripples through the water that her light-form echo doesn't create, emphasizing the distinction between physical and projected, between what is and what could be.

Her echo-image moves in the opposite direction, positioning itself at the chamber's center where the distortion of The Adversary's presence waits. The two Miras create a geometry of intention, original and reflection positioned to enact whatever plan she's conceived in the depths of communion with forces beyond human comprehension.

Vincent lunges forward, water splashing around his knees, his hand reaching for her arm, her shoulder, any part of her that might anchor her to this moment, this reality, this simple human need for her to stay. "Mira, don't leave...don't..." The words tangle in his throat, too many competing for expression, none adequate to convey the magnitude of loss he feels approaching.

She turns to him with movements that seem to cost her enormous effort, as if she's already partially committed to whatever transformation awaits. Her hand rises to touch his where he's grabbed her arm, her fingers trembling against his with fever heat that speaks of internal battles being waged at cellular levels. Through that contact, he feels the war in her body, between human and other, between singular existence and distributed consciousness, between the girl he's in love with and this new form.

"I'm not leaving," she says, and her smile wavers like candleflame in wind, beautiful and fragile and about to be extinguished. "I'm becoming."

Her fingers tighten briefly on his, pressure that feels like goodbye dressed in the language of greeting. The light beneath her skin flares brighter, making her seem for an instant like stained glass with the sun behind it, every vein and bone visible through translucent flesh.

"One of me to rest," she whispers, the words meant for him alone despite the chamber's perfect acoustics. "One of me to stop him."

The simplicity of her plan strikes Vincent with terrible clarity. She won't fight the Titan or The Adversary directly. Instead, she'll become two solutions to two problems, splitting herself across states of being to address threats that exist in different dimensions of reality. One version to give the Titan the consciousness it needs to choose sleep over destruction. Another to stand as barrier between The Adversary and his goal of possession, of using her as gateway to physical reality.

It's brilliant. It's impossible. It's going to destroy everything she was in favor of everything she might prevent. Vincent's hand tightens on hers, trying to communicate through pressure what words fail to convey, that there must be another way, that sacrifice isn't always the answer, that sometimes love is enough to hold against the dark. But even as he grips her fingers, he feels her slipping away, not physically but essentially, her attention dividing between the two forms she's manifested, her consciousness stretching across impossible distances to inhabit both versions simultaneously.

The hum shifts to a higher pitch, climbing toward frequencies that make the air itself seem to vibrate, and through it The Adversary's voice flows like honey over broken glass, sweet and dangerous in equal measure. "Yes, join me," he murmurs, the words rippling through the roots in waves of intensified light. The invitation carries weight beyond language, a gravitational pull that tries to draw everything toward the center where Mira's echo-self stands luminous and waiting.

Mira releases Vincent's hand with gentle finality, her fingers sliding through his grasp like water, like light, like every goodbye he's never wanted to say. She moves toward the massive root cluster with steps that leave no ripples now, as if she's already begun transitioning from physical to something else. Her palm presses flat against the largest root, its bark rough and fever-hot against her skin, and immediately light begins to flow.

The illumination doesn't simply pass from her to the root but weaves between them, threads of gold and red that braid together. Vincent watches her body become translucent at the edges, her outline blurring as whatever she is spreads into the wooden flesh she touches. Through her skin, he can see her bones briefly, outlined in light like an x-ray made of fire, before even that distinction begins to fade.

"I am joining," she whispers, and her voice comes from multiple sources now, from her physical form, from her echo-self, from the roots themselves that have begun to speak with her intonation. The words carry a terrible joy, the satisfaction of a plan coming together despite its cost. "Just not with you."

Her echo-self turns to face the distortion where The Adversary's presence concentrates, and Vincent sees what Mira has done. This projection isn't truly her but a hollow version, empty of everything except the shape of her existence. It's a shell, a decoy, a barrier made of light and memory that carries none of her actual consciousness. It stands as guardian and gateway both, positioned to intercept whatever The Adversary attempts, to be the bridge he seeks while offering no actual crossing.

The Adversary's presence shifts, coils, suddenly understanding the trap. His voice stutters through frequencies that make the chamber's walls crack, stone splitting with sounds like breaking teeth. "No... no, that is not the bridge. That is not..." But his protest comes too late, his realization arriving after commitment, after he's already reached toward what he thought was Mira's essence and found only echo, only light arranged in her likeness but containing nothing of what he needs.

The real Mira sinks into the roots with the inevitability of water finding its level. Her body doesn't disappear so much as integrate, her flesh becoming one with the wood, her consciousness flooding through the root system like water through empty veins. Vincent watches her features soften, blur, begin to merge with the bark's patterns until he can barely distinguish where she ends and the Titan's infrastructure begins. She's not being consumed or destroyed but grafted, her awareness spreading through miles of underground network, carrying with it something the Titan has never possessed: the ability to choose.

Through the root system, her presence races outward, downward, in directions that don't correspond to physical space. She touches the Titan's vast incomprehensible core with human consciousness, with will shaped by love and loss and the desperate need to protect. She gives it what it's never had: enough sense of self to understand the difference between sleep and waking, between stillness and action, between existence and agency. And with that understanding comes choice, immediate and irreversible.

The chamber's red glow collapses inward like a star dying,

light condensing to points of brilliance before winking out entirely. The hum that has tortured them buckles, the smooth frequency breaking into discordant notes that clash against each other like an orchestra falling down stairs. Vincent feels the sound as fracture, as breaking, as something vast and patient choosing to return to dormancy rather than wake to purpose that was never its own.

The Adversary shrieks, the sound thin as wire, sharp as the space between seconds. "What have you done?" The question carries genuine incomprehension, the confusion of something ancient encountering an outcome it never imagined possible. His presence thrashes against Mira's echo-self, trying to break through, to find the real her, but the hollow guardian holds, empty and therefore unbreakable, offering nothing but surface where he needs depth.

Through the fading light, through the collapsing hum, through the sound of roots hardening to something denser than wood, Mira's voice drifts like smoke, gentle and impossibly far away. "Given it silence," she says, the words coming from everywhere and nowhere, from the walls, from the water, from the very air that has gone suddenly thin. "And sealed your doorway."

The roots begin to petrify with unnatural speed, their surfaces going gray, then white, then taking on the appearance of stone. The transformation spreads from where Mira disappeared into them, racing outward through every tendril, every fiber, every connection. The chamber fills with the sound of organic matter crystallizing, a grinding roar that makes Vincent cover his ears though it does nothing to muffle the noise that comes through body as much as air.

The echo-Mira flickers, her light-form beginning to fade as whatever animates it loses cohesion. She turns toward Vincent one last time, and though this projection carries nothing of Mira's actual consciousness, something in its expression seems to acknowledge him, to offer comfort that exists only in his interpretation of empty light. Then she dissolves, not dramatically but gently, like morning mist touched by sun, leaving only afterimages that burn purple behind his eyelids when he blinks.

The Adversary's presence recoils, contracts, begins to pull away from this space that no longer serves his purpose. His voice comes one final time, no longer smooth or seductive but raw with thwarted desire. "This isn't over. There are other doors, other bridges, other ways through. Humans provide multitudes." But the threat sounds hollow, the rage of something denied rather than something still capable. His presence fades like smoke in wind, leaving only the sensation of having been watched by something that has finally, reluctantly, looked away.

The chamber stands in darkness now, the red glow extinguished, the roots turned to stone, the water at their feet going still as glass. Vincent stands in that darkness, his hand still extended toward where Mira vanished, his fingers grasping air that no longer carries her warmth. Somewhere in the petrified root system, her consciousness has spread too thin to ever gather again, become part of something too vast to ever be simply human. She's given the Titan the gift of choice and chosen sleep for it, chosen silence, chosen the long quiet that might last until the earth itself ends. Chosen peace.

They emerge from the Iron Gate like survivors from a mine collapse, blinking against even the storm's dim light, their bodies remembering how to exist in a world with horizons, with sky, with rain that falls according to gravity's simple rules rather than the negotiated physics of that underground chamber. Vincent stumbles on the threshold, his legs uncertain after witnessing transformations that tore holes in his soul. Behind him, Owen and June follow in silence, the kind that comes after sound too large for processing, after experiences that will take years to integrate or perhaps never fully will.

The storm has changed in their absence. Where before it carried malevolence, intention, the signature of something using weather as weapon, now it's simply rain. Heavy, clean rain that falls straight down through air gone still, no longer twisted by impossible winds or lit by geometric lightning. It soaks through Vincent's already damp clothes in seconds, but this water carries no charge, no temperature that defies season, no metallic taste that speaks of things dissolved that shouldn't be. It's just water, blessed in its simplicity, washing over Duswood like absolution.

Vincent stands in it with his face tilted toward the hidden sky, letting the rain mix with what might be tears or might be just the general moisture that saturates everything. His body trembles with more than cold, with more than exhaustion, with the specific variety of shock that comes from losing someone who's still technically present but transformed beyond recognition or recovery. His hands shake at his sides, fingers still curved from trying to hold onto Mira, muscle memory insisting she should be there even as every other sense confirms her absence.

Owen's hand finds his shoulder, the touch uncertain but present, the gesture of someone who doesn't know what comfort looks like but understands it's needed. His face has lost all its certainty, replaced by something rawer, more honest. His worldview hasn't just cracked but shattered completely, leaving him with awe that borders on religious experience, though what god would claim what they've witnessed remains unclear. His equipment hangs forgotten from his shoulder, thousands of dollars of sensors and meters that proved ultimately useless in measuring what mattered.

June stands beside them, her tears flowing without shame or attempt to stop them. Her camera dangles from its strap, unused now, as if she's understood that some moments shouldn't be captured, that some sacrifices deserve to exist only in memory where they can soften with time rather than remain sharp in photographic permanence. Her shoulders shake with silent sobs that might be grief for Mira, might be relief for Duswood, might be the simple human response to brushing against forces too large for comprehension.

The ground beneath their feet has gone still. Not just quiet but truly motionless for the first time in months. The constant vibration that became Duswood's heartbeat, that deep hum that infiltrated dreams and turned thoughts toward lower frequencies, has vanished completely. Vincent feels its absence like sudden deafness, his body still braced for tremors that will never come. The soil accepts the rain without pulse, without response, with the passive reception of earth that's just earth, not the skin of something vast and waiting.

Through the rain, Vincent can see the town spread below them, and already the changes are visible. The red glow that has seeped from cracks and foundations for weeks has vanished, leaving only clean darkness between buildings. Street lights burn normal yellow without the interference that made them flicker and dim. The construction site sits quiet and ordinary, just displaced dirt and machinery rather than a wound that breathes. Even the air tastes different, missing that iron tang that coated every breath, that organic sweetness of decay that shouldn't exist above ground.

The natural sounds of the world return gradually, as if they've been waiting for permission. Rain hitting earth creates its ancient percussion. Wind moves through cedar branches with whispers that carry no meaning beyond the friction of air and wood. Somewhere a dog barks, the sound carrying across the distance without distortion, without the echo that suggested vast spaces below. These simple noises feel like miracles after weeks of supernatural interference, evidence that the world can still function according to comprehensible rules.

Behind them, the Iron Gate has sealed itself. Not with the

desperate steel plates that humans installed seventy years ago, but with something more final. The entrance has collapsed, or transformed, or simply ceased. Where the breathing tunnel mouth gaped just minutes ago, now solid rock faces them, streaming with rainwater that follows the stone's contours like tears on a monument. The metal framework that marked it as human construction has been absorbed, integrated into geology that looks as if it's stood undisturbed for millennia.

Vincent reaches out to touch the wet stone, needing confirmation that it's real, that the passage to that impossible chamber has truly closed. The rock feels cold, inert, carrying no trace of the warmth that pulsed through everything when the Titan stirred. His palm comes away marked only with water and the faintest residue of ordinary minerals, no red staining, no impossible heat, no vibration that speaks of things better left buried.

They stand there as the storm continues its cleansing, three witnesses to sacrifice that saved a town, perhaps saved more than a town. The rain washes away the red clay from their clothes, from their skin, carrying it down the embankment toward Lake Michigan, which accepts it without response, its surface returning to the normal patterns of wind and wave. The water runs clear after a while, no longer tinted with the rust of disturbed depths, just rain returning to the lake as it has for thousands of years before humans arrived to dig and build and wake things that preferred sleep.

Vincent turns away from the sealed stone eventually, though part of him wants to stay, to maintain vigil at this spot where Mira transformed from girl to guardian to something distributed too wide to ever gather back into human shape. But Owen and June need to return to town, need to process what they've seen, need to begin the slow work of living in a world where they know such things are possible. And Vincent needs... he doesn't know what he needs, except that standing here won't bring her back, won't restore her to the girl who kissed him in the backyard last night, who existed in one place at one time and could be held.

As they begin the walk back toward the car, Vincent carries the weight of understanding that some healings require breaking, that some silences are bought with voices that will never speak again, that some forms of salvation look exactly like loss to those left behind. The town spreads before them, quiet and still and safe, purchased with a price that only three people will ever fully comprehend. And somewhere, spread through stone and root and the deep places where human thought can't follow, Mira exists in a form that might be called peace if peace can describe the vast quiet she's chosen, the silence she's become, the rest she's given to something that never asked to wake.

CHAPTER
TWENTY

Vincent's knuckles press into dough that yields and springs back, familiar as breathing, the rhythm of fold and push requiring no thought after a year of afternoon shifts at Cedar Lagoon, where flour dust hangs in slanted light through the front windows and the radio plays songs nobody really hears anymore. His hands move through the practiced motion while his mind drifts elsewhere, to places memory keeps returning despite his attempts to anchor himself in the present moment of yeast and warmth and simple labor.

Joe slides another ball of dough across the prep counter, then another, creating work where none needs to exist. The after-school rush ended an hour ago, and they have enough bases prepared for dinner already, but the older man keeps producing tasks with the determination of someone who understands that idle hands make room for thoughts better left unexamined. He points to the stack of empty sauce containers that need filling, to the cheese that requires grating, to the vegetables waiting to be sliced into precise portions.

The pizzeria wraps around them with its familiar embrace of oregano and baking bread, the sweet tang of tomato sauce that has simmered for hours, the underlying note of olive oil that seasons every surface after decades of use. These scents layer into something that feel like home.

Joe watches from the doorway, his weathered face carefully neutral, the expression of someone who has learned which questions not to ask. He doesn't mention the way Vincent hesitates at the threshold, doesn't comment on the pause before stepping fully outside. Instead, he hands over another stack of pizza boxes that need folding, the cardboard crisp and waiting to be shaped into containers for meals that will feed families who have already begun forgetting what their town almost became.

Through the front windows, Vincent views in the distant Duswood High, the building so new its brick still carries that raw red color that will take seasons to weather into something that belongs. Glass panels catch afternoon sun and throw it back in sheets of gold, modern architecture rising where the sinkhole once opened like a mouth. The courtyard holds cedar saplings, their trunks no thicker than Vincent's wrist, their crowns barely reaching the first-floor windows. They seem impossibly fragile against the memory of the massive trees that once stood before there was a town.

Joe clears his throat, the sound pulling Vincent back to the present, to the counter where his hands have stilled on the dough. "Need you to check the inventory sheets before you leave," Joe says, his gruff voice maintaining normalcy. "And I'm putting you on the schedule for Saturday night. Martinez called in sick for the third time this month."

The words carry no weight beyond their surface meaning, no acknowledgment of the space between what they discuss. Vincent nods, returns to kneading, lets the repetition of the work create a buffer against the pull of memory. His phone buzzes against his hip.

Owen's text appears on the screen, the same two words he sends every few days like a pulse check, like a ritual that confirms what they all need to know: "Any hum?"

Vincent types back "No". The phone screen holds his attention longer than those two letters require, his fingers hovering over keys that might form other words, might ask Owen how the research is going at Michigan Tech, might acknowledge what they experienced together in that red-lit chamber beneath the earth. But those conversations belong to late-night calls when sleep won't come, not to afternoon shifts where the pretense of normal life requires maintenance.

He pockets the phone and returns to the dough, shaping it into circles that will hold sauce and cheese and the simple satisfactions of ordinary hunger, while outside the iron scent fades completely and the cedar saplings reach toward a sky that no longer pulses with unnatural lightning, no longer carries the weight of something vast and stirring, no longer threatens to crack open and reveal what should stay hidden.

———

June frames the shot carefully, the tennis team's green and gold uniforms bright against the new brick, their raised rackets catching afternoon sun while behind them the fresh landscaping spreads in manufactured perfection. Through her viewfinder, she sees what others miss: the way shadows pool too dark in certain corners, how some sections of sod have taken root with unusual vigor while others struggle despite identical care. Her finger presses the shutter release, capturing smiles and victory signs, but her eye has already moved to the margins where interesting things hide.

She packs up late, after the last match, careful not to jostle her bag and risk damaging the lenses. The rest of the year-book staff has already scattered, leaving behind scraps of draft layouts marked in blue pen, the remains of a half-eaten jelly donut, and two still-damp soda cans sweating onto the table. Before she tucks her camera away, she checks a few photos from earlier that day. One makes her smile with a mix of pride of a good shot and nostalgia not yet fully realized. The colors bleeding just enough to hint at movement, a blur of two students walking arm in arm away from the gym, their laughter echoing through the newly polished halls.

Outside, she finds the parking lot surprisingly empty, just a few scattered cars and the distant buzz of a mower working the football field. She heads toward the sidewalk, backpack dragging on one shoulder, the weight making her sore from yesterday's coverage of the track meet. Past the admin wing, the air holds that raw, chemical-green smell of fresh-cut grass, and beneath it, a tinge of something sweeter, like wet cedar or the inside of a new pencil case. She slows at the edge of the lawn, scanning for the source.

A sapling planted beside the main entrance struggles to reach the sky. It's one of dozens scattered across the new grounds, each no taller than June herself, their thin trunks staked against wind that might snap them. But this one holds light differently. Through her lens, the air around it bends, a subtle distortion that creates what almost looks like a second trunk, a shadow that doesn't match the tree's actual form. She adjusts her angle, trying to capture the effect, and for just a moment the distortion solidifies into something that might be a silhouette, human-shaped, standing beside the young cedar with one hand resting against its bark.

"Getting good shots?"

Vincent's voice makes her lower the camera, though she doesn't startle. She's learned to sense approach without looking, a skill developed in months of documenting things that prefer not to be seen. He looks tired, flour dust still visible on his jeans despite what must have been attempts to brush it clean. The afternoon shift at Cedar Lagoon leaves its marks in more than just the lingering scent of oregano.

"The usual," she says, suggesting students posing with foam fingers and painted faces. "Team spirit and teenage joy."

They climb the bleachers together, finding seats high enough to observe most of the grounds. June pulls up the images on her camera's display screen, scrolling past conventional rally photos to find what she really captured. Vincent leans closer, his shoulder brushing hers as he studies each frame with the attention of someone who knows what to look for.

She stops on the sapling photo, the one where light creates that second presence. Vincent's breathing slows as he examines it, his finger hovering over the screen without quite touching, as if contact might disturb whatever the image has preserved. His breath catches, unable to speak.

"Sometimes I think I see her," June admits, her voice pitched low. She doesn't look at Vincent, keeps her eyes on the camera screen where that impossible shadow stands patient beside living wood.

Vincent doesn't answer immediately. His silence carries neither agreement nor denial, just the weight of someone who might see the same things but has chosen not to name them. After a moment, he shifts the conversation.

"Owen sent his weekly check-in," he says, accepting June's unspoken need to move past her admission. "Still measuring background frequencies at Michigan Tech. He says the readings have been normal for weeks."

"Normal," June repeats, tasting the word like something foreign. "Strange how quiet everything feels now. Like the town's holding a string, waiting for permission to cut it."

As they descend the bleachers and cross the field toward the parking lot, Vincent observes how June moves through the space. She steps around certain patches of ground without seeming aware of the avoidance, her path curving in small arcs that make no sense unless you understand what she's not stepping on. The spots where grass grows too thick. The places where soil seems to breathe. The ground that remembers even if the danger has passed.

The habit persists, this careful navigation of a landscape that might be safe but will never be innocent. Vincent follows her lead, matching her steps, avoiding the same patches through shared instinct. Neither mentions the deliberate path they weave between memories embedded in the earth, the way they both still listen for vibrations that no longer come, still taste the air for iron that has mostly faded.

Behind them, the sapling stands in late afternoon light, its shadow stretching long across new grass, sometimes looking like one trunk, sometimes like two, depending on the angle and the observer and the willingness to see what shouldn't be there but somehow, sometimes, is.

———

The path to the north bluff barely visible now, overtaken by blackberry vines and young alders that have claimed the space where dozens of feet once wore the trail bare. Vincent pushes through carefully, his hands finding the gaps between thorns through memory more than sight. The evening has settled into that particular quiet that comes when day creatures yield to night. His boots find the ghost of the trail beneath the overgrowth, that slight depression in the earth that remembers being traveled, being important, being the route to something that demanded witness.

The collapsed entrance reveals itself gradually, first as an interruption in the foliage, then as a tumble of stone and earth that has already begun to look natural, as if the hillside simply decided to slump inward one day without human cause. Wildflowers push through every crack and crevice, their petals white in the failing light, some variety June would know the name of but Vincent simply appreciates for their persistence. They've transformed what was once industrial scarring into something that could be mistaken for untouched forest floor if you didn't know what to look for.

Vincent finds the fallen log where he would sit over the weeks since, its surface worn smooth by his visits, by rain, by the slow work of decomposition that will eventually return it to soil. The bark has mostly peeled away, leaving wood the color of bone, warm still from afternoon sun though shadows have claimed this hollow completely. He settles onto it with the careful movements of someone whose body has learned the exact balance point, the spot where the log won't roll, won't crack, won't betray his weight to the slow drop toward the lake below.

Lake Michigan spreads before him like hammered silver, its surface carrying the last light of sunset in ripples that could be waves or could be the memory of waves, the distinction unclear at this distance. The horizon has gone soft, that blurred line where water becomes sky becomes the possibility of something beyond either. An ore boat moves there, its long shape just beginning to show, but it seems less real than the immediate presence of cedar scent and cooling air and the absence of vibration in the ground beneath him.

The metallic tang that once saturated every breath has faded to something barely there, a ghost of iron that might be imagination or might be the last traces of what seeped up from disturbed depths. Vincent breathes deeply, parsing the air for that familiar taste, finding only hints that could be the blood from where a blackberry thorn caught his palm or could be memory insisting something should be there. The wind moves through the trees with a sound like breathing, like something vast and patient drawing air through wooden lungs, releasing it in sighs that rustle needle and leaf.

Movement catches his peripheral vision, there by the old fence line where rusted wire still marks some forgotten property boundary. Vincent turns his head slowly, afraid that sudden motion might disturb what shouldn't be there but is. Or might be. The figure stands perhaps twenty feet away, barefoot despite the rough ground, wearing something light that could be a dress or could be fog taking form in evening air. Hair lifts in wind that doesn't touch the grass around her feet, dark strands moving with their own current, their own logic.

She watches the lake with the stillness of someone who has all the time in the world, or perhaps exists outside time's normal flow. Her face turns slightly toward him, and though the distance and dimness should make features impossible to distinguish, he sees her smile. Not the tight, pained expression from those final days when she fought against transformation, but something peaceful, knowing, complete. The smile of someone who has found what they were looking for, even if that finding required becoming something else entirely.

Vincent closes his eyes, not from fear but from the need to hold this moment without the questions sight brings. In the darkness behind his lids, the hum returns, so faint he might be imagining it, a vibration that rises through the log, through his bones, through the spaces where memory lives. It doesn't carry threat or warning now, just presence, just the confirmation that something vast still rests beneath the earth, choosing sleep, choosing silence, choosing peace.

A voice whispers through the hum, through the wind, through the space between heartbeats where impossible things sometimes speak. "I'm here...resting." The words fade even as he hears them, dissolving like morning frost touched by sun, leaving only the impression of warmth, of comfort, of a message delivered across distances that can't be measured in miles.

When Vincent opens his eyes, the fence line holds only shadows and the small shapes of saplings that have sprouted there, their trunks thin as wrists, their crowns catching the last gold of sunset. They shine with moisture though no rain has fallen, each leaf holding light like tiny mirrors, reflecting something that might be sky or might be something else watching through them. The air has gone still, even the eternal cedar whisper pausing as if the forest itself waits for what comes next.

"Mira," Vincent whispers, the name emerging without thought, without plan, just the natural response to presence felt if not seen. The word hangs in the air for a moment, visible as breath in the cooling evening, then disperses into nothing.

The earth beneath him remains still, no pulse, no vibration, no answer from the depths. But in the wind that returns gradually, building from silence back to gentle movement through the trees, something drifts that might be laughter. Not sound exactly, but the feeling of laughter, the lightness of it, the joy of someone who has found peace in transformation, who exists now in spaces between rather than trapped in single form.

Vincent sits until full darkness claims the bluff, until the lake becomes invisible, until the air grows cold enough that his body insists on movement. When he finally stands to leave, his hand brushes the log in farewell. The wood feels warm beneath his palm, warmer than evening air should allow, carrying heat that might come from absorbed sunshine or might come from something deeper, something that rests but hasn't forgotten, something that dreams in frequencies too low for human ears but perfect for human hearts to feel.

The walk back through darkness doesn't frighten him anymore. His feet find the path with certainty born of repetition, of acceptance, of understanding that some hauntings are just love wearing different shapes. Behind him, the collapsed entrance keeps its secrets, the wildflowers close their petals for the night, and somewhere distributed through root and stone and the deep places where consciousness can spread like water, something that was once a girl named Mira continues its eternal rest, present everywhere and nowhere, gone and remaining, lost and somehow, impossibly, still found.

AFTERWORD

The *Stonebound* trilogy began with a town that avoided looking too closely at what hurt, and it ends with people who finally do. What started in silence does not end in answers, but in understanding. Not everything needs to be named to be held.

This was never a story about monsters. It was about the ways people bind themselves to one another, and the cost of holding on too tightly or not tightly enough. It was about grief that lingers when words fail, about faith that survives doubt, and about the courage it takes to let something rest without trying to fix it.

Across these books, loss is not an interruption to life but a part of it. What matters is not what is taken, but what is remembered. The moments shared. The promises kept or broken. The quiet choices to stay, to listen, to love even when the outcome is uncertain.

If there is mercy here, it is found in connection. In learning that cherishing something does not mean possessing it, and that some endings are not meant to be fought. They are meant to be honored.

Thank you for walking with these characters to the end. I hope what they found stays with you.

NOTE FROM N.B. CROSS

Thank you for reading *Root Sleep*, the conclusion of the *Stonebound Trilogy*.

If you enjoyed your time in Duswood, I'd be so grateful if you'd leave an honest review. Just a few sentences makes a big difference for indie authors like me.

Your feedback helps this story reach more readers and helps me keep writing.

You can also follow the series, get early access to upcoming releases, exclusive merch, or receive behind-the-scenes updates by signing up here:

https://nbcrossauthor.com/newsletter-signup.html

With gratitude,

N.B. Cross

https://nbcrossauthor.com/

COMING SOON

As of January 2026, I am working on a standalone novel about a father's search for his missing daughter. He fractures into a descent through grief, repetition, and surrender, where time bends, memory corrodes, and the cost of refusing to let go becomes more terrifying than any answer.

I plan to release it in the first quarter of 2026. Check my Instagram and in my newsletter for updates.

ABOUT THE AUTHOR

N.B. Cross writes quiet horror and dark fiction rooted in small towns, haunted landscapes, and the shadows that live between memory and grief. His short story collection, *Static Between the Trees*, introduced readers to his blend of atmosphere and unease. *Hollow Stone, Quiet Bloom*, and *Root Sleep* are the books in his *Stonebound Trilogy*.

Learn more at nbcrossauthor.com and join the Signals from the Static newsletter for a free story, exclusive merch, and upcoming announcements.

Follow at instagram.com/n.b.cross/

ALSO BY N.B. CROSS

Static Between the Trees (short story collection)

Hollow Stone (Stonebound Book 1)

Quiet Bloom (Stonebound Book 2)